ASIMOV'S FOUNDATIONS! (*Part three*)

The three-volume Panther edition of THE EARLY ASIMOV contains twenty-seven stories by the greatest name in twentieth-century science fiction which have never before been collected in book form. They span the formative years of Isaac Asimov's writing career, from 1939 when he sold the second story he ever wrote to the magazine *Astonishing Stories* to 1949 when, with most of his famous robot stories and the greater part of his epic *Foundation* saga already published, Asimov was firmly established among science fiction readers the world over as the foremost living SF author.

This third volume contains seven brilliant Asimov stories, from *Author! Author!* (an early victim of wartime paper shortage!) to *Mother Earth* (first published in *Astounding Science Fiction* in May 1949).

Each volume of THE EARLY ASIMOV will be an essential addition to the library of every true science fiction connoisseur and – as always with Isaac Asimov – first-rate reading entertainment in its own right.

D1471145

Also by Isaac Asimov in Panther Science Fiction

Earth is Room Enough
The Stars Like Dust
The Martian Way
The Currents of Space
The End of Eternity
The Caves of Steel
The Naked Sun
I, Robot
The Rest of the Robots
Asimov's Mysteries
Nightfall One
Nightfall Two
The Gods Themselves

THE FOUNDATION TRILOGY
Foundation
Foundation and Empire
Second Foundation
The Early Asimov: volume 1
The Early Asimov: volume 2

Isaac Asimov

The Early Asimov

or, Eleven Years of Trying
Volume 3

Panther

Granada Publishing Limited
Published in 1974 by Panther Books Ltd
Frogmore, St Albans, Herts AL2 2NF

The Early Asimov first published in Great Britain
(in one volume) by Victor Gollancz Ltd 1973
Copyright © Isaac Asimov 1972
Made and printed in Great Britain by
Richard Clay (The Chaucer Press) Ltd
Bungay, Suffolk
Set in Linotype Times

To the memory of
John Wood Campbell, Jr. (1910–1971)
for reasons that this book will make
amply obvious

CONTENTS

After 'Time Pussy'* there followed a two-month period during which I wrote nothing.

The reasons were twofold. In the first place, Pearl Harbor put the United States in the war the day I wrote 'Time Pussy,' and those first two months after the débâcle were too disastrous and heartbreaking to allow much in the way of fiction composing.

If that in itself weren't enough, the time had come to try, once again, the qualifying examinations that would, or would not, grant me permission to do research. I very much felt myself to be dangling over the abyss. A second failure to pass would probably mean an end for me at Columbia. Consequently, during those hours when I wasn't working in my father's candy store or hanging over the radio, I had to be studying. There was time for nothing else at all.

Hedging my bets rather desperately, I registered for graduate work at New York University, just in case I did not pass once again. After I took my qualifying examinations, at the end of January 1942, I actually attended a few classes at N.Y.U. while waiting for the results to be announced. – But I won't keep you in suspense. On Friday, the thirteenth of February, the results were announced. I had passed, this time.

During the interval between the taking of the qualifying examinations and the annunciation, I managed to do 'Victory Unintentional.' This was a positronic robot story that was a sequel to 'Not Final!' which had *not* been a positronic robot story. Obviously I was trying to ride the series notion all I could, in the hope of surer sales.

I submitted it to Campbell on February 9, 1942, and if I thought Campbell would find himself unable to reject a series story, I was roundly disabused. Nor was he so impressed by 'Nightfall' and by my 'Foundation' series as to find himself incapable of making the rejection a severe one.

On February 13, the very day of my passing into the sacred list of those permitted to do research toward their Ph.D., my spirits were somewhat dashed when I received 'Victory Unintentional' back with a cryptic rejection, which consisted of the

* The last story in *The Early Asimov: Volume 2*.

following, in toto, 'CH₃C₂CH₂CH₂SH.' Campbell very well knew that this was the formula for 'butyl mercaptan,' which gives the skunk its smell, and I very well knew it, too, and Campbell very well knew I knew.

Oh, well! I managed to sell it anyway, to *Super Science Stories* under its post-Pohl editor, on March 16, 1942, and it appeared in the August 1942 issue of that magazine. Though I did not include it in *I, Robot,* I did include it, of necessity, in *The Rest of the Robots.*

After that, though, there came another dry period, the longest I was ever to experience. Once 'Victory Unintentional' was finished, fourteen months (!) were to pass before I turned back to the typewriter. It was not the conventional 'writer's block,' of course, for that I have never experienced. Rather, it was the coming of a vast, triple change in my life.

The first change was the fact that I was now beginning chemical research in earnest under Professor Charles R. Dawson. Research is a full-time job and I still had to work it around, somehow, my duties in my father's candy store, so there was bound to be very little time for writing.

Then, as though that weren't enough, a second change took place simultaneously —

In January 1942 I joined an organization called 'The Brooklyn Writers' Club,' which had sent me a postcard of invitation. I took the invitation to be a recognition of my status as a 'writer' and I couldn't possibly have refused.

The first meeting I attended was on January 19, 1942. It turned out to be rather pleasant. I welcomed the chance to get my mind off the qualifying examinations and the war disasters (though I remember spending part of that first meeting discussing the possibility that New York might be bombed).

Most of the members of the club were no further advanced in the profession than I was; nor were any of them, aside from myself, science fiction writers. The chief activity consisted of reading from our own manuscripts so that criticism from the others might be invited. Since it was quickly discovered that I read 'with expression,' I became chief reader, a role I enjoyed. (It was to be eight years yet before I discovered that I had a natural flair for the lecture platform.)

On February 9, 1942, the third meeting I attended, there was present a young man, Joseph Goldberger, whom I had not met

10

before. He was a couple of years older than I was. I did most of the reading that day and Goldberger was sufficiently impressed to suggest, after the meeting had adjourned, that the two of us, with our girls, go out on a double date and get to know each other. Embarrassed, I had to explain that I had no girl. With an expansive gesture, he said he would get one for me.

And so he did. On February 14, 1942, (Valentine's Day and the day after I had passed my qualifying examinations) I met him at the Astor Hotel at 8.30 p.m. With him was his girl-friend, and with her was *her* girl-friend, Gertrude Blugerman, who was going to be my blind date. – I fell in love, and when I wasn't thinking of research I was thinking of her.

But there was also a third change, in a way the most drastic —

With war, the job situation suddenly changed: technically trained men of all sorts were in demand.

Robert Heinlein, for instance, was an engineer who had been trained at Annapolis. His health had retired him from active service in the Navy and had kept him retired, but his Annapolis connections made it possible for him to work as a civilian engineer at the Naval Air Experimental Station of the U.S. Navy Yard in Philadelphia. He cast about for other qualified people he might persuade to join him there, particularly among his fellow science fiction writers.

He got L. Sprague de Camp to come to the N.A.E.S., and on March 30, 1942, I received a letter from the navy yard asking if I would consider joining them.

I am rather single-minded and, having labored toward my Ph.D. for a year and a half, I would not ordinarily have considered letting go for anything short of a major force. – But the major force was there. I was in love and I wanted to get married even more than I wanted my degree. It occurred to me that I could suspend work toward my Ph.D. with the full approval of the school, thanks to the war emergency, and that I could also get full permission to resume after the war. And by taking a job and postponing – merely *postponing* – my research, I could get married.

I went down to Philadelphia for an interview on April 10 and apparently met their requirements. I took the job, and on May 14, having left my father's candy store at last and (at least as a worker) forever, I moved to Philadelphia. Fortunately, Philadelphia was only an hour and a half from New York by train (in those days, I couldn't drive a car and, even if I could, I wouldn't have been able to get the gasoline because of rationing). I was therefore back in New York every weekend.

By the twenty-fourth of the month I had persuaded Gertrude to agree to marry me, and on July 26 we were married.

During those months it did not bother me that I was doing no writing. I had too much to think of — first the war, then research, then the job, then the marriage.

Besides, in the years up to early 1942, I never thought of my writing as anything but a way to help out with my college tuition. It was fun; it was exciting; and such success as I managed to achieve was deeply satisfying — but it had been done to serve a purpose and that purpose had been served. I had no notion that writing could be my career; that it could ever *possibly* be my career.

My career was to be chemistry. All the time I was writing and selling stories, I was also slaving away at Columbia. Once I earned my Ph.D., I intended to make my living by doing chemical research for some large industry at some munificent salary such as a hundred dollars a week. (As the son of a candy-store keeper, brought up in the depression, I suffered dizzy spells if I tried to think of more than a hundred dollars a week, so I confined my ambitions to that.)

My Philadelphia job, to be sure, paid me only fifty dollars a week at the beginning, but a young couple could live on that, those days, with taxes very small, with an apartment costing $42.50 a month and dinner for two at a restaurant coming to two dollars (including tip).

It wasn't the height of my dreams, but it was only a temporary war job, after all. Once the war was over, I would go back to my research and get my Ph.D. and a better job. Meanwhile, even a salary of $2,600 a year seemed to make it unnecessary for me to write. By my marriage day, I had written forty-two stories, of which twenty-eight had been sold (and three more were yet to sell). My total bachelor earnings over a space of four years had been $1,788.50 for those twenty-eight stories. This amounted to an average earning of just under $8.60 per week or $64 per story.

I never dreamed at that time that I could ever do much

better. I had no intention of ever writing anything but science fiction or fantasy for the pulp magazines, which paid one cent a word at most – a cent and a quarter with bonus.

To make even the feeble fifty dollars a week that my job paid me would make it necessary for me to write and sell some forty stories a year, and, at that time, that didn't seem conceivable to me.

It had been all right to labor at the typewriter to pay my way through school, when I had no other source of income, but for what purpose ought I to be writing now? And with a six-day, fifty-four hour week, and the excitement of a new marriage, who had time?

The very existence of science fiction seemed to fade. I had left my magazine collection in New York; I no longer saw Campbell regularly, or Pohl, or any of my science fiction cronies. I scarcely even read the current magazines as they came out.

I might have let science fiction die altogether, and my writing career with it, except that there were little reminders from the outside world, and little itchings inside me that meant (though I didn't know it at the time) that writing was a great deal more to me than just a handy device to make a little spare cash.

I had hardly begun to work at the N.A.E.S., for instance, when the June 1942 issue of *Astounding* came out with my story 'Bridle and Saddle.' And it made the cover.

It was quite beyond my power to resist the temptation to take a copy to work and show it around. I couldn't help but feel the status I gained as a 'writer.' Later that summer and fall, three other stories were published: 'Victory Unintentional' and 'The Imaginary' in the post-Pohl *Super Science Stories* and 'The Hazing' in *Thrilling Wonder Stories*. Each kept the science fiction world alive for me.

And although my New York coterie of science fiction editors, writers and readers were gone, I was left not entirely bereft.

Working with me at the N.A.E.S. were Robert Heinlein and L. Sprague de Camp, and I kept up a close social relationship with both. To be sure, each had quit writing for the duration but they were far more successful writers than I was and I hero-worshipped them. In addition, John D. Clark, who was an ardent science fiction fan and who had written and published a couple of stories in 1937, was living in Philadelphia at the time and we frequently saw one another. All three kept the science fiction atmosphere about me.

It was on January 5, 1943, though, that the real trigger came. On that day I received a letter from Fred Pohl to the effect that he was planning to rewrite 'Legal Rites' and was going to try to sell it again. That was exciting. He wasn't to succeed in selling the story for six more years, but of course I had no way of telling that. To me it seemed that another sale was in the offing and that I was an as-yet-active writer.

Besides, 'Legal Rites' was a fantasy and I had never yet satisfied that long-standing desire to write and sell a fantasy to *Unknown*. Five times I had tried, and five times I had failed.

On January 13, quite suddenly, a week after the letter had come and fourteen months after my last-written story, the urge overwhelmed me. I sat down to write a fantasy called 'Author! Author!'

Quickly I found there was something lacking. It was the first time I had ever tried to write something for Campbell without conferences with him. I missed the inspiration that invariably came through talks with him; I missed his encouragement. In fact, I wasn't sure that I could write at all without him. So the story limped and there were dry spells. I didn't finish the first draft till March 5, and the final version wasn't ready for mailing till April 4, 1943.

It had taken me nearly three months to write the story. To be sure, it was twelve thousand words long, but 'Bridle and Saddle,' which was half again as long, had taken me only three weeks.

Perhaps if 'Author! Author!' had been rejected, it might have been a long time before I would have had the courage to try again. Fortunately, that was never put to the test. I mailed the story to Campbell on April 6, 1943 (the first time I ever *mailed* him a story instead of handing it to him), and on the twelfth the check of acceptance arrived. There was not even a revision requested, and what's more, Campbell paid me a bonus for the first time since 'Nightfall.' I received one and a quarter cents a word, or $150 in all. My sixth try at *Unknown* had succeeded.

It was the equivalent of three weeks' pay at the N.A.E.S. for something that had taken me, off and on, three months. However, the three months' work on 'Author! Author!' had been of a totally different kind than the three weeks' work at the N.A.E.S. would have been, and the receipt of the $150 check was infinitely more exciting than picking up a similar check, or even a larger one, earned in the course of a punch-the-time-clock job. (Yes, indeed, I punched a time clock at the N.A.E.S.)

As it happened though, the happy excitement with which I greeted the sale was premature. I had scaled the heights of *Unknown* too late, and though I had the money, I didn't have the magazine. Robert Heinlein brought me the sad news on August 2, less than four months after the sale.

Unknown had been having a difficult time of it. Sales weren't high enough, and after its first two years of operation it had had to switch from monthly to bimonthly issues. Now the war had introduced a paper shortage and Street & Smith Publications decided to save what paper it could receive for the more successful *Astounding* and let *Unknown* go.

At the time I made my sale, there were only three more issues of *Unknown* fated to be issued and there was no room in any of them for 'Author! Author!' The story remained in the vaults of Street & Smith indefinitely; a story sold, but not published; and the $150 check was deprived of most of its fun as a result.

There is, however, a happy ending. Twenty years later, Don Bensen of Pyramid Publications was publishing a paperback anthology of stories from *Unknown*, he asked me for an introduction. With glad nostalgia I complied, writing it on January 15, 1963, almost twenty years to the day after I had started writing the only story I ever sold to the magazine. In the course of the introduction, I referred to the sad story of my attempts to write for *Unknown*.

The 1960s were not the 1940s. In 1963, the mere mention of an existing Asimov story that had never been published produced excitement, and Bensen wrote to me within three days, asking to see the story. I dug out the manuscript (I saved them now, you see, even for twenty years) and sent it to him.

He asked permission to include it in a second anthology of *Unknown* stories (pointing out that it had been accepted by the magazine). I explained he would also need permission from Campbell and the publisher. They very kindly granted the permission, and in January 1964, twenty-one years after it was written, 'Author! Author!' was finally published and I finally – after a fashion, and glancingly – made *Unknown*.

21: Author! Author!

It occurred to Graham Dorn, and not for the first time, either, that there was one serious disadvantage in swearing you'll go through fire and water for a girl, however beloved. Sometimes she takes you at your miserable word.

This is one way of saying that he had been waylaid, shanghaied and dragooned by his fiancée into speaking at her maiden aunt's Literary Society. Don't laugh! It's not funny from the speaker's rostrum. Some of the faces you have to look at!

To race through the details, Graham Dorn had been jerked onto a platform and forced upright. He had read a speech on 'The Place of the Mystery Novel in American Literature' in an appalled tone. Not even the fact that his own eternally precious June had written it (part of the bribe to get him to speak in the first place) could mask the fact that it was essentially tripe.

And then when he was weltering, figuratively speaking, in his own mental gore, the harpies closed in, for lo, it was time for the informal discussion and assorted feminine gush.

— Oh, Mr. Dorn, do you work from inspiration? I mean, do you just sit down and then an idea strikes you – all at once? And you must sit up all night and drink black coffee to keep you awake till you get it down?

— Oh, yes. Certainly. (His working hours were two to four in the afternoon every other day, and he drank milk.)

— Oh, Mr. Dorn, you must do the most awful research to get all those bizarre murders. About how much must you do before you can write a story?

— About six months, usually. (The only reference books he ever used were a six-volume encyclopedia and year-before-last's World Almanac.)

— Oh, Mr. Dorn, did you make up your Reginald de Meister from a real character? You must have. He's oh, so convincing in his every detail.

— He's modeled after a very dear boyhood chum of mine. (Dorn had never known *anyone* like de Meister. He lived in

The Unknown 5, edited by D. R. Bensen
Copyright © 1964 by Isaac Asimov

continual fear of meeting someone like him. He had even a cunningly fashioned ring containing a subtle Oriental poison for use just in case he did. So much for de Meister.)

Somewhere past the knot of women, June Billings sat in her seat and smiled with sickening and proprietary pride.

Graham passed a finger over his throat and went through the pantomime of choking to death as unobtrusively as possible. June smiled, nodded, threw him a delicate kiss, and did nothing.

Graham decided to pass a stern, lonely, woman-less life and to have nothing but villainesses in his stories forever after.

He was answering in monosyllables, alternating yesses and noes. Yes, he did take cocaine on occasion. He found it helped the creative urge. No, he didn't think he could allow Hollywood to take over de Meister. He thought movies weren't true expressions of real Art. Besides, they were just a passing fad. Yes, he would read Miss Crum's manuscripts if she brought them. Only too glad to. Reading amateur manuscripts was such fun, and editors are really such brutes.

And then refreshments were announced, and there was a sudden vacuum. It took a split-second for Graham's head to clear. The mass of femininity had coalesced into a single specimen. She was four feet ten and about eighty-five pounds in weight. Graham was six-two and two hundred ten worth of brawn. He could probably have handled her without difficulty, especially since both her arms were occupied with a pachyderm of a purse. Still, he felt a little delicate, to say nothing of queasy, about knocking her down. It didn't seem quite the thing to do.

She was advancing, with admiration and fervor disgustingly clear in her eyes, and Graham felt the wall behind him. There was no doorway within armreach on either side.

'Oh, Mr. de Meister – do, do please let me call you Mr. de Meister. Your creation is so real to me, that I can't think of you as simply Graham Dorn. You don't mind, do you?'

'No, no, of course not,' gargled Graham, as well as he could through thirty-two teeth simultaneously set on edge. 'I often think of myself as Reginald in my more frivolous moments.'

'Thank you. You can have no idea, *dear* Mr. de Meister, how I have looked *forward* to meeting you. I have read *all* your works, and I think they are wonderful.'

'I'm glad you think so.' He went automatically into the

17

modesty routine. 'Really nothing, you know. Ha, ha, ha! Like to please the readers, but lots of room for improvement. Ha, ha, ha!'

'But you really are, you know.' This was said with intense earnestness. 'I mean good, *really* good. I think it is wonderful to be an author like you. It must be almost like being God.'

Graham stared blankly. 'Not to editors, sister.'

Sister didn't get the whisper. She continued, 'To be able to create living characters out of nothing; to unfold souls to all the world; to put thoughts into words; to build pictures and create worlds. I have often thought than an author was the most graciously gifted person in creation. Better an inspired author starving in a garret than a king upon his throne. Don't you think so?'

'Definitely,' lied Graham.

'What are the crass material goods of the world to the wonders of weaving emotions and deeds into a little world of its own?'

'What, indeed?'

'And posterity, think of posterity!'

'Yes, yes. I often do.'

She seized his hand. 'There's only one little request. You might,' she blushed faintly, 'you might give poor Reginald – if you will allow me to call him that just once – a chance to marry Letitia Reynolds. You make her just a little too cruel to him. I'm sure I weep over it for hours together sometimes. But then he is too, too real to me.'

And from somewhere, a lacy frill of handkerchief made its appearance, and went to her eyes. She removed it, smiled bravely, and scurried away. Graham Dorn inhaled, closed his eyes, and gently collapsed into June's arms.

His eyes opened with a jerk. 'You may consider,' he said severely, 'our engagement frazzled to the breaking point. Only my consideration for your poor, aged parents prevents your being known henceforward as the ex-fiancée of Graham Dorn.'

'Darling, you are so noble.' She massaged his sleeve with her cheeks. 'Come, I'll take you home and bathe your poor wounds.'

'All right, but you'll have to carry me. Has your precious, loveable aunt got an axe?'

'But why?'

'For one thing, she had the gall to introduce me as the brain-father, God help me, of the famous Reginald de Meister.'

'And aren't you?'

'Let's get out of this creep-joint. And get this. I'm no relative by brain or otherwise, of that character. I disown him. I cast him into the darkness. I spit upon him. I declare him an illegitimate son, a foul degenerate, and the offspring of a hound, and I'll be damned if he ever pokes his lousy patrician nose into my typewriter again.'

They were in the taxi, and June straightened his tie. 'All right, Sonny, let's see the letter.'

'What letter?'

She held out her hand. 'The one from the publishers.'

Graham snarled and flipped it out of his jacket pocket. 'I've thought of inviting myself to his house for tea, the damned flintheart. He's got a rendezvous with a pinch of strychnine.'

'You may rave later. What does he say? Hmm – uh-huh – "doesn't quite come up to what is expected – feel that de Meister isn't in his usual form – a little revision perhaps towards – feel sure the novel can be adjusted – are returning under separate cover —"'

She tossed it aside. 'I told you you shouldn't have killed off Sancha Rodriguez. She was what you needed. You're getting skimpy on the love interest.'

'You write it! I'm through with de Meister. It's getting so club-women call me Mr. de Meister, and my picture is printed in newspapers with the caption Mr. de Meister. I have no individuality. No one ever heard of Graham Dorn. I'm always: Dorn, Dorn, you know, the guy who writes the de Meister stuff, you know.'

June squealed, 'Silly! You're jealous of your own detective.'

'I am not jealous of my own character. Listen! I hate detective stories. I never read them after I got into the two-syllable words. I wrote the first as a clever, trenchant, biting satire. It was to blast the entire false school of mystery writers. That's why I invented this de Meister. He was the detective to end all detectives. The Compleat Ass, by Graham Dorn.

'So the public, along with snakes, vipers and ungrateful children takes this filth to its bosom. I wrote mystery after mystery trying to convert the public —'

Graham Dorn drooped a little at the futility of it all.

'Oh, well.' He smiled wanly, and the great soul rose above adversity. 'Don't you see? I've got to write other things. I can't waste my life. But who's going to read a serious novel by Graham Dorn, now that I'm so thoroughly identified with de Meister?'

'You can use a pseudonym.'

'I will not use a pseudonym. I'm proud of my name.'

'But you can't drop de Meister. Be sensible, dear.'

'A normal fiancée,' Graham said bitterly, 'would want her future husband to write something really worthwhile and become a great name in literature.'

'Well, I do want you to, Graham. But just a little de Meister once in a while to pay the bills that accumulate.'

'Ha!' Graham knocked his hat over his eyes to hide the sufferings of a strong spirit in agony. 'Now you say that I can't reach prominence unless I prostitute my art to that unmentionable. Here's your place. Get out. I'm going home and write a good scorching letter on asbestos to our senile Mr. MacDunlap.'

'Do exactly as you want to, cookie,' soothed June. 'And tomorrow when you feel better, you'll come and cry on my shoulder, and we'll plan a revision of *Death on the Third Deck* together, shall we?'

'The engagement,' said Graham, loftily, 'is broken.'

'Yes, dear. I'll be home tomorrow at eight.'

'That is of no possible interest to me. Good-bye!'

Publishers and editors are untouchables, of course. Theirs is a heritage of the outstretched hand and the well-toothed smile; the nod of the head and the slap of the back.

But perhaps somewhere, in the privacy of the holes to which authors scurry when the night falls, a private revenge it taken. There, phrases may be uttered where no one can overhear, and letters may be written that need not be mailed, and perhaps a picture of an editor, smiling pensively, is enshrined above the typewriter to act the part of bulls-eye in an occasional game of darts.

Such a picture of MacDunlap, so used, enlightened Graham Dorn's room. And Graham Dorn himself, in his usual writing costume (street-clothes and typewriter), scowled at the fifth sheet of paper in his typewriter. The other four were draped over the edge of the waste-basket, condemned for their milk-and-watery mildness.

He began:

'Dear Sir —' and added slowly and viciously, 'or Madam, as the case may be.'

He typed furiously as the inspiration caught him, disregarding the faint wisp of smoke curling upward from the overheated keys:

'You say you don't think much of de Meister in this story. Well, I don't think much of de Meister, period. You can handcuff your slimy carcass to his and jump off the Brooklyn Bridge. And I hope they drain the East River just before you jump.

'From now on, my works will be aimed higher than your scurvy press. And the day will come when I can look back on this period of my career with the loathing that is its just —'

Someone had been tapping Graham on the shoulder during the last paragraph. Graham twitched it angrily and ineffectively at intervals.

Now he stopped, turned around, and addressed the stranger in his room courteously: 'Who the devilish damnation are you? And you can leave without bothering to answer. I won't think you rude.'

The newcomer smiled graciously. His nod wafted the delicate aroma of some unobtrusive hair-oil toward Graham. His lean, hard-bitten jaw stood out keenly, and he said in a well-modulated voice:

'De Meister is the name. Reginald de Meister.'

Graham rocked to his mental foundations and heard them creak.

'Glub,' he said.

'Pardon?'

Graham recovered. 'I said, "glub," a little code word meaning *which* de Meister.'

'*The* de Meister,' explained de Meister, kindly.

'My character? My detective?'

De Meister helped himself to a seat, and his finely-chiseled features assumed that air of well-bred boredom so admired in the best circles. He lit a Turkish cigarette, which Graham at once recognized as his detective's favorite brand, tapping it slowly and carefully against the back of his hand first, a mannerism equally characteristic.

'Really, old man,' said de Meister. 'This is really excruciatin'ly funny. I suppose I am your character, y'know, but let's not work on that basis. It would be so devastatin'ly awkward.'

'Glub,' said Graham again, by way of a rejoinder.

His mind was feverishly setting up alternatives. He didn't drink, more, at the moment, was the pity, so he wasn't drunk. He had a chrome-steel digestion and he wasn't overheated, so it wasn't a hallucination. He never dreamed, and his imagination – as befitted a paying commodity – was under strict control. And since, like all authors, he was widely considered more than half a screwball, insanity was out of the question.

Which left de Meister simply an impossibility, and Graham felt relieved. It's a very poor author indeed who hasn't learned the fine art of ignoring impossibilities in writing a book.

He said smoothly, 'I have here a volume of my latest work. Do you mind naming your page and crawling back into it. I'm a busy man and God knows I have enough of you in the tripe I write.'

'But I'm here on business, old chap. I've got to come to a friendly arrangement with you first. Things are deucedly uncomfortable as they are.'

'Look, do you know you're bothering me? I'm not in the habit of talking to mythical characters. As a general thing, I don't pal around with them. Beside which, it's time your mother told you that you really don't exist.'

'My dear fellow, I always existed. Existence is such a subjective thing. What a mind thinks exists, *does* exist. I existed in your mind, for instance, ever since you first thought of me.'

Graham shuddered. 'But the question is, what are you doing *out* of my mind? Getting a little narrow for you? Want elbow room?'

'Not at all. Rather satisfact'ry mind in its way, but I achieved a more concrete existence only this afternoon, and so I seize the opportunity to engage you face to face in the aforementioned business conversation. You see, that thin, sentimental lady of your society —'

'What society?' questioned Graham hollowly. It was all awfully clear to him now.

'The one at which you made a speech' – de Meister shuddered in his turn – 'on the detective novel. She believed in my existence, so naturally, I exist.'

He finished his cigarette and flicked it out with a negligent twist of the wrist.

'The logic,' declared Graham, 'is inescapable. Now, what do

you want and the answer is no.'

'Do you realize, old man, that if you stop writing de Meister stories, my existence will become that dull, wraithlike one of all superannuated fictional detectives. I'd have to gibber through the gray mists of Limbo with Holmes, Lecocoq and Dupin.'

'A very fascinating thought, I think. A very fitting fate.'

Reginald de Meister's eyes turned icy, and Graham suddenly remembered the passage on page 123 of *The Case of the Broken Ashtray*:

His eyes, hitherto lazy and unattentive, hardened into twin pools of blue ice and transfixed the butler, who staggered back, a stifled cry on his lips.

Evidently, de Meister lost none of his characteristics out of the novels he adorned.

Graham staggered back, a stifled cry on his lips.

De Meister said menacingly, 'It would be better for you if the de Meister mysteries continue. Do you understand?'

Graham recovered and summoned a feeble indignation. 'Now, wait a while. You're getting out of hand. Remember: in a way, I'm your father. That's right. Your mental father. You can't hand me ultimatums or make threats. It isn't filial. It's lacking in the proper respect and love.'

'And another thing.' said de Meister, unmoved. 'We've got to straighten out this business of Letitia Reynolds. It's gettin' deucedly borin', y'know.'

'Now you're getting silly. My love scenes have been widely heralded as miracles of tenderness and sentiment not found in one murder mystery out of a thousand. – Wait, I'll get you a few reviews. I don't mind your attempts to dictate my actions so much, but I'm damned if you'll criticize my writing.'

'Forget the reviews. Tenderness and all that rot is what I don't want. I've been driftin' after the fair lady for five volumes now, and behavin' the most insufferable ass. This has got to stop.'

'In what way?'

'I've got to marry her in your present story. Either that, or make her a good, respectable mistress. And you'll have to stop making me so damned Victorian and gentlemanly towards ladies. I'm only human, old man.'

'Impossible!' said Graham, 'and that includes your last re-mark.'

De Meister grew severe. 'Really, old chap, for an author, you display the most appallin' lack of concern for the well-bein' of a character who has supported you for a good many years.'

Graham choked eloquently. 'Supported me? In other words, you think I couldn't sell real novels, hey? Well, I'll show you. I wouldn't write another de Meister story for a million dollars. Not even for a fifty percent royalty and all television rights. How's that?'

De Meister frowned and uttered those words that had been the sound of doom to so many criminals: 'We shall see, but you are not yet done with me.'

With firmly jutting jaw, he vanished.

Graham's twisted face straightened out, and slowly – very slowly – he brought his hands up to his cranium and felt care-fully.

For the first time in a long and reasonably ribald mental life, he felt that his enemies were right and that a good dry cleaning would not hurt his mind at all.

The *things* that existed in it!

Graham Dorn shoved the doorbell with his elbow a second time. He distinctly remembered her saying she would be home at eight.

The peep-hole shoved open. 'Hello!'

'Hello!'

Silence!

Graham said plaintively, 'It's raining outside. Can't I come in to dry?'

'I don't know. Are we engaged, Mr. Dorn?'

'If I'm not,' was the stiff reply, 'then I've been turning down the frenzied advances of a hundred passion-stricken girls – beautiful ones, all of them – for no apparent reason.'

'Yesterday, you said —'

'Ah, but who listens to what I say? I'm just quaint that way. Look, I brought you posies.' He flourished roses before the peep-hole.

June opened the door. 'Roses! How plebeian. Come in, cookie, and sully the sofa. Whoa, whoa, before you move a step, what have you got under the other arm? Not the manuscript of *Death on the Third Deck*?'

'Correct. Not that excrescence of a manuscript. This is something different.'

June's tone chilled. 'That isn't your precious novel, is it?'

Graham flung his head up, 'How did you know about it?'

'You slobbered the plot all over me at MacDunlap's silver anniversary party.'

'I did not. I couldn't unless I were drunk.'

'Oh, but you were. Stinking is the term. And on two cocktails too.'

'Well, if I was drunk, I couldn't have told you the right plot.'

'Is the setting a coal-mine district?'

'– Uh – yes.'

'And are the people concerned real, earthy, unartificial, down-to-earth characters, speaking and thinking just like you and me? Is it a story of basic economic forces? Are the human characters lifted up and thrown down and whirled around, all at the mercy of the coal mine and mechanized industry of today?'

'– Uh – yes.'

She nodded her head retrospectively. 'I remember distinctly. First, you got drunk and were sick. Then you got better, and told me the first few chapters. Then I got sick.'

She approached the glowering author. 'Graham.' She leant her golden head upon his shoulder and cooed softly. 'Why don't you continue with the de Meister stories? You get such pretty checks out of them.'

Graham writhed out of her grasp. 'You are a mercenary wretch, incapable of understanding an author's soul. You may consider our engagement broken.'

He sat down hard on the sofa, and folded his arms. 'Unless you will consent to read the script of my novel and give me the usual story analysis.'

'May I give you my analysis of *Death on the Third Deck* first?'

'No.'

'Good! In the first place, your love interest is becoming sickening.'

'It is not.' Graham pointed his finger indignantly. 'It breathes a sweet and sentimental fragrance, as of an older day. I've got the review here that says it.' He fumbled in his wallet.

25

'Oh, bullfeathers. Are you going to start quoting that guy in the Pillsboro (Okla.) Clarion? He's probably your second cousin. You know that your last two novels were completely below par in royalties. And *Third Deck* isn't even being sold.'

'So much the better – Ow!' He rubbed his head violently. 'What did you do that for?'

'Because the only place I could hit as hard as I wanted to, without disabling you, was your head. Listen! The public is tired of your corny Letitia Reynolds. Why don't you let her soak her "gleaming golden crown of hair" in kerosene and get familiar with a match?'

'But June, that character is drawn from life. From you!'

'Graham Dorn! I am not here to listen to insults. The mystery market today is swinging toward action and hot, honest love and you're still in the sweet, sentimental stickiness of five years ago.'

'But that's Reginald de Meister's character.'

'Well, change his character. Listen! You introduce Sancha Rodriguez. That's fine. I approve of her. She's Mexican, flaming, passionate, sultry and in love with him. So what do you do? First he behaves the impeccable gentleman, and then you kill her off in the middle of the story.'

'Hmm, I see — You really think it would improve things to have de Meister forget himself. A kiss or so —'

June clenched her lovely teeth and her lovely fists. 'Oh, darling, how glad I am love is blind! If it ever peeked one tiny little bit, I couldn't stand it. Look, you squirrel's blue plate special, you're going to have de Meister and Rodriguez fall in love. They're going to have an affair through the entire book and you can put your horrible Letitia into a nunnery. She would probably be happier there from the way you make her sound.'

'That's all *you* know about it, my sweet. It so happens that Reginald de Meister is in love with Letitia Reynolds and wants *her*, not this Rodriguez person.'

'And what makes you think that?'

'He told me so.'

'Who told you so?'

'Reginald de Meister.'

'What Reginald de Meister?'

'*My* Reginald de Meister.'

'What do you mean, your Reginald de Meister?'

'My *character*, Reginald de Meister.'

June got up, indulged in some deep-breathing and then said in a very calm voice, 'Let's start all over.'

She disappeared for a moment and returned with an aspirin. 'Your Reginald de Meister, from your books, told you, in person, he was in love with Letitia Reynolds?'

'That's right.'

June swallowed the aspirin.

'Well, I'll explain, June, the way he explained it to me. All characters really exist – at least, in the minds of the authors. But when people really begin to believe in them, they begin to exist in reality, because what people believe in, is, so far as they're concerned, and what is existence anyway?'

June's lips trembled. 'Oh, Gramie, please don't. Mother will never let me marry you if they put you in an asylum.'

'Don't call me Gramie, June, for God's sake. I tell you he was there, trying to tell me what to write and how to write it. He was almost as bad as you. Aw, come on, Baby, don't cry.'

'I can't help it. I always thought you were crazy, but I never thought you were *crazy*!'

'All right, what's the difference? Let's not talk about it any more. I'm never going to write another mystery novel. After all' – (he indulged in a bit of indignation) – 'when it gets so that my own character – my *own* character – tries to tell me what to do, it's going too far.'

June looked over her handkerchief. 'How do you know it was really de Meister?'

'Oh, golly. As soon as he tapped his Turkish cigarette on the back of his hand and started dropping g's like snowflakes in a blizzard, I knew the worst had come.'

The telephone rang. June leaped up. 'Don't answer, Graham. It's probably from the asylum. I'll tell them you're not here. Hello. Hello. Oh, Mr. MacDunlap.' She heaved a sigh of relief, then covered the mouthpiece and whispered hoarsely, 'It might be a trap.'

'Hello, Mr. MacDunlap! ... No, he's not here.... Yes, I think I can get in touch with him.... At Martin's tomorrow, noon.... I'll tell him ... With who? ... With who???' She hung up suddenly.

'Graham, you're to lunch with MacDunlap tomorrow.'

'At his expense! Only at his expense!'

Her great blue eyes got greater and bluer, 'And Reginald de

27

Meister is to dine with you.'

'What Reginald de Meister?'

'Your Reginald de Meister.'

'*My* Reg —'

'Oh, Gramie, *don't*.' Her eyes misted, 'Don't you see, Gramie, now they'll put us both in an insane asylum – and Mr. MacDunlap, too. And they'll probably put us all in the same padded cell. Oh, Gramie, three is such a dreadful crowd.'

And her face crumpled into tears.

Grew S. MacDunlap (that the S. stands for 'Some' is a vile untruth spread by his enemies) was alone at the table when Graham Dorn entered. Out of this fact, Graham extracted a few fleeting drops of pleasure.

It was not so much, you understand, the presence of MacDunlap that did it, as the absence of de Meister.

MacDunlap looked at him over his spectacles and swallowed a liver pill, his favorite sweetmeat.

'Aha. You're here. What is this corny joke you're putting over on me? You had no right to mix me up with a person like de Meister without warning me he was real. I might have taken precautions. I could have hired a bodyguard. I could have bought a revolver.'

'He's *not* real. God damn it! Half of him was *your* idea.'

'That,' returned MacDunlap with heat, 'is libel. And what do you mean, he's not real? When he introduced himself, I took three liver pills at once and he didn't disappear. Do you know what three pills are? Three pills, the kind I've got (the doctor should only drop dead), could make an elephant disappear – if he weren't real. I *know*.'

Graham said wearily, 'Just the same, he exists only in my mind.'

'In your mind, I know he exists. Your mind should be investigated by the Pure Food and Drugs Act.'

The several polite rejoinders that occurred simultaneously to Graham were dismissed almost immediately as containing too great a proportion of pithy Anglo-Saxon expletives. After all – ha, ha – a publisher is a publisher however Anglo-Saxony he may be.

Graham said, 'The question arises, then, how we're to get rid of de Meister.'

'Get rid of de Meister?' MacDunlap jerked the glasses off

his nose in his sudden start, and caught them in one hand. His voice thickened with emotion. 'Who wants to get rid of him?'

'Do you want him around?'

'God forbid,' MacDunlap said between shudders. 'Next to him, my brother-in-law is an angel.'

'He has no business outside my books.'

'For my part, he has no business inside them. Since I started reading your manuscripts, my doctor added kidney pills and cough syrups to my medicines.' He looked at his watch, and took a kidney pill. 'My worst enemy should be a book publisher only a year.'

'Then why,' asked Graham patiently, 'don't you want to get rid of de Meister?'

'Because he is publicity.'

Graham stared blankly.

'Look! What other writer has a real detective? All the others are fictional. Everyone knows that. But yours – *yours* is real. We can let him solve cases and have big newspaper write-ups. He'll make the Police Department look silly. He'll make —'

'That,' interrupted Graham, categorically, 'is by all odds the most obscene proposal I have ever had my ears manured with.'

'It will make money.'

'Money isn't everything.'

'Name one thing it isn't. . . . Shh!' He kicked a near-fracture into Graham's left ankle and rose to his feet with a convulsive smile, 'Mr. de Meister!'

'Sorry, old dear,' came a lethargic voice. 'Couldn't quite make it, you know. Loads of engagements. Must have been most borin' for you.'

Graham Dorn's ears quivered spasmodically. He looked over his shoulder and reeled backward as far as a person could reel while in a sitting position. Reginald de Meister had sprouted a monocle since his last visitation, and his monocular glance was calculated to freeze blood.

De Meister's greeting was casual. 'My dear Watson! So glad to meet you. Overjoyed deucedly.'

'Why don't you go to hell?' Graham asked curiously.

'My dear fellow. Oh, my dear fellow.'

MacDunlap crackled, 'That's what I like. Jokes! Fun! Makes everything pleasant to start with. Now shall we get down to business?'

'Certainly. The dinner is on the way, I trust? Then I'll just order a bottle of wine. The usual, Henry.' The waiter ceased hovering, flew away, and skimmed back with a bottle that opened and gurgled into a glass.

De Meister sipped delicately, 'So nice of you, old chap, to make me a habitué of this place in your stories. It holds true even now, and it is most convenient. The waiters all know me. Mr. MacDunlap, I take it you have convinced Mr. Dorn of the necessity of continuing the de Meister stories.'

'Yes,' said MacDunlap.

'No,' said Graham.

'Don't mind him,' said MacDunlap. 'He's temperamental. You know these authors.'

'Don't mind him,' said Graham. 'He's microcephalic. You know these publishers.'

'Look, old chappie. I take it MacDunlap hasn't pointed out to you the unpleasanter side of acting stubborn.'

'For instance what, old stinkie?' asked Graham, courteously.

'Well, have you ever been haunted?'

'Like coming behind me and saying, Boo!'

'My dear fellow, I say. I'm much more subtle than that. I can really haunt one in modern, up-to-date methods. For instance, have you ever had your individuality submerged?'

He snickered.

There was something familiar about that snicker. Graham suddenly remembered. It was on page 103 of *Murder Rides the Range*:

His lazy eyelids flicked down and up. He laughed lightly and melodiously, and though he said not a word, Hank Marslowe cowered. There was hidden menace and hidden power in that light laugh, and somehow the burly rancher did not dare reach for his guns.

To Graham it still sounded like a nasty snicker, but he cowered, and did not dare reach for his guns.

MacDunlap plunged through the hole the momentary silence had created.

'You see, Graham. Why play around with ghosts? Ghosts aren't reasonable things. They're not *human*! If it's more royalties, you want—'

Graham fired up. 'Will you refrain from speaking of money? From now on, I write only great novels of tearing human emotions.'

MacDunlap's flushed face changed suddenly.

'No,' he said.

'In fact, to change the subject just a moment' – and Graham's tone became surpassingly sweet, as the words got all sticky with maple syrup – 'I have a manuscript here for you to look at.'

He grasped the perspiring MacDunlap by the lapel firmly. 'It is a novel that is the work of five years. A novel that will grip you with its intensity. A novel that will shake you to the core of your being. A novel that will open a new world. A novel that will —'

'No,' said MacDunlap.

'A novel that will blast the falseness of this world. A novel that pierces to the truth. A novel —'

MacDunlap, being able to stretch his hand no higher, took the manuscript.

'No,' he said.

'Why the bloody hell don't you read it?' inquired Graham. 'Now?'

'Well, start it.'

'Look, supposing I read it tomorrow, or even the next day. I have to take my cough syrup now.'

'You haven't coughed once since I got here.'

'I'll let you know immediately —'

'This,' said Graham, 'is the first page. Why don't you begin it? It will grip you instantly.'

MacDunlap read two paragraphs and said, 'Is this laid in a coal-mining town?'

'Yes.'

'Then I can't read it. I'm allergic to coal dust.'

'But it's not real coal dust, MacIdiot.'

'That,' pointed out MacDunlap, 'is what you said about de Meister.'

Reginald de Meister tapped a cigarette carefully on the back of his hand in a subtle manner which Graham immediately recognized as betokening a sudden decision.

'That is all devastatin'ly borin', you know. Not quite gettin' to the point, you might say. Go ahead, MacDunlap, this is no time for half measures.'

MacDunlap girded his spiritual loins and said, 'All right Mister Dorn, with you it's no use being nice. Instead of de Meister, I'm getting coal dust. Instead of the best publicity in fifty years, I'm getting social significance. All right, Mister Smartaleck Dorn, if in one week you don't come to terms with me, *good* terms, you will be blacklisted in every reputable publishing firm in the United States and foreign parts.' He shook his finger and added in a shout, 'Including Scandinavian.'

Graham Dorn laughed lightly, 'Pish,' he said, 'tush. I happen to be an officer of the Author's Union, and if you try to push me around I'll have *you* blacklisted. How do you like that?'

'I like it fine. Because supposing I can prove you're a plagiarist.'

'Me,' gasped Graham, recovering narrowly from merry suffocation. 'Me, the most original writer of the decade.'

'Is that so? And maybe you don't remember that in each case you write up, you casually mention de Meister's notebooks on previous cases.'

'So what?'

'So he has them. Reginald, my boy, show Mister Dorn your notebook of your last case. – You see that. That's *Mystery of the Milestones* and it has, in detail, every incident in your book – and dated the year before the book was published. Very authentic.'

'Again so what?'

'Have you maybe got the right to copy his notebook and call it an original murder mystery?'

'Why, you case of mental poliomyelitis, that notebook is my invention.'

'Who says so? It's de Meister's handwriting, as any expert can prove. And maybe you have a piece of paper, some little contract or agreement, you know, that gives you the right to use his notebooks?'

'How can I have an agreement with a mythical personage?'

'What mythical personage?'

'You and I know de Meister doesn't exist.'

'Ah, but does the jury know? When I testify that I took three strong liver pills and he didn't disappear, what twelve men will say he doesn't exist?'

'This is blackmail.'

'Certainly. I'll give you a week. Or in other words, seven days.'

Graham Dorn turned desperately to de Meister. 'You're in on this, too. In my books I give you the keenest sense of honor. Is this honorable?'

De Meister shrugged. 'My dear fellow. All this – and haunting, too.'

Graham rose.

'Where are you going?'

'Home to write you a letter.' Graham's brows beetled defiantly. 'And this time I'll mail it. I'm not giving in. I'll fight to the last ditch. And, de Meister, you let loose with one single little haunt and I'll rip your head out of its socket and spurt the blood all over MacDunlap's new suit.'

He stalked out, and as he disappeared through the door, de Meister disappeared through nothing at all.

MacDunlap let out a soft yelp and then took a liver pill, a kidney pill, and a tablespoon of cough syrup in rapid succession.

Graham Dorn sat in June's front parlor, and having long since consumed his fingernails, was starting on the first knuckles.

June, at the moment, was not present, and this, Graham felt, was just as well. A dear girl; in fact, a dear, sweet girl. But his mind was not on her.

It was concerned instead with a miasmic series of flashbacks over the preceding six days:

— Say, Graham, I met your side-kick at the club yesterday. You know, de Meister. Got an awful shock. I always had the idea he was a sort of Sherlock Holmes that didn't exist. That's one on me, boy. Didn't know — Hey, where are you going?

— Hey, Dorn, I hear your boss de Meister is back in town. Ought to have material for more stories soon. You're lucky you've got someone to grind out your plots ready-made — Huh? Well, good-bye.

— Why, Graham, darling, wherever were you last night? Ann's affair didn't get *anywhere* without you; or at least, it wouldn't have, if it hadn't been for Reggie de Meister. He asked after you; but then, I guess he felt lost without his Watson. It must feel wonderful to Watson for such— *Mister* Dorn! And the same to you, sir!

— You put one over on me. I thought you made up those wild things. Well, truth is stranger than fiction, ha, ha!

— Police officials deny that the famous amateur criminologist Reginald de Meister has interested himself in this case. Mr. de Meister himself could not be reached by our reporters for comment. Mr. de Meister is best known to the public for his brilliant solutions to over a dozen crimes, as chronicled in fiction form by his so-called 'Watson,' Mr. Grayle Doone.

Graham quivered and his arms trembled in an awful desire for blood. De Meister was haunting him – but good. He was losing his individuality, exactly as had been threatened.

It gradually dawned upon Graham that the monotonous ringing noise he heard was not in his head, but, on the contrary, from the front door.

Such seemed likewise the opinion of Miss June Billings, whose piercing call shot down the stairs and biffed Graham a sharp uppercut to the ear-drums.

'Hey, dope, see who's at the front door, before the vibration tears the house down. I'll be down in half an hour.'

'Yes, dear!'

Graham shuffled his way to the front door and opened it.

'Ah, there. Greetin's,' said de Meister, and brushed past.

Graham's dull eyes stared, and then fired high, as an animal snarl burst from his lips. He took up that gorilla posture, so comforting to red-blooded American males at moments like this, and circled the slightly-confused detective.

'My dear fellow, are you ill?'

'I,' explained Graham, 'am not ill, but you will soon be past all interest in that, for I am going to bathe my hands in your heart's reddest blood.'

'But I say, you'll only have to wash them afterwards. It would be such an obvious clue, wouldn't it?'

'Enough of this gay banter. Have you any last words?'

'Not particularly.'

'It's just as well. I'm not interested in your last words.'

He thundered into action, bearing down upon the unfortunate de Meister like a bull elephant. De Meister faded to the left, shot out an arm and a foot, and Graham described a parabolic arc that ended in the total destruction of an end table, a vase of flowers, a fish-bowl, and a five-foot section of wall.

Graham blinked, and brushed away a curious goldfish from his left eyebrow.

'My dear fellow,' murmured de Meister, 'oh, my dear fellow.'

Too late, Graham remembered that passage in *Pistol Parade*:

De Meister's arms were whipcord lightning, as with sure, rapid thrusts, he rendered the two thugs helpless. Not by brute force, but by his expert knowledge of judo, he defeated them easily without hastening his breath. The thugs groaned in pain.

Graham groaned in pain.

He lifted his right thigh an inch or so to let his femur slip back into place.

'Hadn't you better get up, old chap?'

'I will stay here,' said Graham with dignity, 'and contemplate the floor in profile view, until such time as it suits me or until such time as I find myself capable of moving a muscle. I don't care which. And now, before I proceed to take further measures with you, what the hell do you want?'

Reginald de Meister adjusted his monocle to a nicety. 'You know, I suppose, that MacDunlap's ultimatum expires tomorrow?'

'And you and he with it, I trust.'

'You will not reconsider.'

'Ha!'

'Really,' de Meister sighed, 'this is borin' no end. You have made things comfortable for me in this world. After all, in your books you've made me well-known in all the clubs and better restaurants, the bosom friend, y'know, of the mayor and commissioner of police, the owner of a Park Avenue penthouse and a magnificent art collection. And it all lingers over, old chap. Really quite affectin'.'

'It is remarkable,' mused Graham, 'the intensity with which I am not listening and the distinctness with which I do not hear a word you say.'

'Still,' said de Meister, 'there is no denyin' my book world suits me better. It is somehow more fascinatin', freer from dull logic, more apart from the necessities of the world. In short, I must go back, and to active participation. You have till tomorrow!'

Graham hummed a gay little tune with flat little notes.

'Is this a new threat, de Meister?'

'It is the old threat intensified. I'm going to rob you of every vestige of your personality. And eventually public opinion will force you to write as, to paraphrase you, de Meister's Compleat Stooge. Did you see the name the newspaper chappies pinned on you today, old man?'

'Yes, Mr. Filthy de Meister, and did you read a half-column item on page ten in the same paper. I'll read it *for* you: "Noted Criminologist in 1-A. Will be inducted shortly draft board says." '

For a moment, de Meister said and did nothing. And then, one after another, he did the following things: removed his monocle slowly, sat down heavily, rubbed his chin abstractedly, and lit a cigarette after long and careful tamping. Each of these, Graham Dorn's trained authorial eye recognized as singly representing perturbation and distress on the part of his character.

And never, in any of his books, did Graham remember a time when de Meister had gone through all four consecutively.

Finally, de Meister spoke. 'Why you had to bring up draft registrations in your last book, I really don't know. This urge to be topical; this fiendish desire to be up to the minute with the news is the curse of the mystery novel. A true mystery is timeless; should have no relation to current events; should —'

'There is one way,' said Graham, 'to escape induction —'

'You might at least have mentioned a deferred classification on some vital ground.'

'There is one way,' said Graham, 'to escape induction —'

'Criminal negligence,' said de Meister.

'Look! Go back to the books and you'll never be filled with lead.'

'Write them and I'll do it.'

'Think of the war.'

'Think of your ego.'

Two strong men stood face to face (or would have, if Graham weren't still horizontal) and neither flinched.

Impasse!

And the sweet, feminine voice of June Billings interrupted and snapped the tension:

'May I ask, Graham Dorn, what you are doing on the floor. It's been swept today and you're not complimenting me by attempting to improve the job.'

'I am not sweeping the floor. If you looked carefully,' replied Graham gently, 'you would see that your own adored fiancé is lying here a mass of bruises and a hotbed of pains and aches.'

'You've ruined my end table!'

'I've broken my leg.'

'And my best lamp.'

'And two ribs.'

'And my fishbowl.'

'And my Adam's apple.'

'And you haven't introduced your friend.'

'And my cervical verte — What friend?'

'This friend.'

'Friend! Ha!' And a mist came over his eyes. She was so young, so fragile to come into contact with hard, brutal facts of life. 'This,' he muttered brokenly, 'is Reginald de Meister.'

De Meister at this point broke a cigarette sharply in two, a gesture pregnant with the deepest emotion.

June said slowly. 'Why – why, you're different from what I had thought.'

'How had you expected me to look?' asked de Meister, in soft, thrilling tones.

'I don't know. Differently than you do – from the stories I heard.'

'You remind me, somehow, Miss Billings, of Letitia Reynolds.'

'I think so. Graham said he drew her from me.'

'A very poor imitation, Miss Billings. Devastatin'ly poor.'

They were six inches apart now, eyes fixed with a mutual glue, and Graham yelled sharply. He sprang upright as memory smote him a nasty smite on the forehead.

A passage from *Case of the Muddy Overshoe* occurred to him. Likewise one from *The Primrose Murders*. Also one from *The Tragedy of Hartley Manor, Death of a Hunter, White Scorpion* and, to put it in a small nutshell, from every one of the others.

The passage read:

There was a certain fascination about de Meister that appealed irresistibly to women.

And June Billings was – as it had often, in Graham's idler moments, occurred to him – a woman.

And fascination simply gooed out of her ears and coated the floor six inches deep.

'Get out of this room, June,' he ordered.

'I will not.'

'There is something I must discuss with Mr. de Meister, man to man. I demand that you leave this room.'

'Please go, Miss Billings,' said de Meister.

June hesitated, and in a very small voice said, 'Very well.'

'Hold on,' shouted Graham. 'Don't let him order you about. I demand that you stay.'

She closed the door very gently behind her.

The two men faced each other. There was that in either pair of eyes that indicated a strong man brought to bay. There was stubborn, undying antagonism; no quarter; no compromise. It was exactly the sort of situation Graham Dorn always presented his readers with, when two strong men fought for one hand, one heart, one girl.

The two said simultaneously, 'Let's make a deal!'

Graham said, 'You have convinced me, Reggie. Our public needs us. Tomorrow I shall begin another de Meister story. Let us shake hands and forget the past.'

De Meister struggled with his emotion. He laid his hand on Graham's lapel, 'My dear fellow, it is I who have been convinced by your logic. I can't allow you to sacrifice yourself for me. There are great things in you that must be brought out. Write your coal-mining novels. They count, not I.'

'I couldn't, old chap. Not after all you've done for me, and all you've meant to me. Tomorrow we start anew.'

'Graham, my – my spiritual father, I couldn't allow it. Do you think I have no feelings, *filial* feelings – in a spiritual sort of way.'

'But the war, think of the war. Mangled limbs. Blood. All that.'

'I must stay. My country needs me.'

'But if I stop writing, eventually you will stop existing. I can't allow that.'

'Oh, that!' De Meister laughed with a careless elegance. 'Things have changed since. So many people believe in my existence now that my grip upon actual existence has become too firm to be broken. I don't have to worry about Limbo any more.'

'Oh.' Graham clenched his teeth and spoke in searing sibilants: 'So that's your scheme, you snake. Do you suppose I don't see you're stuck on June?'

'Look here, old chap,' said de Meister haughtily. 'I can't

permit you to speak slightingly of a true and honest love. I love June and she loves me – I know it. And if you're going to be stuffy and Victorian about it, you can swallow some nitro-glycerine and tap yourself with a hammer.'

'I'll nitro-glycerine you! Because I'm going home tonight and beginning another de Meister story. You'll be part of it and you'll get back into it, and what do you think of that?'

'Nothing, because you can't write another de Meister story. I'm too real now, and you can't control me just like *that*. And what do you think of that?'

It took Graham Dorn a week to make up his mind what to think of that, and then his thoughts were completely and startlingly unprintable.

In fact, it was impossible to write.

That is, startling ideas occurred to him for great novels, emotional dramas, epic poems, brilliant essays – but he couldn't write anything about Reginald de Meister.

The typewriter was simply fresh out of Capital R's.

Graham wept, cursed, tore his hair, and anointed his finger tips with liniment. He tried typewriter, pen, pencil, crayon, charcoal and blood.

He could not write.

The doorbell rang, and Graham threw it open.

MacDunlap stumbled in, falling over the first drifts of torn paper directly into Graham's arms.

Graham let him drop. 'Ha!' he said, with frozen dignity.

'My heart!' said MacDunlap, and fumbled for his liver pills.

'Don't die there,' suggested Graham, courteously. 'The management won't permit me to drop human flesh into the incinerator.'

'Graham, my boy,' MacDunlap said, emotionally, 'no more ultimatums! No more threats! I come now to appeal to your finer feelings, Graham' – he went through a slight choking interlude – 'I love you like a son. This skunk de Meister must disappear. You must write more de Meister stories for my sake. Graham – I will tell you something in private. My wife is in love with this detective. She tells me I am not romantic. I! Not romantic! Can you understand it?'

'I can,' was the tragic response. 'He fascinates all women.'

'With that face? With that monocle?'

'It says so in all my books.'

MacDunlap stiffened. 'Ah ha. You again. Dope! If only you

ever stopped long enough to let your mind know what your typewriter was saying.'

'You insisted. Feminine trade.' Graham didn't care any more. Women! He snickered bitterly. Nothing wrong with any of them that a block-buster wouldn't fix.

MacDunlap hemmed. 'Well, feminine trade. Very necessary. – But Graham, what shall I do? It's not only my wife. She owns fifty shares in MacDunlap, Inc. in her own name. If she leaves me, I lose control. Think of it, Graham. The catastrophe to the publishing world.'

'Grew, old chap,' Graham sighed a sigh so deep, his toenails quivered sympathetically. 'I might as well tell you. June, my fiancée, you know, loves this worm. And he loves her because she is the prototype of Letitia Reynolds.'

'The what of Letitia?' asked MacDunlap, vaguely suspecting an insult.

'Never mind. My life is ruined.' He smiled bravely and choked back the unmanly tears, after the first two had dripped off the end of his nose.

'My poor boy!' The two gripped hands convulsively.

'Caught in a vise by this foul monster,' said Graham.

'Trapped like a German in Russia,' said MacDunlap.

'Victim of an inhuman fiend,' said Graham.

'Exactly,' said MacDunlap. He wrung Graham's hand as if he were milking a cow. 'You've got to write de Meister stories and get him back where, next to Hell, he most belongs. Right?'

'Right! But there's one little catch.'

'What?'

'I can't write. He's so real now, I *can't* put him into a book.'

MacDunlap caught the significance of the massed drifts of used paper on the floor. He held his head and groaned, 'My corporation! My wife!'

'There's always the Army,' said Graham.

MacDunlap looked up. 'What about *Death on the Third Deck*, the novel I rejected three weeks ago?'

'That doesn't count. It's past history. It's already affected him.'

'Without being published?'

'Sure. That's the story I mentioned his draft board in. The one that put him in 1-A.'

'I could think of better places to put him.'

'MacDunlap!' Graham Dorn jumped up, and grappled Mac-

Dunlap's lapel. 'Maybe it can be revised.'

MacDunlap coughed hackingly, and stifled out a dim grunt.

'We can put anything we want into it.'

MacDunlap choked a bit.

'We can fix things up.'

MacDunlap turned blue in the face.

Graham shook the lapel and everything thereto attached, 'Say something, won't you?'

MacDunlap wrenched away and took a tablespoon of cough syrup. He held his hand over his heart and patted it a bit. He shook his head and gestured with his eyebrows.

Graham shrugged. 'Well, if you just want to be sullen, go ahead. I'll revise it without you.'

He located the manuscript and tried his fingers gingerly on the typewriter. They went smoothly, with practically no creaking at the joints. He put on speed, more speed, and then went into his usual race, with the portable jouncing along merrily under the accustomed head of steam.

'It's working,' he shouted. 'I can't write new stories, but I can revise old, unpublished ones.'

MacDunlap watched over his shoulder. He breathed only at odd moments.

'Faster,' said MacDunlap, 'faster!'

'Faster than thirty-five?' said Graham, sternly. 'OPA* forbid! Five more minutes.'

'Will he be there?'

'He's always there. He's been at her house every evening this week.' He spat out the fine ivory dust into which he had ground the last inch of his incisors. 'But God help you if your secretary falls down on the job.'

'My boy, on my secretary you can depend.'

'She's got to read that revision by nine.'

'If she doesn't drop dead.'

'With my luck, she will. Will she believe it?'

'Every word. She's seen de Meister. She *knows* he exists.'

Brakes screeched, and Graham's soul cringed in sympathy with every molecule of rubber frictioned off the tires.

He bounded up the stairs, MacDunlap hobbling after.

He rang the bell and burst in at the door. Reginald de

* The Office of Price Administration was in charge of gasoline rationing at this period. Remember 'A' stickers? D.R.B.

Meister standing directly inside received the full impact of a pointing finger, and only a rapid backward movement of the head kept him from becoming a one-eyed mythical character.

June Billings stood aside, silent and uncomfortable.

'Reginald de Meister,' growled Graham, in sinister tones, 'prepare to meet your doom.'

'Oh, boy,' said MacDunlap, 'are you going to get it.'

'And to what,' asked de Meister, 'am I indebted for your dramatic but unilluminatin' statement? Confusin', don't you know.' He lit a cigarette with a fine gesture and smiled.

'Hello, Gramie,' said June, tearfully.

'Scram, vile woman.'

June sniffed. She felt like a heroine out of a book, torn by her own emotions. Naturally, she was having the time of her life.

So she let the tears dribble and looked forlorn.

'To return to the subject, what is this all about?' asked de Meister, wearily.

'I have rewritten *Death on the Third Deck*.'

'Well?'

'The revision,' continued Graham, 'is at present in the hands of MacDunlap's secretary, a girl on the style of Miss Billings, my fiancée that was. That is, she is a girl who aspires to the status of a moron, but has not yet quite attained it. She'll believe every word.'

'Well?'

Graham's voice grew ominous, 'You remember, perhaps, Sancha Rodriguez?'

For the first time, Reginald de Meister shuddered. He caught his cigarette as it dropped. 'She was killed by Sam Blake in the sixth chapter. She was in love with me. Really, old fellow, what messes you get me into.'

'Not half the mess you're in now, old chap. Sancha Rodriguez did *not* die in the revision.'

'Die!' came a sharp, but clear female voice. 'I'll show him if I died. And where have *you* been this last month, you two-crosser?'

De Meister did not catch his cigarette this time. He didn't even try. He recognized the apparition. To an unprejudiced observer, it might have been merely a svelte Latin girl equipped with dark, flashing eyes, and long, glittering fingernails, but to de Meister, it was Sancha Rodriguez – *undead!*

MacDunlap's secretary had read and believed.

'Miss Rodriguez,' throbbed de Meister, charmingly, 'how fascinatin' to see you.'

'Mrs. de Meister to you, you double-timer, you two-crosser, you scum of the ground, you scorpion of the grass. And who is this woman?'

June retreated with dignity behind the nearest chair.

'*Mrs.* de Meister,' said Reginald pleadingly, and turned helplessly to Graham Dorn.

'Oh, you have forgotten, have you, you smooth talker, you low dog. I'll show you what it means to deceive a weak woman. I'll make you mince-meat with my fingernails.'

De Meister back-pedaled furiously. 'But darling —'

'Don't you make sweet talk. What are you doing with this woman?'

'But, darling —'

'Don't give me any explanation. What are you doing with this woman?'

'But darling —'

'Shut up! What are you doing with this woman?'

Reginald de Meister was up in a corner, and Mrs. de Meister shook her fists at him. 'Answer me!'

De Meister disappeared.

Mrs. de Meister disappeared right after him.

June Billings collapsed into real tears.

Graham Dorn folded his arms and looked sternly at her.

MacDunlap rubbed his hands and took a kidney pill.

'It wasn't my fault, Gramie,' said June. 'You said in your books he fascinated all women, so I couldn't help it. Deep inside, I hated him all along. You believe me, don't you?'

'A likely story!' said Graham, sitting down next to her on the sofa. 'A likely story. But I forgive you, maybe.'

MacDunlap said tremulously, 'My boy, you have saved my stocks. Also, my wife, of course. And remember – you promised me one de Meister story each year.'

Graham gritted, 'Just one, and I'll henpeck him to death, and keep one unpublished story forever on hand, just in case. And you're publishing my novel, aren't you, Grew, old boy?'

'Glug,' said MacDunlap.

'Aren't you?'

'Yes, Graham. Of course, Graham. Definitely, Graham. Positively, Graham.'

'Then leave us now. There are matters of importance I must discuss with my fiancée.'

MacDunlap smiled and tiptoed out the door.

Ah, love, love, he mused, as he took a liver pill and followed it up by a cough-syrup chaser.

THE END

I might make two points about 'Author! Author!' It seems to me that I was rather easier about handling romance in this story than in any previous one. Perhaps this is a reflection of the fact that it was the first story I ever wrote as a married man.

Secondly, there are the very dated references to rationing, the draft, and other social phenomena much on the mind of anyone living through World War II. I had warned Bensen of the existence of these references and of the inability of getting them out of the story by revision since they were integral to the plot. Bensen, however, shrugged them off and in his short introduction to the story said to the readers, 'And don't worry about the references to the OPA and Selective Service – consider them as part of the historical setting, just as you would a bodkin or a furbelow in a story of an earlier time.'

And I second that statement here.

Had I rested on the pink cloud of gratification that came with the sale of 'Author! Author!' for a few months, the death of *Unknown* might have disheartened me. It might have seemed to prove that I was not fated to reignite my career after all, and perhaps – again – everything would have turned out differently.

However, within three weeks of the sale I was at the typewriter again. The new story was 'Death Sentence' and it was science fiction. Writing was still slow work; seven weeks to do a 7,200-word story. On June 29, 1943, however, I sent it off to Campbell, and on July 8, it was accepted – one and a quarter cents per word again.

This meant that when the news of *Unknown*'s demise arrived, it was cushioned by the fact that I already had another story written and sold.

Brand Gorla smiled uncomfortably, 'These things exaggerate, you know.'

'No, no, no!' The little man's albino-pink eyes snapped. 'Dorlis was great when no human had ever entered the Vegan System. It was the capital of a Galactic Confederation greater than ours.'

'Well, then, let's say it was an ancient capital. I'll admit that and leave the rest to an archaeologist.'

'Archaeologists are no use. What I've discovered needs a specialist in its own field. And you're on the Board.'

Brand Gorla looked doubtful. He remembered Theo Realo in senior year – a little white misfit of a human who skulked somewhere in the background of his reminiscences. It had been a long time ago, but the albino had been queer. *That* was easy to remember. And he was still queer.

'I'll try to help,' Brand said, 'if you'll tell me what you want.'

Theor watched intently, 'I want you to place certain facts before the Board. Will you promise that?'

Brand hedged, 'Even if I help you along, Theor, I'll have to remind you that I'm junior member of the Psychological Board. I haven't much influence.'

'You must do your best. The facts will speak for themselves.' The albino's hands were trembling.

'Go ahead.' Brand resigned himself. The man was an old school fellow. You couldn't be *too* arbitrary about things.

Brand Gorla leaned back and relaxed. The light of Arcturus shone through the ceiling-high windows, diffused and mellowed by the polarizing glass. Even this diluted version of sunlight was too much for the pink eyes of the other, and he shaded his eyes as he spoke.

'I've lived on Dorlis twenty-five years, Brand,' he said, 'I've poked into places no one today knew existed, and I've found things. Dorlis was the scientific and cultural capital of a civilization greater than ours. Yes it was, and particularly in psychology.'

Astounding Science Fiction, November 1943
Copyright © 1943 by Street and Smith Publications, Inc.
Copyright renewed © 1970 by Isaac Asimov

'Things in the past always seem greater.' Brand condescended a smile. 'There is a theorem to that effect which you'll find in any elementary text. Freshmen invariably call it the 'GOD Theorem.' Stands for "Good-Old-Days," you know. But go on.'

Theor frowned at the digression. He hid the beginning of a sneer, 'You can always dismiss an uncomfortable fact by pinning a dowdy label to it. But tell me this. What do you know of Psychological Engineering?'

Brand shrugged, 'No such thing. Anyway, not in the strict mathematical sense. All propaganda and advertising is a crude form of hit-and-miss Psych Engineering – and pretty effective sometimes. Maybe that's what you mean.'

'Not at all. I mean actual experimentation, with masses of people, under controlled conditions, and over a period of years.'

'Such things have been discussed. It's not feasible in practice. Our social structure couldn't stand much of it, and we don't know enough to set up effective controls.'

Theor suppressed excitement, 'But the ancients *did* know enough. And they *did* set up controls.'

Brand considered phlegmatically, 'Startling and interesting, but how do you know?'

'Because I found the documents relating to it.' He paused breathlessly. 'An entire planet, Brand. A complete world picked to suit, peopled with beings under strict control from every angle. Studied, and charted, and experimented upon. Don't you get the picture?'

Brand noted none of the usual stigmata of mental uncontrol. A closer investigation, perhaps —

He said evenly, 'You must have been misled. It's thoroughly impossible. You can't control humans like that. Too many variables.'

'And that's the point, Brand. They weren't humans.'

'What?'

'They were robots, positronic robots. A whole world of them, Brand, with nothing to do but live and react and be observed by a set of psychologists that were *real* psychologists.'

'That's mad!'

'I have proof – because that robot world still exists. The First Confederation went to pieces, but that robot world kept on going. It still exists.'

'And how do you know?'

Theor Realo stood up. 'Because I've been there these last twenty-five years!'

The Board Master threw his formal red-edged gown aside and reached into a pocket for a long, gnarled and decidedly unofficial cigar.

'Preposterous,' he grunted, 'and thoroughly insane.'

'Exactly,' said Brand, 'and I can't spring it on the Board just like that. They wouldn't listen. I've got to get this across to you first, and then, if you can put your authority behind it —'

'Oh, nuts? I never heard anything as — Who is the fellow?'

Brand sighed, 'A crank, I'll admit that. He was in my class at Arcturus U. and a crack-pot albino even then. Maladjusted as the devil, hipped on ancient history, and just the kind that gets an idea and goes through with it by plain, dumb plugging. He's poked about in Dorlis for twenty-five years, he says. He's got the complete records of practically an entire civilization.'

The Board Master puffed furiously. 'Yeah, I know. In the telestat serials, the brilliant amateur always uncovers the great things. The free lance. The lone wolf. Nuts! Have you consulted the Department of Archaeology?'

'Certainly. And the result was interesting. No one bothers with Dorlis. This isn't just ancient history, you see. It's a matter of fifteen thousand years. It's practically myth. Reputable archaeologists don't waste too much time with it. It's just the thing a book-struck layman with a single-track mind *would* uncover. After this, of course, if the business turns out right, Dorlis will become an archaeologist's paradise.'

The Board Master screwed his homely face into an appalling grimace. 'It's very unflattering to the ego. If there's any truth in all this, the so-called First Confederation must have had a grasp of psychology so far past ours, as to make us out to be blithering imbeciles. Too, they'd have to build positronic robots that would be about seventy-five orders of magnitude above anything we've even blueprinted. Galaxy! Think of the mathematics involved.'

'Look, sir, I've consulted just about everybody. I wouldn't bring this thing to you if I weren't certain that I had every angle checked. I went to Blak just about the first thing, and he's consultant mathematician to United Robots. He says there's no limit to these things. Given the time, the money, and the *advance in psychology* – get that – robots like that could be built right now.'

'What proof has he?'

'Who, Blak?'

'No, no! Your friend. The albino. You said he had papers.'

'He has. I've got them here. He's got documents – and there's no denying their antiquity. I've had that checked every way from Sunday. I can't read them, of course. I don't know if anyone can, except Theor Realo.'

'That's stacking the deck, isn't it? We have to take his say-so.'

'Yes, in a way. But he doesn't claim to be able to decipher more than portions. He says it is related to ancient Centaurian, and I've put linguists to work on it. It can be cracked and if his translation isn't accurate, we'll know about it.'

'All right. Let's see it.'

Brand Gorla brought out the plastic-mounted documents. The Board Master tossed them aside and reached for the translation. Smoke billowed as he read.

'Humph,' was his comment. 'Further details are on Dorlis, I suppose.'

'Theor claims that there are some hundred to two hundred tons of blueprints altogether, on the brain plan of the positronic robots alone. They're still there in the original vault. But that's the least of it. He's been on the robot world itself. He's got photocasts, teletype recordings, all sorts of details. They're not integrated, and obviously the work of a layman who knows next to nothing about psychology. Even so, he's managed to get enough data to prove pretty conclusively that the world he was on wasn't . . . uh . . . natural.'

'You've got that with you, too.'

'All of it. Most of it's on microfilm, but I've brought the projector. Here are your eyepieces.'

An hour later, the Board Master said, 'I'll call a Board Meeting tomorrow and push this through.'

Brand Gorla grinned tightly, 'We'll send a commission to Dorlis?'

'When,' said the Board Master dryly, 'and if we can get an appropriation out of the University for such an affair. Leave this material with me for the while, please. I want to study it a little more.'

*

Theoretically, the Governmental Department of Science and Technology exercises administrative control over all scientific investigation. Actually, however, the pure research groups of the large universities are thoroughly autonomous bodies, and, as a general rule, the Government does not care to dispute that. But a general rule is not necessarily a universal rule.

And so, although the Board Master scowled and fumed and swore, there was no way of refusing Wynne Murry an interview. To give Murry his complete title, he was under secretary in charge of psychology, psychopathy and mental technology. And he was a pretty fair psychologist in his own right.

So the Board Master might glare, but that was all.

Secretary Murry ignored the glare cheerfully. He rubbed his long chin against the grain and said, 'It amounts to a case of insufficient information. Shall we put it that way?'

The Board Master said frigidly, 'I don't see what information you want. The government's say in university appropriations is purely advisory, and in this case, I might say, the advice is unwelcome.'

Murry shrugged, 'I have no quarrel with the appropriation. But you're not going to leave the planet without government permit. That's where the insufficient information comes in.'

'There is no information other than we've given you.'

'But things have leaked out. All this is childish and rather unnecessary secrecy.'

The old psychologist flushed. 'Secrecy! If you don't know the academic way of life, I can't help you. Investigations, especially those of major importance, aren't, and can't be, made public, until definite progress has been made. When we get back, we'll send you copies of whatever papers we publish.'

Murry shook his head, 'Uh-uh. Not enough. You're going to Dorlis, aren't you?'

'We've informed the Department of Science of that.'

'Why?'

'Why do you want to know?'

'Because it's big, or the Board Master wouldn't go himself. What's this about an older civilization and a world of robots?'

'Well, then, you know.'

'Only vague notions we've been able to scrabble up. I want the details.'

'There are none that we know now. We won't know until

49

we're on Dorlis.'

'Then I'm going with you.'

'What!'

'You see, I want the details, too.'

'Why?'

'Ah,' Murry unfolded his legs and stood up, 'now *you're* asking the questions. It's no use, now. I know that the universities aren't keen on government supervision; and I know that I can expect no willing help from *any* academic source. But, by Arcturus, I'm going to get help this time, and I don't care how you fight it. Your expedition is going nowhere, unless I go with you – representing the government.'

Dorlis, as a world, is not impressive. It's importance to Galactic economy is nil, its position far off the great trade routes, its natives backward and unenlightened, its history obscure. And yet somewhere in the heaps of rubble that clutter an ancient world, there is obscure evidence of an influx of flame and destruction that destroyed the Dorlis of an earlier day – the greater capital of a greater Federation.

And somewhere in that rubble, men of a newer world poked and probed and tried to understand.

The Board Master shook his head and then pushed back his grizzling hair. He hadn't shaved in a week.

'The trouble is,' he said, 'that we have no point of reference. The language can be broken, I suppose, but nothing can be done with the notation.'

'I think a great deal has been done.'

'Stabs in the dark! Guessing games based on the translations of your albino friend. I won't base any hopes on that.'

Brand said, 'Nuts! You spent two years on the Nimian Anomaly, and so far only two months on this, which happens to be a hundred thousand times the job. It's something else that's getting you.' He smiled grimly. 'It doesn't take a psychologist to see that the government man is in your hair.'

The Board Master bit the end off a cigar and spat it four feet. He said slowly, 'There are three things about the mule-headed idiot that make me sore. First, I don't like government interference. Second, I don't like a stranger sniffing about when we're on top of the biggest thing in the history of psychology. Third, what in the Galaxy does he want? *What is he after?*'

'I don't know.'

'What *should* he be after? Have you thought of it at all?'

'No. Frankly, I don't care. I'd ignore him if I were you.'

'You would,' said the Board Master violently. 'You would! You think the government's entrance into this affair need only be ignored. I suppose you know that this Murry calls himself a psychologist?'

'I know that.'

'And I suppose you know he's been displaying a devouring interest in all that we've been doing.'

'That, I should say, would be natural.'

'Oh! And you know further —' His voice dropped with startling suddenness. 'All right, Murry's at the door. Take it easy.'

Wynne Murry grinned a greeting, but the Board Master nodded unsmilingly.

'Well, sir,' said Murry bluffly, 'do you know I've been on my feet for forty-eight hours? You've *got* something here. Something big.'

'Thank you.'

'No, no. I'm serious. The robot world exists.'

'Did you think it didn't?'

The secretary shrugged amiably. 'One has a certain natural skepticism. What are your future plans?'

'Why do you ask?' The Board Master grunted his words as if they were being squeezed out singly.

'To see if they jibe with my own.'

'And what are your own?'

The secretary smiled. 'No, no. You take precedence. How long do you intend staying here?'

'As long as it takes to make a fair beginning on the documents involved.'

'That's no answer. What do you mean by a fair beginning?'

'I haven't the slightest idea. It might take years.'

'Oh, damnation.'

The Board Master raised his eyebrows and said nothing.

The secretary looked at his nails. 'I take it you know the location of this robot world.'

'Naturally. Theor Realo was there. His information up to now has proven very accurate.'

'That's right. The albino. Well, why not go there?'

'Go there! Impossible!'

'May I ask why?'

'Look,' said the Board Master with restrained impatience, 'you're not here by our invitation, and we're not asking you to dictate our course of actions, but just to show you that I'm not looking for a fight, I'll give you a little metaphorical treatment of our case. Suppose we were presented with a huge and complicated machine, composed of principles and materials of which we knew next to nothing. It is so vast we can't even make out the relationship of the parts, let alone the purpose of the whole. Now, would you advise me to begin attacking the delicate mysterious moving parts of the machine with a detonating ray before I know what it's all about?'

'I see your point, of course, but you're becoming a mystic. The metaphor is farfetched.'

'Not at all. These positronic robots were constructed along lines we know nothing of as yet and were intended to follow lines with which we are entirely unacquainted. About the only thing we know is that the robots were put aside in complete isolation, to work out their destiny by themselves. To ruin that isolation would be to ruin the experiment. If we go there in a body, introducing new, unforeseen factors, inducing unintended reactions, everything is ruined. The littlest disturbance —'

'Poppycock! Theor Realo has already gone there.'

The Board Master lost his temper suddenly. 'Don't you suppose I know that? Do you suppose it would ever have happened if that cursed albino hadn't been an ignorant fanatic without any knowledge of psychology at all? Galaxy knows what the idiot has done in the way of damage.'

There was a silence. The secretary clicked his teeth with a thoughtful fingernail. 'I don't know. . . . I don't know. But I've got to find out. And I can't wait years.'

He left, and the Board Master turned seethingly to Brand, 'And how are we going to stop him from going to the robot world if he wants to?'

'I don't see how he can go if we don't let him. *He* doesn't head the expedition.'

'Oh, doesn't he? *That's* what I was about to tell you just before he came in. Ten ships of the fleet have landed on Dorlis since we arrived.'

'*What!*'

'Just that.'

'But what for?'

'That, my boy, is what I don't understand, either.'

'Mind if I drop in?' said Wynne Murry, pleasantly, and Theor Realo looked up in sudden anxiety from the papers that lay in hopeless disarray on the desk before him.

'Come in. I'll clear off a seat for you.' The albino hustled the mess off one of the two chairs in a state of twittering nerves.

Murry sat down and swung one long leg over the other. 'Are you assigned a job here, too?' He nodded at the desk.

Theor shook his head and smiled feebly. Almost automatically, he brushed the papers together in a heap and turned them face down.

In the months since he had returned to Dorlis with a hundred psychologists of various degrees of renown. he had felt himself pushed farther and farther from the center of things. There was room for him no longer. Except to answer questions on the actual state of things upon the robot world, which he alone had visited, he played no part. And even there he detected, or seemed to detect, anger that *he* should have gone, and not a competent scientist.

It was a thing to be resented. Yet, somehow, it had always been like that.

'Pardon me?' He had let Murry's next remark slip.

The secretary repeated, 'I say it's surprising you're *not* put to work, then. You made the original discovery, didn't you?'

'Yes,' the albino brightened. 'But it went out of my hands. It got beyond me.'

'You were on the robot world, though.'

'That was a mistake, they tell me. I might have ruined everything.'

Murry grimaced. 'What really gets them, I guess, is that you've got a lot of first-hand dope that they didn't. Don't let their fancy titles fool you into thinking you're a nobody. A layman with common sense is better than a blind specialist. You and I – I'm a layman, too, you know – have to stand up for our rights. Here, have a cigarette.'

'I don't sm — I'll take one, thank you.' The albino felt himself warming to the long-bodied man opposite. He turned the papers face upward again, and lit up, bravely but uncertainly.

'Twenty-five years.' Theor spoke carefully, skirting around urgent coughs.

'Would you answer a few questions about the world?'

'I suppose so. That's all they ever ask me about. But hadn't you better ask *them*? They've probably got it all worked out now.' He blew the smoke as far from himself as possible.

Murry said, 'Frankly, they haven't even begun, and I want the information without benefit of confusing psychological translation. First of all, what kind of people – or things – are these robots? You haven't a photocast of one of them, have you?'

'Well, no. I didn't like to take 'casts of them. But they're not things. They're *people*!'

'No? Do they look like – people?'

'Yes – mostly. Outside, anyway. I brought some microscopic studies of the cellular structure that I got hold of. The Board Master has them. They're different inside, you know, greatly simplified. But you'd never know that. They're interesting – and nice.'

'Are they simpler than the other life of the planet?'

'Oh, no. It's a very primitive planet. And ... and,' he was interrupted by a spasm of coughing and crushed the cigarette to death as unobtrusively as possible. 'They've got a protoplasmic base, you know. I don't think they have the slightest idea they're robots.'

'No. I don't suppose they would have. What about their science?'

'I don't know. I never got a chance to see. And everything was so different. I guess it would take an expert to understand.'

'Did they have machines?'

The albino looked surprised. 'Well, of course. A good many, of all sorts.'

'Large cities?'

'Yes!'

The secretary's eyes grew thoughtful. 'And you like them. Why?'

Theor Realo was brought up sharply. 'I don't know. They were just likable. We got along. They didn't bother me so. It's nothing I can put my finger on. Maybe it's because I have it so hard getting along back home, and they weren't as difficult as real people.'

'They were more friendly?'

'N-no. Can't say so. They never quite accepted me. I was a stranger, didn't know their language at first – all that. But' – he looked up with sudden brightness – 'I understood them better. I could tell what they were thinking better. I — But I don't know why.'

'Hm-m-m. Well – another cigarette? No? I've got to be walloping the pillow now. It's getting late. How about a twosome at golf tomorrow? I've worked up a little course. It'll do. Come on out. The exercise will put hair on your chest.'

He grinned and left.

He mumbled one sentence to himself: 'It looks like a death sentence' – and whistled thoughtfully as he passed along to his own quarters.

He repeated the phrase to himself when he faced the Board Master the next day, with the sash of office about his waist. He did not sit down.

'Again?' said the Board Master, wearily.

'Again!' assented the secretary. 'But real business this time. I may have to take over direction of your expedition.'

'What! Impossible, sir! I will listen to no such proposition.'

'I have my authority.' Wynne Murry presented the metalloid cylinder that snapped open at a flick of the thumb. 'I have full powers and full discretion as to their use. It is signed, as you will observe, by the chairman of the Congress of the Federation.'

'So — But why?' The Board Master, by an effort, breathed normally. 'Short of arbitrary tyranny, is there a reason?'

'A very good one, sir. All along, we have viewed this expedition from different angles. The Department of Science and Technology views the robot world not from the point of view of a scientific curiosity, but from the standpoint of its interference with the peace of the Federation. I don't think you've ever stopped to consider the danger inherent in this robot world.'

'None that I can see. It is thoroughly isolated and thoroughly harmless.'

'How can you know?'

'From the very nature of the experiment,' shouted the Board Master angrily. 'The original planners wanted as nearly a completely closed system as possible. Here they are, just as far off the trade routes as possible, in a thinly populated region of space. The whole idea was to have the robots develop free of interference.'

Murry smiled. 'I disagree with you there. Look, the whole trouble with you is that you're a theoretical man. You look at things the way they ought to be and I, a practical man, look at things as they are. No experiment can be set up and allowed to run indefinitely under its own power. It is taken for granted that somewhere there is at least an observer who watches and *modifies* as circumstances warrant.'

'Well?' said the Board Master stolidly.

'Well, the observers in this experiment, the original psychologists of Dorlis, passed away with the First Confederation, and for fifteen thousand years the experiment has proceeded by itself. Little errors have added up and become big ones and introduced alien factors which induced still other errors. It's a geometric progression. And there's been no one to halt it.'

'Pure hypothesis.'

'Maybe. But you're interested only in the robot world, and I've got to think of the entire Federation.'

'And just what possible danger can the robot world be to the Federation? I don't know *what* in Arcturus you're driving at, man.'

Murry sighed. 'I'll be simple, but don't blame me if I sound melodramatic. The Federation hasn't had any internal warfare for centuries. What will happen if we come into contact with these robots?'

'Are you afraid of one world?'

'Could be. What about their science? Robots can do funny things sometimes.'

'What science can they have? They're not metal-electricity supermen. They're weak protoplasmic creatures, a poor imitation of actual humanity, built around a positronic brain adjusted to a set of simplified human psychological laws. If the word "robot" is scaring you —'

'No, it isn't, but I've talked to Theor Realo. He's the only one who's seen them, you know.'

The Board Master cursed silently and fluently. It came of letting a weak-minded freak of a layman get underfoot where he could babble and do harm.

He said, 'We've got Realo's full story, and we've evaluated it fully and capably. I assure you, no harm exists in them. The experiment is so thoroughly academic, I wouldn't spend two days on it if it weren't for the broad scope of the thing. From what we see, the whole idea was to build up a positronic brain containing modifications of one or two of the fundamental axioms. We haven't worked out the details, but they must be minor, as it was the first experiment of this nature ever tried, and even the great mythical psychologists of that day had to progress stepwise. Those robots, I tell you, are neither supermen nor beasts. I assure you – as a psychologist.'

'Sorry! I'm a psychologist, too. A little more rule-of-thumb, I'm afraid. That's all. But even little modifications! Take the general spirit of combativeness. That isn't the scientific term, but I've no patience for that. You know what I mean. We humans used to be combative. But it's being bred out of us. A stable political and economic system doesn't encourage the waste energy of combat. It's not a survival factor. But suppose the robots are combative. Suppose as the result of a wrong turn during the millennia they've been unwatched, they've become far more combative than ever their first makers intended. They'd be uncomfortable things to be with.'

'And suppose all the stars in the Galaxy became novae at the same time. Let's *really* start worrying.'

'And there's another point.' Murry ignored the other's heavy sarcasm. 'Theor Realo liked those robots. He liked robots better than he likes real people. He felt that he fitted there, and we all know he's been a bad misfit in his own world.'

'And what,' asked the Board Master, 'is the significance of that?'

'You don't see it?' Wynne Murry lifted his eyebrows. 'Theor Realo likes those robots because he is *like* them, obviously. I'll guarantee right now that a complete psychic analysis of Theor Realo will show a modification of several fundamental axioms, and the same ones as in the robots.

'And,' the secretary drove on without a pause, 'Theor Realo worked for a quarter of a century to prove a point, when all science would have laughed him to death if they had known about it. There's fanaticism there; good, honest, *inhuman* perseverance. *Those robots are probably like that!*'

'You're advancing no logic. You're arguing like a maniac, like a moon-struck idiot.'

'I don't need strict mathematical proof. Reasonable doubt is sufficient. I've got to protect the Federation. Look, it *is* reasonable, you know. The psychologists of Dorlis weren't as super as all that. They had to advance stepwise, as you yourself pointed out. Their humanoids – let's not call them robots – were only imitations of human beings and they could be good ones. Humans possess certain very, *very* complicated reaction systems – things like social consciousness, and a tendency toward the establishment of ethical systems; and more ordinary things like chivalry, generosity, fair play and so on, that simply can't possibly be duplicated. I don't think those humanoids can have them. But they *must* have perseverance, which practically implies stubbornness and combativeness, if my notion on Theor Realo holds good. Well, if their science is anywhere at all, then I don't want to have them running loose in the Galaxy, if our numbers are a thousand or million times theirs. And I don't intend to permit them to do so!'

The Board Master's face was rigid. 'What are your immediate intentions?'

'As yet undecided. But I think I am going to organize a small-scale landing on the planet.'

'Now, wait.' The old psychologist was up and around the desk. He seized the secretary's elbow. 'Are you quite certain you know what you're doing? The potentialities in this massive experiment are beyond any possible precalculation by you or me. You can't know what you're destroying.'

'I know. Do you think I enjoy what I'm doing? This isn't a hero's job. I'm enough of a psychologist to want to know what's going on, but I've been sent here to protect the Federation, and to the best of my ability I intend doing it – and a dirty job it is. But I can't help it.'

'You can't have thought it out. What can you know of the insight it will give us into the basic ideas of psychology? This will amount to a fusion of two Galactic systems, that will send us to heights that will make up in knowledge and power a million times the amount of harm the robots could ever do, if they *were* metal-electricity supermen.'

The secretary shrugged. 'Now you're the one that is playing with faint possibilities.'

'Listen, I'll make a deal. Blockade them. Isolate them with your ships. Mount guards. But don't touch them. Give us more time. Give us a chance. You must!'

'I've thought of that. But I would have to get Congress to agree to that. It would be expensive, you know.'

The Board Master flung himself into his chair in wild impatience. 'What kind of expense are you talking about? Do you realize the nature of the repayment if we succeed?'

Murry considered; then, with a half smile, 'What if they develop interstellar travel?'

The Board Master said quickly, 'Then I'll withdraw my objections.'

The secretary rose, 'I'll have it out with Congress.'

Brand Gorla's face was carefully emotionless as he watched the Board Master's stooped back. The cheerful pep talks to the available members of the expedition lacked meat, and he listened to them impatiently.

He said, 'What are we going to do now?'

The Board Master's shoulders twitched and he didn't turn. 'I've sent for Theor Realo. That little fool left for the Eastern Continent last week —'

'Why?'

The older man blazed at the interruption. 'How can I understand anything that freak does! Don't you see that Murry's right? He's a psychic abnormality. We had no business leaving him unwatched. If I had ever thought of looking at him twice, I wouldn't have. He's coming back now, though, and he's going to stay back.' His voice fell to a mumble. 'Should have been back two hours ago.'

'It's an impossible position, sir,' said Brand, flatly.

'Think so?'

'Well — Do *you* think Congress will stand for an indefinite patrol off the robot world? It runs into money, and average Galactic citizens aren't going to see it as worth the taxes. The psychological equations degenerate into the axioms of common sense. In fact, I don't see why Murry agreed to consult Congress.'

'Don't you?' The Board Master finally faced his junior. 'Well, the fool considers himself a psychologist, Galaxy help us, and that's his weak point. He flatters himself that he doesn't want to destroy the robot world in his heart, but that it's the good of the Federation that requires it. And he'll jump at any reasonable compromise. Congress won't agree to it indefinitely, you don't have to point that out to me.' He was talking quietly, patiently. 'But I will ask for ten years, two years, six months – as much as I can get. I'll get something. In that time, we'll learn new facts about the world. Somehow we'll strengthen our case and renew the agreement when it expires. We'll save the

59

project yet.'

There was a short silence and the Board Master added slowly and bitterly, 'And that's where Theor Realo plays a vital part.'

Brand Gorla watched silently, and waited. The Board Master said, 'On that one point, Murry saw what we didn't. Realo is a psychological cripple, and is our real clue to the whole affair. If we study him, we'll have a rough picture of what the robot is like, distorted of course, since his environment has been a hostile, unfriendly one. But we can make allowance for that, estimate his nature in a — Ahh, I'm tired of the whole subject.'

The signal box flashed, and the Board Master sighed. 'Well, he's here. All right, Gorla, sit down, you make me nervous. Let's take a look at him.'

Theor Realo came through the door like a comet and brought himself to a panting halt in the middle of the floor. He looked from one to the other with weak, peering eyes.

'How did all this happen?'

'All what?' said the Board Master coldly. 'Sit down. I want to ask you some questions.'

'No. You first answer *me*.'

'*Sit down!*'

Realo sat. His eyes were brimming. 'They're going to destroy the robot world.'

'Don't worry about that.'

'But you said they could if the robots discovered interstellar travel. You said so. You fool. Don't you see —' He was choking.

The Board Master frowned uneasily. 'Will you calm down and talk sense?'

The albino gritted his teeth and forced the words out. 'But they'll *have* interstellar travel before long.'

And the two psychologists shot toward the little man.

'What!!'

'Well ... well, what do you think?' Realo sprang upward with all the fury of desperation. 'Did you think I landed in a desert or in the middle of an ocean and explored a world all by myself? Do you think life is a storybook? I was captured as soon as I landed and taken to the big city. At least, I think it was a big city. It was different from our kind. It had — But I won't tell you.'

'Never mind the city,' shrieked the Board Master. 'You were captured. Go ahead.'

'They studied *me*. They studied my machine. And then, one night, I left, to tell the Federation. They didn't know I left. They didn't want me to leave.' His voice broke. 'And I would have stayed as soon as not, but the Federation had to know.'

'Did you tell them anything about your ship?'

'How could I? I'm no mechanic. I don't know the theory or construction. But I showed them how to work the controls and let them look at the motors. That's all.'

Brand Gorla said, to himself mostly, 'Then they'll never get it. That isn't enough.'

The albino's voice raised itself in sudden shrieking triumph. 'Oh, yes, they will. I know them. They're machines, you know. They'll work on that problem. And they'll work. And they'll work. And they'll never quit. And they'll get it. They got enough out of me. I'll *bet* they got enough.'

The Board Master looked long, and turned away – wearily. 'Why didn't you tell us?'

'Because you took my world away from me. I discovered it – by myself – all by myself. And after I had done all the real work, and invited you in, you threw me out. All you had for me was complaints that I had landed on the world and might have ruined everything by interference. Why should I tell you? Find out for yourselves if you're so wise, that you could afford to kick me around.'

The Board Master thought bitterly, 'Misfit! Inferiority complex! Persecution mania! Nice! It all fits in, now that we've bothered to take our eyes off the horizon and see what was under our nose. And now it's all ruined.'

He said, 'All right, Realo, we all lose. Go away.'

Brand Gorla said tightly, 'All over? Really all over?'

The Board Master answered, 'Really all over. The original experiment, as such, is over. The distortions created by Realo's visit will easily be large enough to make the plans we are studying here a dead language. And besides – Murry is right. If they have interstellar travel, they're dangerous.'

Realo was shouting, 'But you're not going to destroy them. You can't destroy them. They haven't hurt anyone.'

There was no answer, and he raved on, 'I'm going back. I'll warn them. They'll be prepared. I'll warn them.'

He was backing toward the door, his thin, white hair bristling, his red-rimmed eyes bulging.

The Board Master did not move to stop him when he dashed out.

'Let him go. It was *his* lifetime. I don't care any more.'

Theor Realo smashed toward the robot world at an acceleration that was half choking him.

Somewhere ahead was the dustspeck of an isolated world with artificial imitations of humanity struggling along in an experiment that had died. Struggling blindly toward a new goal of interstellar travel that was to be their death sentence.

He was heading toward that world, toward the same city in which he had been 'studied' the first time. He remembered it well. Its name was the first words of their language he had learned.

New York!

THE END

On July 26, 1943, which was a Monday, I had one of the rare days off I could take during wartime. (It was, after all, my first wedding anniversary.) I was in New York that day, and I visited Campbell just as in the good old days. I discussed with him another story in the 'Foundation' series, as well as another in the 'positronic robot' series. From then on, I always saw Campbell on the rare days when I was in New York on a weekday, and of course we corresponded regularly.

I was definitely back at writing. Output was low, but during the remaining war years I wrote two positronic robot stories, 'Catch That Rabbit' and 'Paradoxical Escape,' which appeared in the February 1944 and August 1945 issues of *Astounding*, respectively. Both were eventually included in *I, Robot*. (The latter story appears in *I, Robot* under the title of 'Escape.' The word 'Paradoxical' had been added by Campbell in one of his few title changes, and I didn't like it.)

I also wrote no less than four stories of the 'Foundation' series during those same years. These were 'The Big and the Little,' 'The Wedge,' 'Dead Hand' and 'The Mule.' All appeared in *Astounding*, of course, the first three in the August 1944, October 1944, and April 1945 issues, respectively.

'The Mule' set several records for me. It was the longest story I had ever written up to that time – fifty thousand words long. Yet even so, and despite the fact that I had to work on it in small scraps of time left over from job and marriage, I managed to complete it in three and a half months. It was submitted on May 21, 1945, and was accepted on the twenty-ninth. (Indeed, throughout the war I never got a single rejection, or even a delayed acceptance. Nor did I submit to anyone but Campbell.)

What's more, at the beginning of 1944 Campbell raised his basic rate to one and a half cents a word and some months later to a cent and three quarters. For 'The Mule' I received a check at the higher rate, for $875. It was by far the largest check I ever received for a single story. By the end of the war, in fact, I was making half as much money writing in my spare time as I was making at my N.A.E.S. job, even though I had been promoted and was receiving sixty dollars a week by the end of the war.

Then, too, 'The Mule' was the first story I ever had published as a serial. It appeared in two parts in the November and December 1945 issues of *Astounding*.

Of the wartime 'Foundation' stories, 'The Big and the Little' and 'The Wedge' are included in *Foundation*, while 'Dead Hand' and 'The Mule,' together, make up all of *Foundation and Empire*.

During the two years between mid-1943 and mid-1945, I wrote only one story that was neither one of the 'Foundation' series nor one of the 'Positronic robot' series, and that one was inspired directly by the N.A.E.S. This story was 'Blind Alley,' which was written during September and early October of 1944. It was submitted to Campbell on October 10, and accepted on the twentieth.

23 : Blind Alley

Only once in Galactic History was an intelligent race of non-Humans discovered —

'Essays on History,'
by Ligurn Vier

(i)

From: Bureau for the Outer Provinces
To: Loodun Antyok, Chief Public Administrator, A-8

Subject: Civilian Supervisor of Cepheus 18, Administrative Position as,
References:
(a) Act of Council 2515, of the year 971 of the Galactic Empire, entitled, 'Appointment of Officials of the Administrative Service, Methods for, Revision of.'
(b) Imperial Directive, Ja 2374, dated 243/975 G.E.
1. By authorization of reference (a), you are hereby appointed to the subject position. The authority of said position as Civilian Supervisor of Cepheus 18 will extend over non-Human subjects of the Emperor living upon the planet under the terms of autonomy set forth in reference (b).
2. The duties of the subject position shall comprise the general supervision of all non-Human internal affairs, co-ordination of authorized government investigating and reporting committees, and the preparation of semiannual reports on all phases of non-Human affairs.

C. Morily, Chief, BuOuProv,
12/977 G.E.

Loodun Antyok had listened carefully, and now he shook his round head mildly, 'Friend, I'd like to help you, but you've grabbed the wrong dog by the ears. You'd better take this up with the Bureau.'

Tomor Zammo flung himself back into his chair, rubbed his beak of a nose fiercely, thought better of whatever he was

Astounding Science Fiction, March 1945
Copyright © 1945 by Street and Smith Publications, Inc.

going to say, and answered quietly, 'Logical, but not practical. I can't make a trip to Trantor now. You're the Bureau's representative on Cepheus 18. Are you entirely helpless?'

'Well, even as Civilian Supervisor, I've got to work within the limits of Bureau policy.'

'Good,' Zammo cried, 'then, tell me what Bureau policy is. I head a scientific investigating committee, under direct Imperial authorization with, supposedly, the widest powers; yet at every angle in the road I am pulled up short by the civilian authorities with only the parrot shriek of "Bureau policy" to justify themselves. What *is* Bureau policy? I haven't received a decent definition yet.'

Antyok's gaze was level and unruffled. He said, 'As I see it – and this is not official, so you can't hold me to it – Bureau policy consists in treating the non-Humans as decently as possible.'

'Then, what authority have they —'

'*Ssh!* No use raising your voice. As a matter of fact, His Imperial Majesty is a humanitarian and a disciple of the philosophy of Aurelion. I can tell you quietly that it is pretty well-known that it is the Emperor himself who first suggested that this world be established. You can bet that Bureau policy will stick pretty close to Imperial notions. And you can bet that I can't paddle my way against *that* sort of current.'

'Well, m'boy,' the physiologist's fleshy eyelids quivered, 'if you take that sort of attitude, you're going to lose your job. No, I won't have you kicked out. That's not what I mean at all. Your job will just fade out from under you, because nothing is going to be accomplished here!'

'Really? Why?' Antyok was short, pink, and pudgy, and his plump-cheeked face usually found it difficult to put on display any expression other than one of bland and cheerful politeness – but it looked grave now.

'You haven't been here long. I have.' Zammo scowled. 'Mind if I smoke?' The cigar in his hand was gnarled and strong and was puffed to life carelessly.

He continued roughly, 'There's no place here for humanitarianism, administrator. You're treating non-Humans as if they were Humans, and it won't work. In fact, I don't like the word "non-Human." They're animals.'

'They're intelligent,' interjected Antyok, softly.

'Well, intelligent animals, then. I presume the two terms are not mutually exclusive. Alien intelligences mingling in the same space won't work, anyway.'

'Do you propose killing them off?'

'Galaxy, no!' He gestured with his cigar. 'I propose we look upon them as objects for study, and only that. We could learn a good deal from these animals if we were allowed to. Knowledge, I might point out, that would be used for the immediate benefit of the human race. *There's* humanity for you. *There's* the good of the masses, if it's this spineless cult of Aurelion that interests you.'

'What, for instance, do you refer to?'

'To take the most obvious — You have heard of their chemistry, I take it?'

'Yes,' Antyok admitted. 'I have leafed through most of the reports on the non-Humans published in the last ten years. I expect to go through more.'

'Hmp. Well — Then, all I need say is that their chemical therapy is extremely thorough. For instance, I have witnessed personally the healing of a broken bone – what passes for a broken bone with them, I mean – by the use of a pill. The bone was whole in fifteen minutes. Naturally, none of their drugs are any earthly use on Humans. Most would kill quickly. But if we found out how they worked on the non-Humans – on the animals —'

'Yes, yes. I see the significance.'

'Oh, you do. Come, that's gratifying. A second point is that these animals communicate in an unknown manner.'

'Telepathy!'

The scientist's mouth twisted, as he ground out, 'Telepathy! Telepathy! Telepathy! Might as well say by witch brew. Nobody knows anything about telepathy except its name. What is the mechanism of telepathy? What is the physiology and the physics of it? I would like to find out, but I can't. Bureau policy, if I listen to you, forbids.'

Antyok's little mouth pursed itself. 'But — Pardon me, doctor, but I don't follow you. How are you prevented? Surely the Civil Administration has made no attempt to hamper scientific investigation of these non-Humans. I cannot speak for my predecessor entirely, of course, but I myself —'

'No direct interference has occurred. I don't speak of that. But by the Galaxy, administrator, we're hampered by the spirit of the entire set-up. You're making us deal with humans. You allow them their own leader and internal autonomy. You pamper them and give them what Aurelion's philosophy would call "rights." I can't deal with their leader.'

'Why not?'

'Because he refuses to allow me a free hand. He refuses to allow experiments on any subject without the subject's own consent. The two or three volunteers we get are not too bright. It's an impossible arrangement.'

Antyok shrugged helplessly.

Zammo continued, 'In addition, it is obviously impossible to learn anything of value concerning the brains, physiology and chemistry of these animals without dissection, dietary experiments and drugs. You know, administrator, scientific investigation is a hard game. Humanity hasn't much place in it.'

Loodun Antyok tapped his chin with a doubtful finger, 'Must it be quite so hard? These are harmless creatures, these non-Humans. Surely, dissection — Perhaps, if you were to approach them a bit differently – I have the idea that you antagonize them. Your attitude might be somewhat overbearing.'

'Overbearing! I am not one of these whining social psychologists who are all the fad these days. I don't believe you can solve a problem that requires dissection by approaching it with what is called the "correct personal attitude" in the cant of the times.'

'I'm sorry you think so. Sociopsychological training is required of all administrators above the grade of A-4.'

Zammo withdrew his cud of a cigar from his mouth and replaced it after a suitably contemptuous interval. 'Then you'd better use a bit of your technique on the Bureau. You know, I *do* have friends at the Imperial Court.'

'Well, now, I *can't* take the matter up with them, not baldly. Basic policy does not fall within my cognizance, and such things can only be initiated by the Bureau. But, you know, we might try an indirect approach on this.' He smiled faintly, 'Strategy.'

'What sort?'

Antyok pointed a sudden finger, while his other hand fell lightly on the rows of gray-bound reports upon the floor just next his chair, 'Now, look, I've gone through most of these. They're dull, but contain *some* facts. For instance, when was the last non-Human infant born on Cepheus 18?'

Zammo spent little time in consideration. 'Don't know. Don't care either.'

'But the Bureau would. There's *never* been a non-Human infant born on Cepheus 18 – not in the two years the world has been established. Do you know the reason?'

The physiologist shrugged, 'Too many possible factors. It would take study.'

'All right, then. Suppose you write a report —'

'Reports! I've written twenty.'

'Write another. Stress the unsolved problems. Tell them you must change your methods. Harp on the birth-rate problem. The Bureau doesn't dare ignore that. If the non-Humans die out, someone will have to answer to the Emperor. You see —'

Zammo stared, his eyes dark, 'That will swing it?'

'I've been working for the Bureau for twenty-seven years. I know its ways.'

'I'll think about it.' Zammo rose and stalked out of the office. The door slammed behind him.

It was later that Zammo said to a co-worker, 'He's a bureaucrat, in the first place. He won't abandon the orthodoxies of paper work and he won't risk sticking his neck out. He'll accomplish little by himself, yet maybe more than a little if we work through him.'

From: Administrative Headquarters, Cepheus 18

To: BuOuProv

Subject: Outer Province Project 2563, Part II – Scientific Investigations of non-Humans of Cepheus 18, Co-ordination of,

References:

(a) BuOuProv letr. Cep-N-CM/jg, 100132, dated 302/975 G.E.

(b) AdHQ-Ceph18 letr. AA-LA/mn, dated 140/977 G.E.

Enclosure:

1. SciGroup 10, Physical & Biochemical Division, Report, entitled, 'Physiologic Characteristics of non-Humans of Cepheus 18, Part XI,' dated 172/977 G.E.

1. Enclosure 1, included herewith, is forwarded for the information of the BuOuProv. It is to be noted that Section XII, paragraphs 1–16 of Encl. 1, concern possible changes in present BuOuProv policy with regard to non-Humans with a view to facilitating physical and chemical investigations at present proceeding under authorization of reference (a)

2. It is brought to the attention of the BuOuProv that reference (b) has already discussed possible changes in investigating

68

methods and that it remains the opinion of AdHQ-Ceph18 that such changes are as yet premature. It is nevertheless suggested that the question of non-Human birth rate be made the subject of a BuOuProv project assigned to AdHQ-Ceph18 in view of the importance attached by SciGroup 10 to the problem, as evidenced in Section V of Enclosure 1.

L. Antyok, Superv. AdHQ-Ceph18,

174/977

From: BuOuProv

To: AdHQ-Ceph18

Subject: Outer Province Project 2563 – Scientific Investigations of non-Humans of Cepheus 18, Co-ordination of,

Reference:

(a) AdHQ-Ceph18 letr. AA-LA/mn, dated 174/977 G.E.

1. In response to the suggestion contained in paragraph 2 of reference (a), it is considered that the question of the non-Human birth rate does not fall within the cognizance of AdHQ-Ceph 18. In view of the fact that SciGroup 10 has reported said sterility to be probably due to a chemical deficiency in the food supply, all investigations in the field are relegated to Sci Group 10 as the proper authority.

2. Investigating procedures by the various SciGroups shall continue according to current directives on the subject. No changes in policy are envisaged.

C. Morily, Chief, BuOuProv,

186/977 G.E.

(ii)

There was a loose-jointed gauntness about the news reporter which made him appear somberly tall. He was Gustiv Bannerd, with whose reputation was combined ability – two things which do not invariably go together despite the maxims of elementary morality.

Loodum Antyok took his measure doubtfully and said, 'There's no use denying that you're right. But the Sci-Group report was confidential. I don't understand how —'

'It leaked,' said Bannerd, callously. 'Everything leaks.'

Antyok was obviously baffled, and his pink face furrowed slightly, 'Then I'll just have to plug the leak here. I can't pass your story. All references to SciGroup complaints have to come out. You see that, don't you?'

'No.' Bannerd was calm enough. 'It's important; and I have my rights under the Imperial directive. I think the Empire should know what's going on.'

'But it isn't going on,' said Antyok, despairingly. 'Your claims are all wrong. The bureau isn't going to change its policy. I showed you the letters.'

'You think you can stand up against Zammo when he puts the pressure on?' the newsman asked derisively.

'I will – if I think he's wrong.'

'If!' stated Bannerd flatly. Then, in a sudden fervor, 'Antyok, the Empire has something great here; something greater by a good deal than the government apparently realizes. They're destroying it. They're treating these creatures like animals.'

'Really —' began Antyok, weakly.

'Don't talk about Cepheus 18. It's a zoo. It's a high-class zoo, with your petrified scientists teasing those poor creatures with their sticks poking through the bars. You throw them chunks of meat, but you cage them up. I know! I've been writing about them for two years now. I've almost been living with them.'

'Zammo says —'

'Zammo!' This with hard contempt.

'Zammo says,' insisted Antyok with worried firmness, 'that we treat them too like humans as it is.'

The newsman's straight, long cheeks were rigid, 'Zammo is rather animallike in his own right. He is a science-worshiper. We can do with less of them. Have you read Aurelion's works?' The last was suddenly posed.

'Umm. Yes. I understand the Emperor —'

'The Emperor tends towards us. That is good – better than the hounding of the last reign.'

'I don't see where you're heading?'

'These aliens have much to teach us. You understand? It is nothing that Zammo and his Sci-Group can use; no chemistry, no telepathy. It's a way of life; a way of thinking. The aliens have no crime, no misfits. What effort is being made to study their philosophy? Or to set them up as a problem in social engineering?'

Antyok grew thoughtful, and his plump face smoothed out, 'It is an interesting consideration. It would be a matter for psychologists —'

'No good. Most of them are quacks. Psychologists point out problems, but their solutions are fallacious. We need men of Aurelion. Men of the Philosophy —'

'But look here, we can't turn Cepheus 18 into ... into a metaphysical study.'

'Why not? It can be done easily.'

'How?'

'Forget your puny test-tube peerings. Allow the aliens to set up a society free of Humans. Give them an untrammeled independence and allow an intermingling of philosophies —'

Antyok's nervous response came, 'That can't be done in a day.'

'We can start in a day.'

The administrator said slowly, 'Well, I can't prevent you from trying to start.' He grew confidential, his mild eyes thoughtful, 'You'll ruin your own game, though, if you publish SciGroup 10's report and denounce it on humanitarian grounds. The Scientists are powerful.'

'And we of The Philosophy as well.'

'Yes, but there's an easy way. You needn't rave. Simply point out that the SciGroup is not solving its problems. Do so unemotionally and let the readers think out your point of view for themselves. Take the birth-rate problem, for instance. *There's* something for you. In a generation, the non-Humans might die out, for all science can do. Point out that a more philosophical approach is required. Or pick some other obvious point. Use your judgment, eh?'

Antyok smiled ingratiatingly as he arose, 'But, for the Galaxy's sake, don't stir up a bad smell.'

Bannerd was stiff and unresponsive, 'You may be right.'

It was later that Bannerd wrote in a capsule message to a friend, 'He is not clever, by any means. He is confused and has no guiding-line through life. Certainly utterly incompetent in his job. But he's a cutter and a trimmer, compromises his way around difficulties, and will yield concessions rather than risk a hard stand. He may prove valuable in that. Yours in Aurelion.'

From: AdHQ-Ceph18

To: BuOuProv

Subject: Birth rate of non-Humans on Cepheus 18, News Report on.

References:

(a) AdHQ-Ceph18 letr. AA-LA/mn, dated 174/977 G.E.

(b) Imperial Directive, Ja2374, dated 243/975 G.E.

Enclosures:

1-G. Bannerd news report, date-lined Cepheus 18, 201/977 G.E.

2-G. Bannerd news report, date-lined Cepheus 18, 203/977 G.E.

1. The sterility of non-Humans on Cepheus 18, reported to the BuOuProv in reference (a), has become the subject of news reports to the galactic press. The news reports in question are submitted herewith for the information of the BuOuProv as Enclosures 1 and 2. Although said reports are based on material considered confidential and closed to the public, the news reporter in question maintained his rights to free expression under the terms of reference (b).

2. In view of the unavoidable publicity and misunderstanding on the part of the general public now inevitable, it is requested that the BuOuProv direct future policy on the problem of non-Human sterility.

L. Antyok, Superv. AdHQ-Ceph18,
209/977 G.E.

From: BuOuProv
To: AdHQ-Ceph18
Subject: Birth rate of non-Humans on Cepheus 18, Investigation of.
References:
(a) AdHQ-Ceph18 letr. AA-LA/mn, dated 209/977 G.E.
(b) AdHQ-Ceph18 letr. AA-LA/mn, dated 174/977 G.E.

1. It is proposed to investigate the causes and the means of precluding the unfavorable birth-rate phenomena mentioned in references (a) and (b). A project is therefore set up, entitled, 'Birth rate of non-Humans on Cepheus 18, Investigation of' to which, in view of the crucial importance of the subject, a priority of AA is given.

2. The number assigned to the subject project is 2910, and all expenses incidental to it shall be assigned to Appropriation number 18/78.

C. Morily, Chief, BuOuProv,
223/977 G.E.

(iii)

If Tomor Zammo's ill-humor lessened within the grounds of SciGroup 10 Experimental Station, his friendliness had not thereby increased. Antyok found himself standing alone at the viewing window into the main field laboratory.

The main field laboratory was a broad court set at the environmental conditions of Cepheus 18 itself for the discomfort of the experimenters and the convenience of the experimentees. Through the burning sand, and the dry, oxygen-rich air, there sparkled the hard brilliance of hot, white sunlight. And under the blaze, the brick-red non-Humans, wrinkled of skin and wiry of build, huddled in their squatting positions of ease, by ones and twos.

Zammo emerged from the laboratory. He paused to drink water thirstily. He looked up, moisture gleaming on his upper lip, 'Like to step in there?'

Antyok shook his head definitely, 'No, thank you. What's the temperature right now?'

'A hundred twenty, if there were shade. And they complain of the cold. It's drinking time now. Want to watch them drink?'

A spray of water shot upward from the fountain in the center of the court, and the little alien figures swayed to their feet and hopped eagerly forward in a queer, springy half-run. They milled about the water, jostling one another. The centers of their faces were suddenly disfigured by the projection of a long and flexible fleshy tube, which thrust forward into the spray and was withdrawn dripping.

It continued for long minutes. The bodies swelled and the wrinkles disappeared. They retreated slowly, backing away, with the drinking tube flicking in and out, before receding finally into a pink, wrinkled mass above a wide, lipless mouth. They went to sleep in groups in the shaded angles, plump and sated.

'Animals!' said Zammo, with contempt.

'How often do they drink?' asked Antyok.

'As often as they want. They can go a week if they have to. We water them every day. They store it under their skin. They eat in the evenings. Vegetarians, you know.'

Antyok smiled chubbily, 'It's nice to get a bit of firsthand information occasionally. Can't read reports all the time.'

'Yes?' – noncommittally. Then, 'What's new? What about the lacy-pants boys on Trantor?'

Antyok shrugged dubiously, 'You can't get the Bureau to commit itself, unfortunately. With the Emperor sympathetic to the Aurelionists, humanitarianism is the order of the day. You know that.'

There was a pause in which the administrator chewed his lip uncertainly. 'But there's this birth-rate problem now. It's finally been assigned to AdHQ, you know – and double A priority, too.'

Zammo muttered wordlessly.

Antyok said, 'You may not realize it, but that project will now take precedence over all other work proceeding on Cepheus 18. It's important.'

He turned back to the viewing window and said thoughtfully with a bald lack of preamble. 'Do you think those creatures might be unhappy?'

'Unhappy!' The word was an explosion.

'Well, then,' Antyok corrected hastily, 'maladjusted. You understand? It's difficult to adjust an environment to a race we know so little of.'

'Say – did you ever see the world we took them from?'

'I've read the reports —'

'Reports!' – infinite contempt. 'I've *seen* it. This may look like desert out there to you, but it's a watery paradise to those devils. They have all the food and water they can get. They have a world to themselves with vegetation and natural water flow, instead of a lump of silica and granite where fungi were force-grown in caves and water had to be steamed out of gypsum rock. In ten years, they would have been dead to the last beast, and we saved them. Unhappy? Ga-a-ah, if they are, they haven't the decency of most animals.'

'Well, perhaps. Yet I have a notion.'

'A notion? What is your notion?' Zammo reached for one of his cigars.

'It's something that might help you. Why not study the creatures in a more integrated fashion? Let them use their initiative. After all, they did have a highly-developed science. Your reports speak of it continually. Give them problems to solve.'

'Such as?'

'Oh ... oh,' Antyok waved his hands helplessly. 'Whatever you think might help most. For instance, spaceships. Get them into the control room and study their reactions.'

'Why?' asked Zammo with dry bluntness.

'Because the reaction of their minds to tools and controls adjusted to the human temperament can teach you a lot. In addition, it will make a more effective bribe, it seems to me, than anything you've yet tried. You'll get more volunteers if they think they'll be doing something interesting.'

'That's your psychology coming out. Hm-m-m. Sounds better than it probably is. I'll sleep on it. And where would I get permission, in any case, to let them handle spaceships? I've none at *my* disposal, and it would take a good deal longer than it was worth to follow down the line of red tape to get one assigned to us.'

Antyok pondered, and his forehead creased lightly, 'It doesn't *have* to be spaceships. But even so – If you would write up another report and make the suggestion yourself – strongly, you understand – I might figure out some way of tying it up with my birth-rate project. A double-A priority can get practically anything, you know, without questions.'

Zammo's interest lacked a bit even of mildness, 'Well, maybe. Meanwhile, I've some basal metabolism tests in progress, and it's getting late. I'll think about it. It's got its points.'

From: AdHQ-Ceph18
To: BuOuProv
Subject: Outer Province Project 2910, Part I – Birth rate of non-Humans on Cepheus 18, Investigation of,
   Reference:
   (a) BuOuProv letr. Ceph-N-CM/car, 115097, 233/977 G.E.
   Enclosure:
   1. SciGroup 10, Physical & Biochemical Division report, Part XV, dated 220/977 G.E.
   1. Enclosure 1 is forwarded herewith for the information of the BuOuProv.
   2. Special attention is directed to Section V, Paragraph 3 of Enclosure 1 in which it is requested that a spaceship be assigned SciGroup 10 for use in expediting investigations authorized by the BuOuProv. It is considered by AdHQ-Ceph18 that such investigations may be of material use in aiding work now in progress on the subject project, authorized by reference (a). It is suggested, in view of the high priority placed by the BuOu Prov upon the subject project, that immediate consideration be given the SciGroup's request.
                    L. Antyok, Superv. AdHQ-Ceph18,
                                        240/977 G.E.

From: BuOuProv
To: AdHQ-Ceph18
Subject: Outer Province Project 2910 – Birth rate of non-Humans on Cepheus 18, Investigation of.
   Reference:
   (a) AdHQ-Ceph18 letr. AA-LA/mn, dated 240/977 G.E.

1. Training Ship *AN-R*-2055 is being placed at the disposal of AdHQ-Ceph18 for use in investigation of non-Humans on Cepheus 18 with respect to the subject project and other authorized OuProv projects, as requested in Enclosure 1 to reference (a).

2. It is urgently requested that work on the subject project be expedited by all available means.

C. Morily, Head, BuOuProv,
251/977 G.E.

(iv)

The little, bricky creature must have been more uncomfortable than his bearing would admit to. He was carefully wrapped in a temperature already adjusted to the point where his human companions steamed in their open shirts.

His speech was high-pitched and careful, 'I find it damp, but not unbearably so at this low temperature.'

Antyok smiled, 'It was nice of you to come. I had planned to visit you, but a trial run in your atmosphere out there —' The smile had become rueful.

'It doesn't matter. You other worldlings have done more for us than ever we were able to do for ourselves. It is an obligation that is but imperfectly returned by the endurance on my part of a trifling discomfort.' His speech seemed always indirect, as if he approached his thoughts sidelong, or as if it were against all etiquette to be blunt.

Gustiv Bannerd, seated in an angle of the room, with one long leg crossing the other, scrawled nimbly and said, 'You don't mind if I record all this?'

The Cepheid non-Human glanced briefly at the journalist, 'I have no objection.'

Antyok's apologetics persisted. 'This is not a purely social affair, sir. I would not have forced discomfort on you for that. There are important questions to be considered, and you are the leader of your people.'

The Cepheid nodded, 'I am satisfied your purposes are kindly. Please proceed.'

The administrator almost wriggled in his difficulty in putting thoughts into words. 'It is a subject,' he said, 'of delicacy, and one I would never bring up if it weren't for the overwhelming importance of the ... uh ... question. I am only the spokesman of my government —'

76

'My people consider the otherworld government a kindly one.'

'Well, yes, they are kindly. For that reason, they are disturbed over the fact that your people no longer breed.'

Antyok paused, and waited with worry for a reaction that did not come. The Cepheid's face was motionless except for the soft, trembling motion of the wrinkled area that was his deflated drinking tube.

Antyok continued, 'It is a question we have hesitated to bring up because of its extremely personal angles. Noninterference is my government's prime aim, and we have done our best to investigate the problem quietly and without disturbing your people. But, frankly, we —'

'Have failed?' finished the Cepheid, at the other's pause.

'Yes. Or at least, we have not discovered a concrete failure to reproduce the exact environment of your original world; with, of course, the necessary modification to make it more livable. Naturally, it is thought there is some chemical shortcoming. And so I ask your voluntary help in the matter. Your people are advanced in the study of your own biochemistry. If you do not choose, or would rather not —'

'No, no, I can help.' The Cepheid seemed cheerful about it. The smooth flat planes of his loose-skinned, hairless skull wrinkled in an alien response to an uncertain emotion. 'It is not a matter that any of us would have thought would have disturbed you other-worldlings. That it does is but another indication of your well-meaning kindness. This world we find congenial, a paradise in comparison to our old. It lacks in nothing. Conditions such as now prevail belong in our legends of the Golden Age.'

'Well —'

'But there is a something; a something you may not understand. We cannot expect different intelligences to think alike.'

'I shall try to understand.'

The Cepheid's voice had grown soft, its liquid undertones more pronounced, 'We were dying on our native world; but we were fighting. Our science, developed through a history older than yours, was losing; but it had not yet lost. Perhaps it was because our science was fundamentally biological, rather than physical as yours is. Your people discovered new forms of energy and reached the stars. Our people discovered new truths of psychology and psychiatry and built up a working society free of disease and crime.

'There is no need to question which of the two angles of approach was the more laudable, but there is no uncertainty as to which proved more successful in the end. In our dying world, without the means of life or sources of power, our biological science could but make the dying easier.

'And yet we fought. For centuries past, we had been groping toward the elements of atomic power, and slowly the spark of hope had glimmered that we might break through the two-dimensional limits of our planetary surface and reach the stars. There were no other planets in our system to serve as stepping stones. Nothing but some twenty light-years to the nearest star, without the knowledge of the possibility of the existence of other planetary systems, but rather of the contrary.

'But there is something in all life that insists on striving; even on useless striving. There were only five thousand of us left in the last days. Only five thousand. And our first ship was ready. It was experimental. It would probably have been a failure. But already we had all the principles of propulsion and navigation correctly worked out.'

There was a long pause, and the Cepheid's small black eyes seemed glazed in retrospect.

The newspaperman put in suddenly, from his corner, 'And then we came?'

'And then you came,' the Cepheid agreed simply. 'It changed everything. Energy was ours for the asking. A new world, congenial and, indeed, ideal, was ours even without asking. If our problems of society had long been solved by ourselves, our more difficult problems of environment were suddenly solved for us, no less completely.'

'Well?' urged Antyok.

'Well – it was somehow not well. For centuries, our ancestors had fought toward the stars, and now the stars suddenly proved to be the property of others. We had fought for life, and it had become a present handed to us by others. There is no longer any reason to fight. There is no longer anything to attain. All the universe is the property of your race.'

'This world is yours,' said Antyok, gently.

'By sufferance. It is a gift. It is not ours by right.'

'You have earned it, in my opinion.'

And now the Cepheid's eyes were sharply fixed on the other's countenance, 'You mean well, but I doubt that you understand. We have nowhere to go, save this gift of a world.

We are in a blind alley. The function of life is striving, and that is taken from us. Life can no longer interest us. We have no offspring – voluntarily. It is our way of removing ourselves from your way.'

Absent-mindedly, Antyok had removed the fluoro-globe from the window seat, and spun it on its base. Its gaudy surface reflected light as it spun, and its three-foot-high bulk floated with incongruous grace and lightness in the air.

Antyok said, 'Is that your only solution? Sterility?'

'We might escape still,' whispered the Cepheid, 'but where in the Galaxy is there place for us? It is all yours.'

'Yes, there is no place for you nearer than the Magellanic Clouds if you wished independence. The Magellanic Clouds —'

'And you would not let us go of yourselves. You mean kindly, I know.'

'Yes, we mean kindly – but we could not let you go.'

'It is a mistaken kindness.'

'Perhaps, but could you not reconcile yourselves? You have a world.'

'It is something past complete explanations. Your mind is different. We could not reconcile ourselves. I believe, administrator, that you have thought of all this before. The concept of the blind alley we find ourselves trapped in is not new to you.'

Antyok looked up, startled, and one hand steadied the fluoro-globe, 'Can you read my mind?'

'It is just a guess. A good one, I think.'

'Yes – but *can* you read my mind? The minds of humans in general, I mean. It is an interesting point. The scientists say you cannot, but sometimes I wonder if it is that you simply will not. Could you answer that? I am detaining you, unduly, perhaps.'

'No ... no —' But the little Cepheid drew his enveloping robe closer, and buried his face in the electrically-heated pad at the collar for a moment. 'You other-worldlings speak of reading minds. It is not so at all, but it is assuredly hopeless to explain.'

Antyok mumbled the old proverb, 'One cannot explain sight to a man blind from birth.'

'Yes, just so. This sense which you call "mind reading," quite erroneously, cannot be applied to us. It is not that we cannot receive the proper sensations, it is that your people do not transmit them, and we have no way of explaining to you how

79

to go about it.'

'Hm-m-m.'

'There are times, of course, of great concentration or emotional tension on the part of an other-worldling when some of us who are more expert in this sense; more sharp-eyed, so to speak; detect vaguely *something*. It is uncertain; yet I myself have at times wondered —'

Carefully, Antyok began spinning the fluoro-globe once more. His pink face was set in thought, and his eyes were fixed upon the Cepheid. Gustiv Bannerd stretched his fingers and reread his notes, his lips moving silently.

The fluoro-globe spun, and slowly the Cepheid seemed to grow tense as well, as his eyes shifted to the colorful sheen of the globe's fragile surface.

The Cepheid said, 'What is that?'

Antyok started, and his face smoothed into an almost chuckling placidity, 'This? A Galactic fad of three years ago; which means that it is a hopelessly old-fashioned relic this year. It is a useless device but it looks pretty. Bannerd, could you adjust the windows to non-transmission?'

There was the soft click of a contact, and the windows became curved regions of darkness, while in the center of the room, the fluoro-globe was suddenly the focus of a rosy effulgence that seemed to leap outward in streamers. Antyok, a scarlet figure in a scarlet room, placed it upon the table and spun it with a hand that dripped red. As it spun, the colors changed with a slowly increasing rapidity, blended and fell apart into more extreme contrasts.

Antyok was speaking in an eerie atmosphere of molten, shifting rainbow, 'The surface is of a material that exhibits variable fluorescence. It is almost weightless, extremely fragile, but gyroscopically balanced so that it rarely falls, with ordinary care. It is rather pretty, don't you think?'

From somewhere the Cepheid's voice came, 'Extremely pretty.'

'But it has outworn its welcome; outlived its fashionable existence.'

The Cepheid's voice was abstracted, 'It is very pretty.'

Bannerd restored the light at a gesture, and the colors faded.

The Cepheid said, 'That is something my people would enjoy.' He stared at the globe with fascination.

And now Antyok rose. 'You had better go. If you stay longer, the atmosphere may have bad effects. I thank you humbly for your kindness.'

'I thank you humbly for yours.' The Cepheid had also risen.

Antyok said, 'Most of your people, by the way, have accepted our offers to them to study the make-up of our modern spaceships. You understand, I suppose, that the purpose was to study the reactions of your people to our technology. I trust that conforms with your sense of propriety.'

'You need not apologize. I, myself, have now the makings of a human pilot. It was most interesting. It recalls our own efforts – and reminds us of how nearly on the right track we were.'

The Cepheid left, and Antyok sat, frowning.

'Well,' he said to Bannerd, a little sharply. 'You remember our agreement, I hope. This interview can't be published.'

Bannerd shrugged, 'Very well.'

Antyok was at his seat, and his fingers fumbled with the small metal figurine upon his desk, 'What do you think of all this, Bannerd?'

'I am sorry for them. I think I understand how they feel. We must educate them out of it. The Philosophy can do it.'

'You think so?'

'Yes.'

'We can't let them go, of course.'

'Oh, no. Out of the question. We have too much to learn from them. This feeling of theirs is only a passing stage. They'll think differently, especially when we allow them the completest independence.'

'Maybe. What do you think of the fluoro-globes, Bannerd? He liked them. It might be a gesture of the right sort to order several thousand of them. The Galaxy knows, they're a drug on the market right now, and cheap enough.'

'Sounds like a good idea,' said Bannerd.

'The Bureau would never agree, though. I know them.'

The newsman's eyes narrowed, 'But it might be just the thing. They need new interests.'

'Yes? Well, we *could* do something. I could include your transcript of the interview as part of a report and just emphasize the matter of the globes a bit. After all, you're a member of the Philosophy and might have influence with important people, whose word with the Bureau might carry much more weight than mine. You understand —?'

'Yes,' mused Bannerd. 'Yes.'

From: AdHQ-Ceph18

To: BuOuProv

Subject: OuProv Project 2910, Part II; Birth rate of non-Humans on Cepheus 18, Investigation of.

Reference:

(a) BuOuProv letr. Cep-N-CM/car, 115097, dated 223/977 G.E.

Enclosure:

1. Transcript of conversation between L. Antyok of AdHQ-Ceph18, and Ni-San, High Judge of the non-Humans on Cepheus 18.

1. Enclosure 1 is forwarded herewith for the information of the BuOuProv.

2. The investigation of the subject undertaken in response to the authorization of reference (a) is being pursued along the new lines indicated in Enclosure 1. The BuOuProv is assured that every means will be used to combat the harmful psychological attitude at present prevalent among the non-Humans.

3. It is to be noted that the High Judge of the non-Humans on Cepheus 18 expressed interest in fluoro-globes. A preliminary investigation into this fact of non-Human psychology has been initiated.

> L. Antyok, Superv. AdHQ-Ceph18,
> 272/977 G.E.

From: BuOuProv

To: AdHQ-Ceph18

Subject: OuProv Project 2910; Birth rate of non-Humans on Cepheus 18, Investigation of.

Reference:

(a) AdHQ-Ceph 18 letr. AA-LA/mn, dated 272/977 G.E.

1. With reference to Enclosure 1 of reference (a), five thousand fluoro-globes have been allocated for shipment to Cepheus 18, by the Department of Trade.

2. It is instructed that AdHQ-Ceph18 make use of all methods of appeasing non-Humans' dissatisfaction, consistent with the necessities of obedience to Imperial proclamations.

> C. Morily, Chief, BuOuProv,
> 283/977 G.E.

The dinner was over, the wine had been brought in and the cigars were out. The groups of talkers had formed, and the captain of the merchant fleet was the center of the largest. His brilliant white uniform quite outsparkled his listeners.

He was almost complacent in his speech: 'The trip was nothing. I've had more than three hundred ships under me before this. Still, I've never had a cargo quite like this. What do you want with five thousand fluoro-globes on this desert, by the Galaxy!'

Loodun Antyok laughed gently. He shrugged, 'For the non-Humans. It wasn't a difficult cargo, I hope.'

'No, not difficult. But bulky. They're fragile, and I couldn't carry more than twenty to a ship, with all the government regulations concerning packing and precautions against breakage. But it's the government's money, I suppose.'

Zammo smiled grimly. 'Is this your first experience with government methods, captain?'

'Galaxy, no,' exploded the spaceman. 'I try to avoid it, of course, but you can't help getting entangled on occasion. And it's an abhorrent thing when you are, and that's the truth. The red tape! The paper work! It's enough to stunt your growth and curdle your circulation. It's a tumor, a cancerous growth on the Galaxy. I'd wipe out the whole mess.'

Antyok said, 'You're unfair, captain. You don't understand.'

'Yes? Well, now, as one of these bureaucrats,' and he smiled amiably at the word, 'suppose you explain your side of the situation, administrator.'

'Well, now,' Antyok seemed confused, 'government is a serious and complicated business. We've got thousands of planets to worry about in this Empire of ours and billions of people. It's almost past human ability to supervise the business of governing without the tightest sort of organization. I think there are something like four hundred million men today in the Imperial Administrative Service alone, and in order to co-ordinate their efforts and to pool their knowledge, you *must* have what you call red tape and paper work. Every bit of it, senseless though it may seem, annoying though it may be, has its uses. Every piece of paper is a thread binding the labors of four hundred million humans. Abolish the Administrative Service and you abolish the Empire; and with it, interstellar peace, order and civilization.'

'Come —' said the captain.

'No. I mean it.' Antyok was earnestly breathless. 'The rules and system of the Administrative set-up must be sufficiently all-embracing and rigid so that in case of incompetent officials, and sometimes one *is* appointed – you may laugh, but there are incompetent scientists, and newsmen, and captains, too – in case of incompetent officials, I say, little harm will be done. For, at the worst, the system can move by itself.'

'Yes,' grunted the captain, sourly, 'and if a capable administrator should be appointed? He is then caught by the same rigid web and is forced into mediocrity.'

'Not at all,' replied Antyok, warmly. 'A capable man can work within the limits of the rules and accomplish what he wishes.'

'How?' asked Bannerd.

'Well ... well —' Antyok was suddenly ill at ease. 'One method is to get yourself an A-priority project, or double-A, if possible.'

The captain leaned his head back for laughter, but never quite made it, for the door was flung open and frightened men were pouring in. The shouts made no sense at first. Then:

'Sir, the ships are gone. These non-Humans have taken them by force.'

'What? All?'

'Every one. Ships and creatures —'

It was two hours later that the four were together again, alone in Antyok's office now.

Antyok said coldly, 'They've made no mistakes. There's not a ship left behind, not even your training ship, Zammo. And there isn't a government ship available in this entire half of the Sector. By the time we organize a pursuit they'll be out of the Galaxy and halfway to the Magellanic Clouds. Captain, it was your responsibility to maintain an adequate guard.'

The captain cried, 'It was our first day out of space. Who could have known —'

Zammo interrupted fiercely, 'Wait a while, captain. I'm beginning to understand. Antyok,' his voice was hard, 'you engineered this.'

'I?' Antyok's expression was strangely cool, almost indifferent.

'You told us this evening that a clever administrator got an

A-priority project assigned to accomplish what he wished. You got such a project in order to help the non-Humans escape.'

'I did? I beg your pardon, but how could that be? It was you yourself in one of your reports that brought up the problem of the failing birth rate. It was Bannerd, here, whose sensational articles frightened the Bureau into making a double A-priority project out of it. I had nothing to do with it.'

'*You* suggested that I mention the birth rate,' said Zammo, violently.

'Did I?' said Antyok, composedly.

'And for that matter,' roared Bannerd, suddenly, 'you suggested that I mention the birth rate in my articles.'

The three ringed him now and hemmed him in. Antyok leaned back in his chair and said easily, 'I don't know what you mean by suggestions. If you are accusing me, please stick to evidence – legal evidence. The laws of the Empire go by written, filmed or transcribed material, or by witnessed statements. All my letters as administrator are on file here, at the Bureau, and at other places. I never asked for an A-priority project. The Bureau assigned it to me, and Zammo and Bannerd are responsible for that. In print, at any rate.'

Zammo's voice was an almost inarticulate growl, 'You hoodwinked me into teaching the creatures how to handle a spaceship.'

'It was *your* suggestion. I have your report proposing they be studied in their reaction to human tools on file. So has the Bureau. The evidence – the *legal* evidence, is plain. I had nothing to do with it.'

'Nor with the globes?' demanded Bannerd.

The captain howled suddenly, 'You had my ships brought here purposely. Five thousand globes! You knew it would require hundreds of craft.'

'I never asked for globes,' said Antyok, coldly. 'That was the Bureau's idea, although I think Bannerd's friends of The Philosphy helped that along.'

Bannerd fairly choked. He spat out, 'You were asking that Cepheid leader if he could read minds. You were telling him to express interest in the globes.'

'Come, now. You prepared the transcript of the conversation yourself, and that, too, is on file. You can't prove it.' He stood up, 'You'll have to excuse me. I must prepare a report for the Bureau.'

At the door, Antyok turned, 'In a way, the problem of the

non-Humans is solved, even if only to their own satisfaction. They'll breed now, and have a world they've earned themselves. It's what they wanted.

'Another thing. Don't accuse me of silly things. I've been in the Service for twenty-seven years, and I assure you that my paper work is proof enough that I have been thoroughly correct in everything I have done. And captain, I'll be glad to continue our discussion of earlier this evening at your convenience and explain how a capable administrator can work through red tape and still get what he wants.'

It was remarkable that such a round, smooth baby-face could wear a smile quite so sardonic.

From: BuOuProv
To: Loodun Antyok, Chief Public Administrator, A-8
Subject: Administrative Service, Standing in.
Reference:
(a) AdServ Court Decision 22874-Q, dated 1/978 G.E.

1. In view of the favorable opinion handed down in reference (a) you are hereby absolved of all responsibility for the flight of non-Humans on Cepheus 18. It is requested that you hold yourself in readiness for your next appointment.

R. Horpritt, Chief, AdServ,
15/978 G.E.

THE END

The letters that form a major part of this story (which contains one of my rare examples of extraterrestrial intelligences) are, you will be glad to know, based on the kind of material that routinely passed in and out of the N.A.E.S. (and, for all I know, still does). The turgid style is not my invention. I couldn't invent it if I tried.

When the story appeared, L. Sprague de Camp happily pointed out one flaw in the letter style: I had carelessly made someone in lower position, who was addressing someone in higher position, say, 'it is requested' instead of 'it is suggested.' The underling can humbly suggest, but only an overling can harshly request.

'Blind Alley' has one distinction I would like to mention.

After the war, there began that flood of science fiction anthologies that has been growing in width and depth ever since. Few, if any, science fiction writers have been anthologized as often as I have and the first one of my stories to be anthologized was not 'Nightfall' or a 'positronic robot' story or a 'Foundation' story. It was 'Blind Alley.'

In early 1946 Groff Conklin was putting out the first of his many science fiction anthologies – one called 'The Best of Science Fiction' – and there you will find 'Blind Alley.' That story, for which Campbell had paid $148.75 ($1\frac{3}{4}$c a word) then earned another $42.50 ($\frac{1}{2}$c a word). This meant that 'Blind Alley' had earned me $2\frac{1}{4}$c a word, which was a record high at the time.

Strictly speaking, the money for the anthologization was paid to Street & Smith, but Street & Smith had the enlightened habit of turning such money over to the author – voluntarily and without legal compulsion. And this was the first indication I ever received, by the way, that a story could earn more money than that which it earned at the time of its original sale.

On May 8, 1945, one week before 'The Mule' was completed, the war ended in Europe. Naturally, there was at once a move to demobilize as many of the men who had been fighting in Europe as possible, and to draft replacements from among those who had luxuriated at home.

All through the war, till then, I had been receiving regular draft deferments as a research chemist working in a position important to the war effort. Periodically, there were revisions of the draft rules, and it was a rare month in which it did not look at one time or another as though I might be drafted. (It kept me on my toes, I can tell you, but I did not feel particularly ill-used. My predominant feeling was that of a sneaking guilt at not being drafted and some shame that I was relieved at my deferment.)

During 1944, the uncertainty went so far that I was called in for a physical examination, and it at once turned out that my nearsightedness was so bad as to render me ineligible for the draft anyway.

After V-E Day, the navy yard was ordered to retain only some percentage of those of its deferred employees, allowing the remainder to be drafted. Presumably, the navy yard would select its most important employees to keep, but they knew a better trick, according to the tale we employees heard. They retained all draftable employees who met the physical requirements, and removed protection from those who did *not* meet them either because of age or physical defect. In this way, they hoped to keep them all – those who were fit, because they were declared necessary, and those who were overage or unfit, because they were overage or unfit.

I, as an unfit employee, was one of those declared non-essential.

And then (you guessed it) the Army lowered its physical requirements. The result was that those navy yard employees with bad eyes or other mild deficiencies were put in imminent peril of the draft, while others, who were in every way equivalent except that they were in good shape, were not. (You may well laugh.)

For four months after V-E Day, it was up and down with me and the draft and I never knew, on one day, whether I might not receive my induction notice on the next. While I waited, the atom bombs were dropping on Hiroshima and Nagasaki and the Japanese formally surrendered on September 2.

On September 7, 1945, I received my notice of induction. I didn't enjoy it, of course, but I tried to be philosophical. The war was over, and, whatever difficulties I might have during the two years I expected to be in, at least no one would be shooting at me. I entered the Army on November 1, 1945, as a buck private.

Naturally, during all the fuss over the draft, culminating in my induction, I did no writing. There was an eight-month hiatus, in fact, the longest in three years.

On January 7, 1946, however, while I was still working my way through basic training in Camp Lee, Virginia, I began another 'positronic robot' story, called 'Evidence.' I made use of a typewriter in one of the administrative buildings.

Naturally, it was slow work. I didn't finish first draft till February 17, and then everything came to a halt when, the very next day, I discovered that I would be among those sent out to the South Pacific to participate in 'Operation Crossroads.' This was the first postwar atom bomb test, on the island of Bikini (which later gave its name to a bathing suit so skimpy as to react on the male constitution – in theory – like an atom bomb). The fact that a week later I received my check for the anthologization of 'Blind Alley' did little to raise my spirits.

We left on March 2, 1946, traveling by train and ship, and arrived in Honolulu on March 15. There then began a long wait before we could go on to Bikini (the atom bomb test was postponed, of course). When time began to hang heavy enough, I returned to 'Evidence.' I persuaded a sympathetic librarian to lock me up in the building when it closed for lunch so that I had an hour each day absolutely alone at the typewriter. I finished the story on April 10, and mailed it off to Campbell the next day.

On April 29, I received word of its acceptance. By that time, the word rate had reached two cents.

I never did go to Bikini, by the way. Some administrative error back home ended the allotment being sent to my wife. I was sent back to the United States on May 28 to inquire into the matter; it was all straightened out by the time I was back at Camp Lee. As long as I was there, however, I applied for a 'research discharge' on the ground that I was going back to my Ph.D work. I was out of the Army, as a corporal, on July 26.

'Evidence' was the only story I wrote while in uniform.

As soon as I got out of the Army I made arrangements to return to Columbia, after an absence of a little over four years, and to resume my work toward my Ph.D. under Professor Dawson.

There was still no question in my mind that chemistry was my career, and my only career. In the four years of my marriage I had written nine science fiction stories and one fantasy and had sold them all – but all the sales had been to Campbell.

Since *Unknown* had died, I was terribly conscious that *Astounding* might die as well. If that happened, or if Campbell retired, I was not at all sure that I could continue selling.

The situation looked better postwar than prewar, to be sure. During the first four years of my marriage, I had earned $2667 as a writer, or an average of under $13 per week. This was about half again as well as I had been doing in my bachelor days, even though I was writing fewer stories.

The word rate had doubled, you see, and there was even the hope of subsidiary rights – extra money for already sold stories. 'Blind Alley' had already placed in an anthology, and on August 30, 1946, only a month after I got out of the Army, I discovered that I had made a second such sale. A new science fiction anthology, 'Adventures in Time and Space,' edited by Raymond J. Healey and J. Francis McComas, was to include 'Nightfall' and I was to receive $66.50 for that.

There was even more than anthologization sales. In that same month of August, the September 1946 issue of *Astounding* hit the stands with 'Evidence' (Had I but known when writing it that by the time it was published I would be safely out of the Army!) Almost at once I received a telegram asking for the movie rights. The gentleman interested turned out to be none other than Orson Welles. In great excitement, I sold him the radio, television and movie rights to the story on September 20, and waited to become famous. (I couldn't become wealthy, because the entire payment in full was only $250.)

Unfortunately, nothing happened. To this day, Mr. Welles has never used the story. But the check was certainly useful toward paying my tuition.

Despite everything, though, it still seemed quite out of the question that I could ever possibly depend on writing for a year-in, year-out living, especially now that I was married and hoped, eventually, to have children.

So back to school it was, with a small savings account to serve as a cushion, with some veterans' benefits supplied by the government, and, of course, with the hope that I would make a little extra cash writing.

In September I wrote still another 'positronic robot' story, 'Little Lost Robot,' racing to complete it before the fall semester started and I grew immersed in my work. Campbell took it promptly and it appeared in the March 1947 issue of *Astounding*. Eventually, it and 'Evidence' were included in *I, Robot*.

Once the semester started, it became difficult to find time to write. Toward the end of 1946, I managed to begin another 'Foundation' story, 'Now You See It —.' I finished it on February 2, 1947, and submitted it to Campbell on the fourth. By that time I was rather sick of the 'Foundation' series and I tried to write 'Now You See It —' in such a way as to make it the last of the series.

Campbell would have none of that. I had to revise the ending to permit a sequel, and on the fourteenth he took it. It appeared in the January 1948 *Astounding* and eventually made up the first third of my book *Second Foundation*.

In May 1947 I wrote a story that, for the first time in over two years, was neither a 'Foundation' story nor a 'positronic robot' story. It was 'No Connection.' I submitted it to Campbell on May 26, and it was accepted on the thirty-first.

24: No Connection

Raph was a typical American of his times. Remarkably ugly, too, by American standards of our times. The bony structure of his jaws was tremendous and the musculature suited it. His nose was arched and wide and his black eyes were small and forced wide apart by the span of said nose. His neck was thick, his body broad, his fingers spatulate, with strongly curved nails.

If he had stood erect, on thick legs with large, well-padded feet, he would have topped two and a half yards. Standing or sitting, his mass neared a quarter of a ton.

Yet his forehead rose in an unrestricted arc and his cranial capacity did not stint. His enormous hand dealt delicately with a pen, and his mind droned comfortably on as he bent over his desk.

In fact, his wife and most of his fellow-Americans found him a fine-looking fellow.

Which shows the alchemy of a long displacement along the time-axis.

Raph, Junior, was a smaller edition of our typical American. He was adolescent and had not yet lost the hairy covering of childhood. It spread in a dark, close-curled mat across his chest and back, but it was already thinning and perhaps within the year he would first don the adult shirt that would cover the proudly-naked skin of manhood.

But, meanwhile, he sat in breeches alone, and scratched idly at a favorite spot just above the diaphragm. He felt curious and just a little bored. It wasn't bad to come with his father to the museum when people were there. Today was a Closed-Day, however, and the empty corridors rang lonesomely when he walked along them.

Besides, he knew everything in it – mostly bones and stones.

Junior said: 'What's that thing?'

'What thing?' Raph lifted his head and looked over his shoulder. Then he looked pleased. 'Oh, that's something quite new. That's a reconstruction of Primate Primeval. It was sent to me from the North River Grouping. Isn't it a nice job, though?' And he returned to his work, in the grip of a momentary twinge of pleasure. Primate Primeval wasn't to go on exhibition for a week at least – not until he prepared an honorable place for it with suitable surroundings, but, for the moment, it was in his office and his own private darling.

Raph looked at the 'nice job' with quite other emotions, however. What he saw was a spindly figure of contemptuous size, with thin legs and arms, hair-covered and owning an ugly, small-featured face with large, protruding eyes.

He said: 'Well, what *is* it, Pa?'

Raph stirred impatiently: 'It's a creature that lived many millions of years ago, we think. That's the way we think it looks.'

'Why?' insisted the youngster.

Raph gave up. Apparently, he would have to root out the subject and do away with it.

'Well, for one thing we can tell about the muscles from the shape of the bones, and the positions where the tendons would fit and where some of the nerves would go. From the teeth we can tell the type of digestive system the animal would have, and from the foot-bones, what type of posture it would have. For the rest, we go by the principle of Analogy, that is, by the outside appearance of creatures that exist today that have the same kind of skeleton. For instance, that's why he's covered with red hair. Most of the Primates today – they're little insignificant creatures, practically extinct – are red-haired, have bare callosities on the rump —'

Junior scurried behind the figure and satisfied himself on that score.

'– have long, fleshy probosces, and short, shriveled ears. Their diets are unspecialized, hence the rather all-purpose teeth, and they are nocturnal, hence the large eyes. It's all simple, really. Now, does that dispose of you, youngster?'

And then Junior, having thought and thought about it, came out with a disparaging: 'He looks just like a Eekah to me, though. Just like an ugly, old Eekah.'

Raph stared at him. Apparently he had missed a point: 'An Eekah?' he said, 'What's an Eekah? Is that an imaginary creature you've been reading about?'

'Imaginary! Say, Pa, don't you *ever* stop at the Recorder's?'

This was an embarrassing question to answer, for 'Pa' never did, or at least, never since his maturity. As a child, the Re-

corder, as custodian of the world's spoken, written and recorded fiction, had, of course, had an unfailing fascination.
But he had grown up —

He said, tolerantly: 'Are there new stories about Eekahs? I
remember none when I was young.'

'You don't get it, Pa.' One would almost suppose that the
young Raph was on the very verge of an exasperation he was
too cautious to express. He explained in wounded fashion:
'The Eekahs are real things. They come from the Other World.
Haven't you heard about *that*? We've been hearing about it in
school, even, and in the Group Magazine. They stand upside
down in their country, only they don't know it, and they look
just like Ol' Primeval there.'

Raph collected his astonished wits. He felt the incongruity
of cross-examining his half-grown child for archaeological
data and he hesitated a moment. After all, he had heard *some*
things. There *had* been word of vast continents existing on the
other hemisphere of Earth. It seemed to him that there were
reports of life on them. It was all hazy – perhaps it wasn't
always wise to stick so closely to the field of one's own interest.

He asked Junior: 'Are there Eekahs here among the Groupings?'

Junior nodded rapidly: 'The Recorder says they can think
as good as us. They got machines that go through the air.
That's how they got here.'

'Junior!' said Raph severely.

'I ain't lying,' Junior cried with aggrieved virtue. 'You ask
the Recorder and see what *he* says.'

Raph slowly gathered his papers together. It was Closed-
Day, but he could find the Recorder at his home, no doubt.

The Recorder was an elderly member of the Red River Gurrow Grouping and few alive could remember a time when he
was not. He had succeeded to the post by general consent and
filled it well, for he was Recorder for the same reason that
Raph was curator of the museum. He liked to be, he wanted to
be, and he could conceive no other life.

The social pattern of the Gurrow Grouping is difficult to
grasp unless born into it, but there was a looseness about it that
almost made the word 'pattern' incongruous. The individual
Gurrow took whatever job he felt an aptitude for, and such

work as was left over and needed to be done was done either in common, or consecutively by each according to an order determined by lot. Put so, it sounds too simple to work, but actually the traditions that had gathered with the five thousand years since the first Voluntary Grouping of Gurrahs was supposed to have been established, made the system complicated, flexible – and workable.

The Recorder was, as Raph had anticipated, at his home, and there was the embarrassment of renewing an old and unjustly neglected acquaintanceship. He had made use of the Recorder's reference library, of course, but always indirectly – yet he had once been a child, an intimate learner at the feet of accumulated wisdom, and he had let the intimacy lapse.

The room he now entered was more or less choked with recordings and, to a lesser degree, with printed material. The Recorder interspersed greetings with apologies.

'Shipments have come from some of the other Groupings,' he said. 'It needs time for cataloguing, you know, and I can't seem to find the time I used to.' He lit a pipe and puffed strongly. 'Seems to me I'll have to find a full-time assistant. What about your son, Raph? He clusters about here the way you did twenty years ago.'

'You remember those times?'

'Better than you do, I think. Think your son would like that?'

'Suppose you talk to him. He might like to. I can't honestly say he's fascinated by archaeology.' Raph picked up a recording at random and looked at the identification tag: 'Um-m-m – from the Joquin Valley Grouping. That's a long way from here.'

'A long way.' The Recorder nodded. 'I have sent them some of ours, of course. The works of our own Grouping are highly regarded throughout the continent,' he said, with proprietary pride. 'In fact' – he pointed the stem of his pipe at the other – 'your own treatise on extinct primates has been distributed everywhere. I've sent out two thousand copies and there are still requests. That's pretty good – for archaeology.'

'Well, archaeology is why I am here – that and what my son says you've been telling him.' Raph had a little trouble starting: 'It seems you have spoken of creatures called Eekahs from the Antipodes, and I would like to have such information as you have on them.'

The Recorder looked thoughtful: 'Well, I could tell you what I know offhand, or we could go to the Library and look up the references.'

'Don't bother opening the Library for me. It's a Closed-Day. Just give me some notion of things and I'll search the references later.'

The Recorder bit at his pipe, shoved his chair back against the wall and de-focused his eyes thoughtfully. 'Well,' he said, 'I suppose it starts with the discovery of the continents on the other side. That was five years ago. You know about that, perhaps?'

'Only the fact of it. I know the continents exist, as everyone does now. I remember once speculating on what a shining new field it would be for archaeological research, but that is all.'

'Ah, then there is much else to tell you of. The new continents were never discovered by us directly, you know. It was five years ago that a group of non-Gurrow creatures arrived at the East Harbor Grouping in a machine that flew – by definite scientific principles, we found out later, based essentially on the buoyancy of air. They spoke a language, were obviously intelligent, and called themselves Eekahs. The Gurrows, of the East Harbor Grouping, learned their language – a simple one though full of unpronounceable sounds – and I have a grammar of it, if you're interested –'

Raph waved that away.

The Recorder continued: 'The Gurrows of the Grouping, with the aid of those of the Iron Mountain Grouping – which specialize in steel works, you know – built duplicates of the flying machine. A flight was made across the ocean, and I should say there are several dozens of volumes on all that – volumes on the flying machine, on a new science called aerodynamics, new geographies, even a new system of philosophy based on the plurality of intelligences. All produced at the East Harbor and Iron Mountain Groupings. Remarkable work for only five years, and all are available here.'

'But the Eekahs – are they still at the East Harbor Groupings?'

'Um-m-m. I'm pretty certain they are. They refused to return to their own continents. They call themselves "political refugees."'

'Politi ... *what*?'

'It's their own language,' said the Recorder, 'and it's the

95

only translation available.'

'Well, why *political* refugees? Why not geological refugees, or oompah refugees. I should think a translation ought to make sense.'

The Recorder shrugged: 'I refer you to the books. They're not criminals, they claim. I know only what I tell you.'

'Well, then, what do they look like? Do you have pictures?'

'At the Library.'

'Did you read my "Principles of Archaeology?" '

'I looked through it.'

'Do you remember the drawings of Primate Primeval?'

'I'm afraid not.'

'Then, look, let's go down to the Library, after all.'

'Well, sure.' The Recorder grunted as he rose.

The Administrator of the Red River Gurrow Grouping held a position in no way different in essentials from that of the Museum Curator, the Recorder or any other voluntary job holder. To expect a difference is to assume a society in which executive ability is rare.

Actually, all jobs in a Gurrow Grouping – where a 'job' is defined as regular work, the fruits of which adhere to others in addition to the worker himself – are divided into two classes: one, Voluntary Jobs, and the other, Involuntary or Community Jobs. All of the first classification are equal. If a Gurrow enjoys the digging of useful ditches, his bent is to be respected and his job to be honored. If no one enjoys such burrowing and yet it is found necessary for comfort, it becomes a Community Job, done by lot or rotation according to convenience – annoying but unavoidable.

And so it was that the Administrator lived in a house no more ample and luxurious than others, sat at the head of no tables, had no particular title other than the name of his job, and was neither envied, hated, nor adored.

He liked to arrange Inter-Group trade, to supervise the common finances of the Group, and to judge the infrequent disagreements that arose. Of course, he received no additional food or energy privileges for doing what he liked.

It was not, therefore, to obtain permission, but to place his accounts in decent order, that Raph stopped in to see the Administrator. The Closed-Day had not yet ended. The Administrator sat peacefully in his after-dinner armchair, with an after-dinner cigar in his mouth, and an after-dinner book in his hand. Although there was something rather timeless about six children and a wife, even they had an after-dinner air about them.

Raph received a multiple greeting upon entering, and raised two hands to his ears, for if the various Administratelets (Only applicable title. Author.) had a job, it was noisemaking. Certainly, it was what they liked to do, and certainly others reaped most of the fruits therefrom, for their own eardrums were apparently impervious.

The Administrator shooed them.

Raph accepted a cigar.

'I intend leaving the Grouping for a time, Lahr,' he said. 'My job necessitates it.'

'We won't enjoy your going, Raph. I hope it will not be for long.'

'I hope not. What have we in Common Units?'

'Oh, ample for your purposes, I'm sure. Where do you intend going?'

'To the East Harbor Grouping.'

The Administrator nodded and blew out a thoughtful puff of smoke: 'Unfortunately, East Harbor has a surplus in their favor registered in our books – I can verify that, if you wish – but the Common Units of Exchange on hand will take care of transportation and necessary expenses.'

'Well, that's fine. But tell me, what is my status on the Community Job Roster?'

'Um-m-m – I'll have to get the rolls. You'll excuse me a moment.' He trundled away, heaving his great weight across the room and out into the hallway. Raph paused to poke at the youngest of the children who rolled up to him, growling in mock ferocity with gleaming teeth – a black little bundle of thick fur, with the long, childish snout that had not yet broadened away from the shape of the animal ancestry of half a million years earlier.

The Administrator returned with a heavy ledger and large spectacles. He opened the ledger meticulously, riffled the pages to the proper place and then drew a careful finger down the columns.

He said: 'There's only the question of water supply, Raph. You're due on the Maintenance gang for this next week. There's nothing else due for at least two months.'

'I'll be back before then. Is there any chance of someone subbing for me on the Water Maintenance?'

'Um-m-m — I'll get someone. I can always send my oldest. He's getting to job age and he might as well taste everything. He may like working on the dam.'

'Yes? You tell me if he does, then. He can replace me, regularly.'

The Administrator smiled gently: 'Don't plan on that, Raph. If he can figure out a way of making sleeping useful to all of us, he'll certainly take it up as a job. And why are you going to East Harbor Grouping, by the way, if it's something you care to talk about?'

'You'll laugh, perhaps, but I have just found out that there exist such things as Eekahs.'

'Eekahs? Yes, I know.' The Administrator pointed a finger. 'Creatures from across the sea! Right?'

'Right! But that's not all. I've come from the Library. I've seen trimensional reproductions, Lahr, and they're *Primate Primeval*, or almost. They're primates, anyway, *intelligent* primates. They've got small eyes, flat noses and completely different jawbones – but they're at least second cousins. I've *got* to see them, Lahr.'

The Administrator shrugged. He felt no interest in the matter himself. 'Why? I ask out of ignorance, Raph. Does it matter, your seeing them?'

'Matter?' Raph was obviously appalled at the question. 'Don't you know what's been going on these last years? Have you read my archaeology book?'

'No,' said the Administrator, definitely, 'I wouldn't read it to save myself a turn at Garbage Disposal.'

Raph said: 'Which probably proves you more suited to Garbage Disposal than archaeology. But never mind. I've been fighting single-handed for nearly ten years in favor of my theory that Primate Primeval was an intelligent creature with a developed civilization. I have nothing on my side so far but logical necessity, which is the last thing most archaeologists will accept. They want something solid. They want the remains of a Grouping, or artifacts, structures, books – get it. All I can give them is a skeleton with a huge brain-pan. Stars above, Lahr, what do they expect to survive in ten million years? Metal dies. Paper dies. Film dies.

'Only stone lasts, Lahr. And bone that's turned to stone. I've got that. A skull with room for a brain. And stone, too, old sharpened knives. Ground flints.'

'Well,' said Lahr, 'there are your artifacts.'

'Those are called eoliths, dawn stones. They won't accept them. They call them natural products, fortuitously shaped by erosion into the shapes they have, the idiots.'

Then he grinned with a scientific ferocity: 'But if the Eekahs are intelligent primates, I've practically proven my case.'

Raph had traveled before, but never eastward, and the decline of agriculture on the road impressed him. In early history, the Gurrow Groupings had been entirely unspecialized. Each had been self-sufficient, and trade was a gesture of friendliness rather than a matter of necessity.

And so it was still in most Groupings. His own Grouping, the Red River, was perhaps typical. Some five hundred miles inland, set in lush farm land, agriculture remained centric. The river yielded some fish and there was a well-developed dairy industry. In fact, it was food exports that provided cause for the healthy state of the store of Common Units.

As they traveled eastward, however, the Groupings through which they passed paid less and less mind to the shallowing soil and more and more to the smoking factory structures.

In the East Harbor Grouping, Raph found a trading center which depended for its prosperity primarily upon ships. It was a more populous Grouping than the average, more densely packed, with houses, on occasion, within a hundred yards of each other.

Raph felt an uncomfortable prickling at the thought of living in such close quarters. The docks were even worse, with Gurrows engaged at the huge Community Jobs of loading and unloading.

The Administrator of this East Harbor Grouping was a young man, new at his job, overwhelmed with the joy of his work, and beside himself with the pleasure of welcoming a distinguished stranger.

Raph sat through an excellent meal, and was treated to a long discourse as to the exact derivation of each dish. To his provincial ears, beef from the Prairie Grouping, potatoes from the Northeast Woods Grouping, coffee from the Isthmus

Grouping, wine from the Pacific Grouping, and fruit from the Central Lakes Grouping were something strange and wonderful.

Over the cigars – South Island Grouping – he brought up the subject of the Eekahs. The East Harbor Administrator grew solemn and a little uneasy.

'The man you want to see is Lernin. He'll be glad to help you all he can. You say you know something of these Eekahs?'

'I say I would *like* to know something. They resemble an extinct species of animal I am familiar with.'

'Then *that* is your field of interest. I see.'

'Perhaps you can tell me some of the details of their arrival, Administrator,' suggested Raph, politely.

'I was not Administrator at the time, friend, so that I lack first-hand information, but the records are plain. This group of Eekahs that arrived in their flying-machine ... you've heard about these aeronautical devices?'

'Yes, yes.'

'Yes. Well ... apparently they were fugitives.'

'So I have heard. Yet they claim not to be criminals. Isn't that so?'

'Yes. Queer, isn't it? They admitted that they had been condemned – this was after long and skillful questioning, once we had learned their language – but denied that they were evildoers. Apparently, they had disagreed with their Administrator on principles of policy.'

Raph nodded his head knowingly: 'Ah, and refused to abide by the common decision. Is that it?'

'More confusing than that. They insist there was no common decision. They claim that the Administrator decided on policy of his own accord.'

'And was not replaced?'

'Apparently those who believe he should are considered criminals – as these were.'

There was a frank pause of disbelief. Then Raph said: 'Does that sound reasonable to you?'

'No, I merely relay to you their words. Of course, the Eekah language is quite a barrier. Some of the sounds can't be pronounced: words have different meanings according to position in the sentence and according to tiny differences in inflection. And it happens often that Eekah words even when best trans-

100

lated are a complete puzzle.'

'They must have been surprised to find Gurrows here,' suggested Raph, 'if they are members of a different genus.'

'Surprised!' The Administrator's voice sank: 'I'll say they were surprised. Now, this information has not been generally published for obvious reasons, so I hope you remember that it's confidential. These Eekahs killed five Gurrows before they could be disarmed. They had an instrument that expelled metal pellets at high speed by means of controlled explosive chemical reaction. We have duplicated it since. Naturally, under the circumstances, we are not branding them criminals, for it is reasonable to assume that they did not realize we were intelligent beings. Apparently,' and the Administrator smiled ruefully, 'we resemble certain animals in their world. Or so they say.'

But Raph was galvanized into a sudden enthusiasm: 'Stars above! They said that, did they? Did they go into details? What kind of animals?'

The Administrator was taken back: 'Well, I don't know. They give names in their language. What meaning has that? They called us giant "bears."'

'Giant what?'

'Bears. I haven't the slightest idea what they are, except presumably that they look like us. I know of no such in America.'

'Bears. Bears.' Raph stumbled over the word. 'That's interesting. It's more than interesting. It's stupendous. Do you know, Administrator, that there is a great dispute among us as to the ancestry of Gurrows? Living animals related to Gurrow sapiens would be of immense importance.' Raph rubbed his huge hands with pleasure.

The Administrator was pleased at the sensation he had caused. He said: 'And a puzzling thing in addition is that they call themselves by two names.'

'Two names?'

'Yes. No one knows the distinction yet, no matter how much the Eekahs explain it to us, except that one is a more general name, and one a more specific. The basis of the difference escapes us.'

'I see. Which is "Eekah"?'

'That is the specific one. The general one is' – the Administrator stumbled slowly over the harsh syllables – 'Chim-pan-zee. There, that's it. There are a group called Eekahs and there are other groups with other names. But they are all called Chim ... what I said before.'

The Administrator sought through his mind for other juicy items of miscellany with which he was acquainted, but Raph interrupted him.

'May I see Lernin tomorrow?'

'Of course.'

'Then I shall do so. Thank you for your courtesy, Administrator.'

Lernin was a slight individual. It is doubtful if he weighed more than two hundred and fifty. There was also an imperfection in his walk, a slight lameness. But neither of these facts made much of an impression on Raph once the conversation had begun, for Lernin was a thinker who could impose his vigor upon others.

It was Raph whose eagerness dominated the first half of the conversation, and Lernin's comments were as luminous and as brief as lightning flashes. And then, there was a sudden whirl of the center of gravity, and Lernin took over.

'You will excuse me, learned friend,' Lernin said with a characteristic stiffness that he could make so amiable, 'if I find your problem unimportant. No, no' – he lifted a long-fingered hand – 'not, in the uncomplicated talk of the times, merely unimportant to myself because my interest lies elsewhere, but unimportant to the Grouping of all the Groupings – to every single Gurrow from end to end of the world.'

The concept was staggering. For a moment, Raph was offended; offended deep in his sense of individuality. It showed in his face.

Lernin added quickly: 'It may sound impolite, crude, uncivilized. But I must explain. I must explain because you are primarily a social scientist and will understand – perhaps better than we ourselves.'

'My life-interest,' said Raph angrily, 'is important to myself. I cannot assume those of others in preference.'

'What I talk about should be the life-interest of all – if only because it may be the means of saving the lives of all of us.'

Raph was beginning to suspect all sorts of things from a queer form of joking to the unbalance of mind that sometimes came with age. Yet Lernin was not old.

Lernin said, with an impressive fervor: 'The Eekahs of the other world are a danger to us, for they are not friendly to us.'

And Raph replied naturally: 'How do you know?'

'No one other than myself, my friend, has lived more closely with these Eekahs who have arrived here, and I find them people with minds of emotional content strange to us. I have collected queer facts which we find difficult to interpret, but which point, at any rate, in disquieting directions.

'I'll list a few: Eekahs in organized groups kill one another periodically for obscure reasons. Eekahs find it impossible to live in manner other than those of ants – that is, in huge conglomerate societies – yet find it impossible to allow for the presence of one another. Or, to use the terminology of the social scientists, they are gregarious without being social, just as we Gurrows are social without being gregarious. They have elaborate codes of behavior, which, we are told, are taught to the young, but which are disobeyed in universal practice, for reasons obscure to us. Et cetera. Et cetera. Et cetera.'

'I am an archaeologist,' said Raph, stiffly. 'These Eekahs are of interest to me biologically only. If the curvature of the thigh bone is known to me, I care little for the curvature of their cultural processes. If I can follow the shape of the skull, it is immaterial to me that the shape of their ethics is mysterious.'

'You don't think that their insanities may affect us here?'

'We are six thousand miles apart, or more, along either ocean,' said Raph. 'We have our world. They have theirs. There is no connection between us.'

'No connection,' mused Lernin, 'so others have said. No connection at all. Yet Eekahs have reached us, and others may follow. We are told that the other world is dominated by a few, who are in turn dominated by their queer need for security which they confuse with an Eekah word called "power," which, apparently, means the prevailing of one's own will over the sum of the will of the community. What if this "power" should extend to us?'

Raph bent his mind to the task. The matter was utterly ridiculous. It seemed impossible to picture the strange concepts.

Lernin said: 'These Eekahs say that their world and ours in the long past were closer together. They say that there is a well-known scientific hypothesis in their world of a continental drift. That may interest you, since otherwise you might find it difficult to reconcile the existence of fossils of Primate Primeval closely related to living Eekahs six thousand miles away.'

And the mists cleared from the archaeologist's brain as he glanced up with a live interest untroubled by insanities: 'Ah, you should have said this sooner.'

'I say it now as an example of what you may achieve for yourself by joining us and helping us. There is another thing. These Eekahs are physical scientists, like ourselves here in East Harbor, but with a difference dictated by their own cultural pattern. Since they live in hives, they think in hives, and their science is the result of an ant-society. Individually, they are slow and unimaginative; collectively, each supplies a crumb different from that supplied by his fellow – so that a vast structure is erected quickly. Here the individual is infinitely brighter, but he works alone. You, for instance, know nothing of chemistry, I imagine.'

'A few of the fundamentals, but nothing else,' admitted Raph. 'I leave that, naturally, to the chemist.'

'Yes, naturally. But I *am* a chemist. Yet these Eekahs, though my mental inferiors, and no chemists in their own world, know more chemistry than I. For instance, did you know that there exist elements that spontaneously disintegrate?'

'Impossible,' exploded Raph. 'Elements are eternal, changeless —'

Lernin laughed: 'So you have been taught. So I have been taught. So I taught others. Yet the Eekahs are right, for in my laboratories I have checked them, and in every detail they are right. Uranium gives rise to a spontaneous radiation. You've heard of uranium, of course? And furthermore, I have detected radiations of energy beyond that produced by uranium which must be due to traces of elements unknown to us but described by the Eekahs. And these missing elements fit well into the so-called Periodic Tables some chemists have tried to foist upon the science. Though I do wrong to use the word "foist" now.'

'Well,' said Raph, 'why do you tell me this? Does this, too, help me in my problem?'

'Perhaps,' said Lernin, ironically, 'you will yet find it a royal bribe. You see, the energy production of uranium is absolutely constant. No known outward change in environment can affect it – and as a result of the loss in energy, uranium slowly turns to lead at an *absolutely constant rate*. A group of our men is even now using this fact as a basis for a method of determining the age of the earth. You see, to determine the age of a stratum of rock in the earth, then, it is but necessary to discover a region in it containing a trace of uranium – a widely spread element – and to determine about it the quantity of lead – and I might here add that the lead produced from uranium differs from ordinary lead and can be easily characterized – and it is then simple to determine the length of time in which that stratum has been solid. And of course, if a fossil is found in that stratum, it is of the same age, am I not correct?'

'Stars above,' and Raph rose to his feet in a tremble, 'you do not deceive me? It is really possible to do this?'

'It is possible. It is even easy. I tell you that our great defense, even at this late date, is co-operation in science. We are a group now of many, my friend, from many Groupings, and we want you among us. If you join us, it would be a simple matter to extend our earthage project to such regions as you may indicate – regions rich in fossils. What do you say?'

'I will help you.'

It is doubtful if the Gurrow Groupings had ever before seen a community venture of such breadth as now took place. East Harbor Grouping, as has been remarked, was a shipping center, and certainly a trans-Atlantic vessel was not beyond the capacity of a Grouping that traded along the full lengths of both coasts of the Americas. What *was* unusual was the vastness of the co-operation of Gurrows from many Groupings, Gurrows of many interests.

Not that they were all happy.

Raph, for instance, on the particular morning that now concerns us, six months from the date of his first arrival in East Harbor, was searching anxiously for Lernin.

Lernin, for his part, was searching for nothing but greater speed.

They met on the docks, where Lernin, biting the end off a cigar and leading the way to a region where smoking was permitted, said: 'And you, my friend, seem concerned. Not, certainly, about the progress of our ocean liner?'

'I am concerned,' said Raph, gravely, 'about the reports I have received of the expedition testing the age of the rocks.'

'Oh — And you are unhappy about it?'

'Unhappy!' exploded Raph. 'Have you seen them?'

'I have received a copy. I have looked at it. I have even read parts of it. But I have had little time and most of it bounced off. Will you please enlighten me?'

'Certainly. In the last several months, three of the regions I have indicated as being fossiliferous have been tested. The first region was in the area of East Harbor Grouping itself. Another was in the Pacific Bay Grouping, and a third in the Central Lakes Grouping. I purposely asked that those be done first because they are the richest areas and because they are widely separated. Do you know, for instance, what age they tell me the rocks upon which we stand are?'

'Two billion years, I think, is the oldest figure I noticed.'

'And that's the figure for the oldest rocks – the basic igneous stratum of basalt. The upper strata, however – the recent sedimentary layers containing dozens of fossils of Primate Primeval – how old do you think *these* are supposed to be? Five – hundred – trillion – years! How is that? Do you understand?'

'Trillion?' Lernin squinted upwards and shook his head. 'That's strange.'

'I'll add to it. The Pacific Coast Grouping is one hundred trillion years old – so I am told – and Central Lakes almost eighty trillion years old.'

Lernin said: 'And the other measurements? The ones that did not involve your strata?'

'That is the most peculiar thing of all. Most of the chosen investigations were carried on in strata that were not particularly fossiliferous. They had their own criteria of choice based on geological reasoning – and they got consistent results – one million to two billion years depending upon the depth and geological history of the particular region tested. Only *my* areas give these strange and impossible vagaries.'

And Lernin said, 'But what do the geologists say about all this? Can there be some error?'

'Undoubtedly. But they have fifty decent, reasonable measurements. For themselves, they have proved the method and are happy. There are three anomalies, to be sure, but they view them with equanimity as involving some unknown factors. I don't see it that way. These three measurements mean everything.' Raph interrupted himself fiercely: 'How sure are you that radioactivity is an absolute constant?'

'Sure? Can one ever be sure? Nothing we know of so far affects it, and such is likewise the definite testimony of our Eekahs. Besides, my friend, if you are implying that radio-activity was more extensive in the past than in the present, why only in your fossil regions? Why not everywhere?'

'Why, indeed? It's another aspect of a problem which is growing more important daily. Consider. We have regions which show a past of abnormal radioactivity. We have regions which show abnormal fossil frequencies. Why should these re-gions coincide, Lernin?'

'One obvious answer suggests itself, my friend. If your Pri-mate Primeval existed at a time when certain regions were highly radioactive, certain individuals would wander into them and die. Radioactive radiation is deadly in excess, of course. Radioactivity and fossils, there you are.'

'Why not other creatures,' demanded Raph. 'Only Primate Primeval occurs in excess, and he was intelligent. He would not be trapped by dangerous radiation.'

'Perhaps he was not intelligent. That is, after all, only your theory and not a proven fact.'

'Certainly, then, he was more intelligent than his small-brained contemporaries.'

'Perhaps not even that. You romanticize too much.'

'Perhaps I do.' Raph spoke in half a whisper. 'It seems to me that I can conjure up visions of a great civilization of a million years back – or more. A great power; a great intelligence – that has vanished completely, except for the tiny whispers of ossi-fied bones which retain that huge cavity in which a brain once existed, and a bony five-fingered hand curving into slender signs of manipulative skill – with an opposing thumb. They *must* have been intelligent.'

'Then, what killed them?' Lernin shrugged: 'Several million species of living things have survived.'

Raph looked up, half in anger: 'I cannot accompany your group, Lernin, on a Voluntary basis. To go to the other world would be useful, yes, if I could engage in my own studies. For your purposes, it can be only a Community Job to me. I cannot give my heart to it.'

But Lernin's jaw was set: 'That arrangement would not be fair. There are many of us, my friend, who are sacrificing our own interests. If we all placed them first and investigated the other world in terms of our own particular provincialisms only, our great purpose would be destroyed. My friend, there is not one of our men that we can spare. We must all work as if our lives depended on our instant solution of the Eekah problem, which, believe me, it does.'

Raph's jaws twisted in distaste. 'On your side, you have a vague apprehension of these weak, stupid little creatures. On my side I have a definite problem of great intellectual attraction to myself. And between the two I can see no connection – no possible connection at all.'

'Nor can I. But listen to me a moment. A small group of our most trusted men returned last week from a visit to the other world. It was not official, as ours will be. It made no contacts. It was a frank piece of espionage, which I am telling you about now. I ask your discretion on the matter.'

'Naturally.'

'Our men possessed themselves of Eekah event-sheets.'

'Pardon me?'

'It is a created name to describe the objects. Printed records are issued daily in the various centers of Eekah population of events and occurrences of the day, and what passes for literary efforts as well.'

Raph was momentarily interested: 'It strikes me as an excellent idea.'

'Yes, in its essence. The Eekah notion of interesting events, however, appears to consist entirely of antisocial events. However, leave that be. My point is that the existence of the Americas is well-known there these days – and it is universally spoken of as a "new land of opportunity." The various divisions of Eekahs eye it with a universal desire. The Eekahs are many, they are crowded, their economy is irrational. They want new land, and that is what this is to them – new and empty land.'

'Not empty,' pointed out Raph, mildly.

'Empty to them,' insisted Lernin terribly. 'That is the vast danger. Lands occupied by Gurrows are to them empty and they mean to take it, all the more so since they have often enough striven to take the lands of one another.'

Raph shrugged: 'Even so, they —'

'Yes. They are weak and stupid. You said that, and so they are. But only singly. They will unite for a purpose. To be sure, they will fall apart when the purpose is done – but momentarily they will join and become strong, which we perhaps cannot do, witness yourself. And their weapons of war have been keened in the fire of conflict. Their flying machines, for instance, are superb war weapons.'

'But we have duplicated it —'

'In quantity? We have also duplicated their chemical explosives, but only in the laboratory, and their firing tubes and armored vehicles, but only in experimental plants. And yet there is more – something developed within the last five years, for our own Eekahs know nothing about it.'

'And what is that?'

'We don't know. Their event-sheets speak of it – the names applied to it mean nothing to us – but the context implies the terror of it, even on the part of these kill-mad Eekahs. There seems no evidence that it has been used, or that all the Eekah groups have it – but it is used as a supreme threat. It will perhaps be clearer to you when all the evidence is presented once our voyage is under way.'

'But what is it? You talk of it as if it were a bogey.'

'Why, *they* talk of it as if it were a bogey. And what *could* be a bogey to an Eekah? That is the most frightening aspect of it. So far, we know only that it involves the bombardment of an element they call plutonium – of which we have never heard and of which our own Eekahs have never heard either – by objects called neutrons, which our Eekahs say are subatomic particles without charge, which seems to us completely ridiculous.'

'And that is all?'

'All. Will you suspend judgment till we show you the sheets?'

Raph nodded reluctantly: 'Very well.'

Raph's leaden thoughts revolved in their worn groove as he stood there alone.

Eekahs and Primate Primeval. A living creature of erratic habits and a dead creature that must have aspired to heights. A sordid present of explosives and neutron bombardments and a glorious, mysterious past —

No connection! No connection!

THE END

By June 1947 I had already been working on my Ph.D. research with near-total concentration (I was no longer working in the candy store; my younger brother, Stanley, had taken over) for nearly a year. I was in the home stretch and beginning to think forward to writing my Ph.D. dissertation. I rather dreaded that, since the obligatory style of dissertations is turgid in the extreme, and I had by now spent nine years trying to write well and was afraid I simply might not be able to write badly enough to qualify for my degree.

The experiments I was doing at the time required me, periodically, to dissolve a compound called catechol in water. The catechol existed in fine, feathery, fluffy needles that dissolved very readily in water. In fact, when I sprinkled catechol into the beaker of water, the individual needles dissolved as soon as they struck the water surface. Idly, it occurred to me that if the catechol were any more soluble than it was, it would dissolve *before* it struck the water surface.

Naturally, I thought at once that this notion might be the basis for an amusing story. It occurred to me, however, that instead of writing an actual story based on the idea, I might write up a fake research paper on the subject and get a little practice in turgid writing.

I did the job on June 8, 1947, even giving it the kind of long-winded title that research papers so often have – 'The Endochronic Properties of Resublimated Thiotimoline' – and added tables, graphs and fake references to non-existent journals.

I was not at all sure that 'Thiotimoline' (no use trying to quote the entire name every time) was publishable. *Astounding*, however, ran serious articles on scientific subjects of particular interest to science fiction readers and I thought it just possible Campbell might be interested in a gag article that would be on the borders of science fiction.

I brought it in to him on the tenth, and he took it almost at once.

25: The Endochronic Properties of Resublimated Thiotimoline

The correlation of the structure of organic molecules with their various properties, physical and chemical, has in recent years afforded much insight into the mechanism of organic reactions, notably in the theories of resonance and mesomerism as developed in the last decade. The solubilities of organic compounds in various solvents has become of particular interest in this connection through the recent discovery of the endochronic nature of thiotimoline.

It has been long known that the solubility of organic compounds in polar solvents such as water is enhanced by the presence upon the hydrocarbon nucleus of hydrophilic – i.e., water-loving – groups, such as the hydroxy (-OH), amino (-NH_2), or sulfonic acid (SO_3H) groups. Where the physical characteristics of two given compounds – particularly the degree of subdivision of the material – are equal, then the time of solution – expressed in seconds per gram of material per milliliter of solvent – decreases with the number of hydrophilic groups present. Catechol, for instance, with two hydroxy groups on the benzene nucleus, dissolves considerably more quickly than does phenol, with only one hydroxy group on the nucleus. Feinschreiber and Hravlek in their studies on the problem have contended that with increasing hydrophilism, the time of solution approaches zero. That this analysis is not entirely correct was shown when it was discovered that the compound thiotimoline will dissolve in water – in the proportions of 1 gm./ml. – in *minus* 1.12 seconds. That is, it will dissolve *before* the water is added.

Previous communications from these laboratories indicated thiotimoline to contain at least fourteen hydroxy groups, two amino groups and one sulfonic acid group. The presence of a nitro group (-NO_2) in addition has not yet been confirmed, and no evidence as yet exists as to the nature of the hydrocarbon nucleus, though an at least partly aromatic structure seems certain.

The Endochronometer – First attempts to measure the time

Astounding Science Fiction, March 1948
Copyright © 1948 by Street & Smith Publications, Inc.

of solution of thiotimoline quantitatively met with considerable difficulty because of the very negative nature of the value. The fact that the chemical dissolved prior to the addition of the water made the attempt natural to withdraw the water after solution and before addition. This, fortunately for the law of Conservation of Mass-Energy, never succeeded, since solution never took place unless the water was eventually added. The question is, of course, instantly raised as to how the thiotimoline can 'know' in advance whether the water will ultimately be added or not. Though this is not properly within our province as physical chemists, much recent material has been published within the last year upon the psychological and philosophical problems thereby posed.

Nevertheless, the chemical difficulties involved rest in the fact that the time of solution varies enormously with the exact mental state of the experimenter. A period of even slight hesitation in adding the water reduces the negative time of solution, not infrequently wiping it out below the limits of detection. To avoid this, a mechanical device has been constructed, the essential design of which has already been reported in a previous communication.[6] This device, termed the endochronometer, consists of a cell 2 cubic centimeters in size into which a desired weight of thiotimoline is placed, making certain that a small hollow extension at the bottom of the solution cell – 1 millimeter in internal diameter – is filled. To the cell is attached an automatic pressure micro-pipette containing a specific volume of the solvent concerned. Five seconds after the circuit is closed, this solvent is automatically delivered into the cell containing the thiotimoline. During the time of action, a ray of light is focused upon the small cell-extension described above, and at the instant of solution, the transmission of this light will no longer be impeded by the presence of solid thiotimoline. Both the instant of solution – at which time the transmission of light is recorded by a photo-electric device – and the instant of solvent addition can be determined with an accuracy of better than 0.01 %. If the first value is subtracted from the second, the time of solution (T) can be determined.

The entire process is conducted in a thermostat maintained at 25.00° C. – to an accuracy of 0.01° C.

Thiotimoline Purity – The extreme sensitivity of this method highlights the deviations resulting from trifling impurities present in thiotimoline. (Since no method of laboratory synthesis of the substance has been devised, it may be practically obtained only through tedious isolation from its natural source, the bark of the shrub *Rosacea Karlsbadensis rugo*.) Great efforts were therefore made to purify the material through repeated recrystallizations from conductivity water – twice redistilled in an all-tin apparatus – and through final sublimations. A comparison of the solution times (T) at various stages of the purification process is shown in Table I.

TABLE I

Purification stage	Average 'T' (12 observations)	'T' extremes	% error
As isolated	−0·72	−0·25; −1·01	34·1
First recrystallization	−0·95	−0·84; −1·09	9·8
Second recrystallization	−1·05	−0·99; −1·10	4·0
Third recrystallization	−1·11	−1·08; −1·13	1·8
Fourth recrystallization	−1·12	−1·10; −1·13	1·7
First resublimation	−1·12	−1·11; −1·13	0·9
Second resublimation	−1·122	−1·12; −1·13	0·7

It is obvious from Table I that for truly quantitative significance, thiotimoline purified as described must be used. After the second resublimation, for instance, the error involved in an even dozen determinations is less than 0.7%, with the extreme values being −1.119 seconds and −1.126 seconds.

In all experiments described subsequently in this study, thiotimoline so purified has been used.

Time of Solution and Volume of Solvent – As would seem reasonable, experiments have shown that increasing the volume of solvent enables the thiotimoline to dissolve more quickly – i.e., with an increasingly negative time of solution. From Figure 1, however, we can see that this increase in endochronic properties levels off rapidly after a volume of solvent of approximately 1.25 ml. This interesting plateau effect has appeared with varying volume of solvent for all varieties of solvents used in these laboratories, just as in all cases the time of solution approaches zero with decreasing volume of solvent.

Time of Solution and Concentration of a Given Ion – In Figure 2, the results are given of the effect of the time of

113

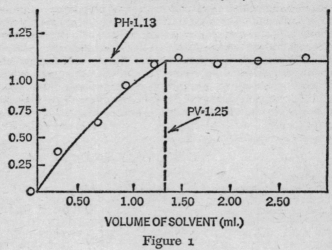

Figure 1

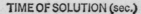

Figure 2

solution (T) of varying the volume of solvent, where the solvent consists of varying concentrations of sodium chloride solution. It can be seen that, although in each case the volume at which this plateau is reached differs markedly with the concentration, the heights of the plateau are constant (i.e. —1.13). The volume at which it is reached, hereinafter termed the Plateau Volume (PV), decreases with decreasing concentration of sodium chloride, approaching the PV for water as the NaCl concentration approaches zero. It is, therefore, obvious that a sodium chloride solution of unknown concentration can be quite accurately characterized by the determination of its PV, where other salts are absent.

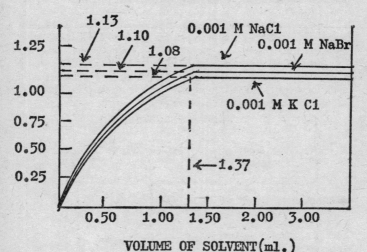

Figure 3

This usefulness of PV extends to other ions as well. Figure 3 gives the endochronic curves for 0.001 molar solutions of sodium chloride, sodium bromide and potassium chloride. Here, the PV in each case is equal within the limits of experimental error — since the concentrations in each case are equal — but the Plateau Heights (PH) *are* different.

A tentative conclusion that might be reached from this experimental data is that the PH is characteristic of the nature of the ions present in solution, whereas the PV is characteristic of the concentration of these ions. Table II gives the values of Plateau Height and Plateau Volume for a wide variety of salts in equal concentrations, when present alone.

The most interesting variation to be noted in Table II is that of the PV with the valence type of the salt present. In the case of salts containing pairs of singly-charged ions – i.e., sodium chloride, potassium chloride and sodium bromide – the PV is constant for all. This holds also for those salts containing one singly charged ion and one double charged ion – i.e. sodium sulphate, calcium chloride and magnesium chloride – where the PV, though equal among the three, varies markedly from those of the first set. The PV is, therefore, apparently a function of the ionic strength of the solution.

This effect also exists in connection with the Plateau Height, though less regularly. In the case of singly charged ions, such as in the first three salts listed in Table II, the PH is fairly close to that of water itself. It falls considerably where doubly charged ions, such as sulphate or calcium, are present. And when the triply charged phosphate ion or ferric ion is present, the value sinks to merely a quarter of its value in water.

TABLE II

Solvent (Salt solutions in 0·001 M concentration)	Plateau Height (PH) seconds	Plateau Volume (PV) milliliters
Water	−1·13	1·25
Sodium Chloride solution	−1·13	1·37
Sodium Bromide Solution	−1·10	1·37
Potassium Chloride solution	−1·08	1·37
Sodium Sulphate solution	−0·72	1·59
Calcium Chloride solution	−0·96	1·59
Magnesium Chloride solution	−0·85	1·59
Calcium Sulphate solution	−0·61	1·72
Sodium Phosphate solution	−0·32	1·97
Ferric Chloride solution	−0·29	1·99

Time of Solution and Mixtures of Ions – Experiments currently in progress in these laboratories are concerned with the extremely important question of the variation of these endochronic properties of thiotimoline in the presence of mixtures of ions. The state of our data at present does not warrant very

116

general conclusions, but even our preliminary work gives hope of the further development of the endochronic methods of analysis. Thus, in Figure 4, we have the endochronic curve where a mixture of 0.001 M Sodium Chloride and 0.001 M Ferric Chloride solutions is the solvent. Here, two sharp changes in slope can be seen: the first at a solution time of −0.29, and the second at −1.13, these being the PH's characteristic of Fer-

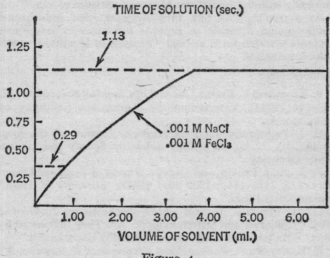

Figure 4

ric Chloride and Sodium Chloride respectively – see Table II. The PH for a given salt would thus appear not to be affected by the presence of other salts.

This is definitely not the case, however, for the PV, and it is to a quantitative elucidation of the variation of PV with impurities in the solvent that our major efforts are now directed.

Summary – Investigations of the endochronic qualities of thiotimoline have shown that:

a – Careful purification of the material is necessary for obtaining quantitative results.

b – Increasing the volume of solvent results in increasing the negative time of solution to a constant value known as the

Plateau Height (PH), at a volume of solvent known as the Plateau Volume (PV).

c – The value of the PH is characteristic of the nature of the ions present in the solvent, varying with the ionic strength of the solution and not varying with the addition of other ions.

d – The value of the PV is characteristic of the concentration of the ions present in the solvent, being constant for different ions in solution of equal ionic strength, but varying markedly with the admixtures of second varieties of ions.

As a result of all this, it is suggested that endochronic methods offer a means of rapid – 2 minutes or less – and accurate – within 0.1 % at least – analysis of inorganic, water-soluble materials.

Bibliography:

P. Krum and L. Eshkin. *Journal of Chemical Solubilities, 27*, 109–114 (1944), 'Concerning the Anomalous Solubility of Thiotimoline.'

E. J. Feinshreiber and Y. Hravlek. *Journal of Chemical Solubilities, 22*, 57–68 (1939), 'Solubility Speeds and Hydrophilic Groupings.'

P. Krum, I. Eshkin, and O. Nile. *Annals of Synthetic Chemistry, 115*, 1122–1145; 1208–1215 (1945), 'Structure of Thiotimoline, Parts I & II.'

G. H. Freudler, *Journal of Psychochemistry, 2*, 476–488 (1945), 'Initiative and Determination: Are They Influenced by Diet? – As tested by Thiotimoline solubility Experiments.'

E. Harley-Short, *Philosophical Proceedings & Reviews, 15*, 125–197 (1946), 'Determinism and Free-Will. The Application of Thiotimoline Solubility to Marxian Dialectic.'

P. Krum, *'Journal of Chemical Solubilities, 29*, 818–819 (1946), 'A Device for the Quantitative Measurement of Thiotimoline Solubility Speed.'

A. Roundin, B. Lev, and Y. J. Prutt, *Proceedings of the Society of Plant Chemistry, 80*, 11–18 (1930), 'Natural Products isolated from shrubs of the genus *Rosacea*.'

Tiotimolin kak Ispitatel Marksciiskoy dilektiki B. Kreschiatika, *Journal Naouki i Sovetskoy Ticorii* Vol. 11, No. 3.

Philossophia Neopredelennosti i Tiotimolin, Molvinski Pogost i Z. Brikalo. *Mir i Kultura* Vol. 2, No. 31.

THE END

When Campbell took the piece, I made one cautious stipulation. I knew it would appear in the spring and I knew that in the spring I would come up for my 'oral examinations' – the last hurdle on the path to my Ph.D. I didn't want any austere member of the examining board to decide I was making fun of chemical research and to be sufficiently offended to vote against me on the grounds that I wasn't temperamentally suited to the high honor of the doctorate. – So I asked Campbell to run it under a pseudonym.

When the magazine with the article finally reached the newsstands, in mid-February 1948, I was appalled to discover that Campbell had utterly forgotten the matter of the pseudonym. The article appeared under my own name and I was scheduled to have my orals within three months. My nervousness was increased when, almost at once, copies of the magazine began circulating in the chemistry department.

On May 20, 1948, I had my orals. The examining board *had* seen the article. After I had been on the grill for an hour and twenty minutes, the last question (asked by Professor Ralph S. Halford) was, 'Mr. Asimov, tell us something about the thermodynamic properties of the compound thiotimoline.'

I broke into hysterical laughter out of sheer relief, for it struck me instantly that they wouldn't play good-natured jokes with me (Professor Halford sounded jovial and everyone else was smiling) if they were going to flunk me. I was led out, still laughing, and after a twenty-minute wait, the examiners emerged, shook my hand, and said, 'Congratulations, Dr. Asimov.'

My fellow students insisted on forcing five Manhattans down my throat that afternoon and, since I am a teetotaler under normal conditions and have no tolerance for alcohol, I was royally drunk at once. It took them three hours to sober me up.

After the official ceremonies, on June 1, 1948, I was Isaac Asimov, Ph.D.

As it turned out, Campbell's non-use of a pseudonym (and I bet he did it deliberately, because he was smarter than I was) was a lucky break indeed. Not only did the examining board *not* take it amiss, but the article became, in a minor way, famous, and I with it.

Although 'Thiotimoline' appeared in *Astounding*, as did all my stories of the time, it received circulation far outside the ordinary science fiction world. It passed from chemist to chemist, by way of the magazine itself, or by reprints in small trade journals, or by copies pirated and mimeographed, even by word of mouth. People who had never heard of me at all as a science fiction writer, heard of thiotimoline. It was the very first time my fame transcended the field.

What's more, although 'Thiotimoline' was essentially a work of fantasy, the *form* was that of non-fiction. Viewed from that standpoint, 'Thiotimoline' was the first piece of non-fiction I had ever published professionally – the harbinger of a vast amount to come.

But what amused me most was that a surprising number of readers actually took the article seriously. I was told that in the weeks after its appearance the librarians at the New York Public Library were driven out of their minds by hordes of eager youngsters who demanded to see copies of the fake journals I had used as pseudo references.

But back to the summer of 1947 —

Over a period of five years I had sold fourteen stories, every one of them to Campbell. This didn't mean that he was the only editor in the field, at all. Almost all the magazines that had been published before the war still existed (although only *Astounding* was really doing well) and would have welcomed submissions from me. Had Campbell rejected any of the stories I had submitted to him, I would certainly have tried one of those other magazines. – But he didn't, so I didn't.

The magazine *Startling Stories*, in which I had published 'Christmas on Ganymede' five and a half years before, published a forty-thousand word 'short novel' in each issue. It wasn't easy to get a publishable story of that length every month though, especially since *Startling*'s rate was only half that of *Astounding*.

Sometimes it was necessary, therefore, for the editor of the magazine, who at that time was Sam Merwin, Jr., to canvass those authors known to be capable of turning out such a story. About the time I was doing 'Thiotimoline,' Merwin approached me with a suggestion that I write a lead short novel.

Startling, he explained, had always published stories with the accent on adventure, but, in imitation of *Astounding*'s success, he had persuaded the publisher to try the experiment of publishing stories with a heavier accent on science. Would I consider, then, doing a lead for *Startling*?

I was terribly flattered. Also, as I said earlier, I was nervous about having become a one-editor author and would have welcomed a chance to prove to myself that I could write beyond Campbell's protective shadow. I agreed, therefore, and a good part of the summer of 1947 (when I wasn't engaged in preparing my experimental data for the upcoming Ph.D. dissertation) was spent in preparing a story I called 'Grow Old with Me.'*

By August 3 I had completed first draft. On August 26, I had the first part of it in final copy and submitted that to Merwin. He approved. On September 23 the entire story was submitted and I had no doubt, whatever, of its acceptance. On October 15, 1947, however, Merwin told me that, alas, *Startling* had decided not to go for heavy science, after all, but for adventure, and that 'Grow Old with Me' would have to be completely rewritten with no guarantee of acceptance after that.

I suppose it is an indication of how things had advanced when I tell you it was the first time that I did not accept a request for revision philosophically. Quite otherwise! It had been five years and more since even Campbell had rejected one of my stories; how, then, dare a comparative nonentity like Merwin do so? Particularly since *he* had approached *me* for the story?

I made no effort to hide my annoyance. In fact, I seized the manuscript and stalked out of the office, and in an obvious rage.† I submitted the story to Campbell, giving him a full account of events. – I have always made it a practice to tell any editor to whom I submit a story of any rejection it has previously received. There is no necessity to do this; it is not, as far as I know, an ethical requirement for a writer. I just do

---

* This was inspired by Robert Browning's poem *Rabbi Ben Ezra* and was a misquotation – which shows you the level of my culture. The first line of the poem is 'Grow old along with me.'
† Years afterwards, as a result of the subsequent history of that story, Merwin took to apologizing for that rejection every time he met me – but he didn't have to, and I kept telling him so. He was editor, and he was completely within his rights to reject the story, and I was being pettily temperamental to be angry about it. I have made every effort, since, to avoid evident anger at any rejection, however unjustified it might seem at the time, and I think I have succeeded.

it, and it has not, again as far as I know, ever cost me an acceptance.

As it happened, Campbell rejected the story, but not, I'm sure, because it had been somewhere else first. He told me enough things wrong with the story to make me feel that perhaps Merwin had not been so arbitrary in rejecting it. I thrust the story in the drawer in disgust and thought no more about it for nearly two years.

The rejection came at a bad time. More and more, I was wrapped up in trying to complete my research, in writing my dissertation, and, most of all, in anxiously looking for a job. There wasn't much time to write, and the rejection had sufficiently disheartened and humiliated me so that I withdrew from writing for nearly a year. This was the third long withdrawal of my writing career, and, to this date, the last.

I did not find a job; my expected Ph.D. degree was no passport to affluence, after all. That was humiliating, too.

I accepted an offer from Professor Robert C. Elderfield to do a year's postdoctoral research for him for $4,500, working on anti-malarial drugs. I accepted, though not with great enthusiasm, and started work for him on June 2, 1948, the day after I had officially gained my Ph.D. – At least it would give me another year to find a job.

By the next month, I had settled down sufficiently to consider writing a science fiction story, 'The Red Queen's Race.' On July 12 it was finished and I submitted it to Campbell. It was accepted on the sixteenth and once again I was back in business.

26: The Red Queen's Race

Here's a puzzle for you, if you like. Is it a crime to translate a chemistry textbook into Greek?

Or let's put it another way. If one of the country's largest atomic power plants is completely ruined in an unauthorized experiment, is an admitted accessory to that act a criminal?

These problems only developed with time, of course. We started with the atomic power plant – drained. I really mean *drained*. I don't know exactly how large the fissionable power source was – but in two flashing microseconds, it had all fissioned.

No explosion. No undue gamma ray density. It was merely that every moving part in the entire structure was fused. The entire main building was mildly hot. Just a dead, useless building which later on took a hundred million dollars to replace.

It happened about three in the morning, and they found Elmer Tywood alone in the central source chamber. The findings of twenty-four close-packed hours can be summarized quickly.

1. Elmer Tywood – Ph.D., Sc.D., Fellow of This and Honorary That, one-time youthful participant of the original Manhattan Project, and now full Professor of Nuclear Physics – was no interloper. He had a Class-A Pass – Unlimited. But no record could be found as to his purpose in being there just then. A table on casters contained equipment which had not been made on any recorded requisition. It, too, was a single fused mass – not quite too hot to touch.

2. Elmer Tywood was dead. He lay next to the table; his face congested, nearly black. No radiation effect. No external force of any sort. The doctor said apoplexy.

3. In Elmer Tywood's office safe were found two puzzling items: i.e. twenty foolscap sheets of apparent mathematics, and a bound folio in a foreign language which turned out to be Greek, the subject matter, on translation, turning out to be chemistry.

The secrecy which poured over the whole mess was some-

Astounding Science Fiction, January 1949
Copyright © 1948 by Street & Smith Publications, Inc.

thing so terrific as to make everything that touched it, *dead*. It's the only word that can describe it. Twenty-seven men and women, all told, including the Secretary of Defense, the Secretary of Science and two or three others so top-notch that they were completely unknown to the public, entered the power plant during the period of investigation. All who had been in the plant that night, the physicist who had identified Tywood, the doctor who had examined him, were retired into virtual home arrest.

No newspaper ever got the story. No inside dopester got it. A few members of Congress got part of it.

And naturally so! Anyone or any group or any country that could suck all the available energy out of the equivalent of perhaps fifty to a hundred pounds of plutonium without exploding it, had America's industry and America's defense so snugly in the palm of the hand that the light and life of one hundred sixty million people could be turned off between yawns.

Was it Tywood? Or Tywood and others? Or just others, through Tywood?

And my job? I was decoy; or front man, if you like. Someone has to hang around the university and ask questions about Tywood. After all, he was missing. It could be amnesia, a hold-up, a kidnapping, a killing, a runaway, insanity, accident – I could busy myself with that for five years and collect black looks, and maybe divert attention. To be sure, it didn't work out that way.

But don't think I was in on the whole case at the start. I wasn't one of the twenty-seven men I mentioned a while back, though my boss was. But I knew a little – enough to get started.

Professor John Keyser was also in Physics. I didn't get to him right away. There was a good deal of routine to cover first in as conscientious a way as I could. Quite meaningless. Quite necessary. But I was in Keyser's office now.

Professors' offices are distinctive. Nobody dusts them except some tired cleaning woman who hobbles in and out at eight in the morning, and the professor never notices the dust anyway. Lots of books without much arrangement. The ones close to the desk are used a lot – lectures are copied out of them. The ones out of reach are wherever a student put them back after borrowing them. Then there are professional journals that look cheap and are darned expensive, which are waiting about and which may some day be read. And plenty of paper on the desk; some of it scribbled on.

Keyser was an elderly man – one of Tywood's generation. His nose was big and rather red, and he smoked a pipe. He had that easy-going and nonpredatory look in his eyes that goes with an academic job – either because that kind of job attracts that kind of man or because that kind of job makes that kind of man.

I said: 'What kind of work is Professor Tywood doing?'

'Research physics.'

Answers like that bounce off me. Some years ago they used to get me mad. Now I just said: 'We know that, professor. It's the details I'm after.'

And he twinkled at me tolerantly: 'Surely the details can't help much unless you're a research physicist yourself. Does it matter – under the circumstances?'

'Maybe not. But he's gone. If anything's happened to him in the way of' – I gestured, and deliberately clinched – 'foul play, his work may have something to do with it – unless he's rich and the motive is money.'

Keyser chuckled dryly: 'College professors are never rich. The commodity we peddle is but lightly considered, seeing how large the supply is.'

I ignored that, too, because I know my looks are against me. Actually, I finished college with a 'very good' translated into Latin so that the college president could understand it, and never played in a football game in my life. But I look rather the reverse.

I said: 'Then we're left with his work to consider.'

'You mean spies? International intrigue?'

'Why not? It's happened before! After all, he's a nuclear physicist, isn't he?'

'He is. But so are others. So am I.'

'Ah, but perhaps he knows something you don't.'

There was a stiffening to the jaw. When caught off-guard, professors can act just like people. He said, stiffly: 'As I recall offhand, Tywood has published papers on the effect of liquid viscosity on the wings of the Rayleigh line, on higher-orbit field equations, and on spin-orbit coupling of two nucleons, but his main work is on quadrupole moments. I am quite competent in these matters.'

'Is he working on quadrupole moments now?' I tried not to bat an eye, and I think I succeeded.

'Yes – in a way.' He almost sneered, 'He may be getting to the experimental stage finally. He's spent most of his life, it seems, working out the mathematical consequences of a special theory of his own.'

'Like this,' and I tossed a sheet of foolscap at him.

The sheet was one of those in the safe in Tywood's office. The chances, of course, were that the bundle meant nothing, if only because it was a professor's safe. That is, things are sometimes put in at the spur of the moment because the logical drawer was filled with unmarked exam papers. And of course, nothing is ever taken out. We had found in that safe dusty little vials of yellowish crystals with scarcely legible labels, some mimeographed booklets dating back to World War II and marked 'Restricted,' a copy of an old college yearbook, and some correspondence concerning a possible position as Director of Research for American Electric, dated ten years back, and, of course, chemistry in Greek.

The foolscap was there, too. It was rolled up like a college diploma with a rubber band about it and had no label or descriptive title. Some twenty sheets were covered with ink marks, meticulous and small —

I had one sheet of that foolscap. I don't think any one man in the world had more than one sheet. And I'm sure that no man in the world but one knew that the loss of his particular sheet and of his particular life would be as nearly simultaneous as the government could make it.

So I tossed the sheet at Keyser, as if it were something I'd found blowing about the campus.

He stared at it and then looked at the back side, which was blank. His eyes moved down from the top to the bottom, then jumped back to the top.

'I don't know what this is about,' he said, and the words seemed sour to his own taste.

I didn't say anything. Just folded the paper and shoved it back into the inside jacket pocket.

Keyser added petulantly: 'It's a fallacy you laymen have that scientists can look at an equation and say, "Ah, yes —" and go on to write a book about it. Mathematics has no existence of its own. It is merely an arbitrary code devised to describe physical observations or philosophical concepts. Every man can adapt it is to his own particular needs. For instance no one can look at a symbol and be sure of what it means. So far, science has used every letter in the alphabet, large, small and italic, each symbolizing many different things. They have used bold-faced letters, Gothic-type letters, Greek letters, both capital and small, subscripts, superscripts, asterisks, even Hebrew letters. Different scientists use different symbols for the same concept and the same symbol for different concepts. So if you show a disconnected page like this to any man, without information as to the subject being investigated or the particular symbology used, he could absolutely not make sense out of it.'

I interrupted: 'But you said he was working on quadrupole moments. Does that make this sensible?' and I tapped the spot on my chest where the foolscap had been slowly scorching a hole in my jacket for two days.

'I can't tell. I saw none of the standard relationships that I'd expect to be involved. At least I recognized none. But I obviously can't commit myself.'

There was a short silence, then he said: 'I'll tell you. Why don't you check with his students?'

I lifted my eyebrows: 'You mean in his classes?'

He seemed annoyed: 'No, for Heaven's sake. His research students! His doctoral candidates! They've been working with him. They'll know the details of that work better than I, or anyone in the faculty, could possibly know it.'

'It's an idea,' I said, casually. It was, too. I don't know why, but I wouldn't have thought of it myself. I guess it's because it's only natural to think that any professor knows more than any student.

Keyser latched onto a lapel as I rose to leave. 'And, besides,' he said, 'I think you're on the wrong track. This is in confidence, you understand, and I wouldn't say it except for the unusual circumstances, but Tywood is not thought of too highly in the profession. Oh, he's an adequate teacher, I'll admit, but his research papers have never commanded respect. There has always been a tendency toward vague theorizing, unsupported by experimental evidence. That paper of yours is probably more of it. No one could possibly want to ... er kidnap him because of it.'

'Is that so? I see. Any ideas, yourself, as to why he's gone, or where he's gone?'

'Nothing concrete,' he said pursing his lips, 'but everyone knows he is a sick man. He had a stroke two years ago that kept him out of classes for a semester. He never did get well. His left side was paralyzed for a while and he still limps. Another stroke would kill him. It could come any time.'

'You think he's dead, then?'

'It's not impossible.'

'But where's the body, then?'

'Well, really – That is *your* job, I think.'

It was, and I left.

I interviewed each one of Tywood's four research students in a volume of chaos called a research laboratory. These student research laboratories usually have two hopefuls working therein, said two constituting a floating population, since every year or so they are alternately replaced.

Consequently, the laboratory has its equipment stack in tiers. On the laboratory benches is the equipment immediately being used, and in three or four of the handiest drawers are replacements or supplements which are likely to be used. In the farther drawers, on the shelves reaching up to the ceiling, in odd corners, are fading remnants of the past student generations – oddments never used and never discarded. It is claimed, in fact, that no research student ever knew all the contents of his laboratory.

All four of Tywood's students were worried. But three were worried mainly by their own status. That is, by the possible effect the absence of Tywood might have on the status of their 'problem.' I dismissed those three – who all have their degrees now, I hope – and called back the fourth.

He had the most haggard look of all, and had been least communicative – which I considered a hopeful sign.

He now sat stiffly in the straight-backed chair at the right of the desk, while I leaned back in a creaky old swivel-chair and pushed my hat off my forehead. His name was Edwin Howe and *he* did get his degree later on; I know that for sure, because he's a big wheel in the Department of Science now.

I said: 'You do the same work the other boys do, I suppose?'

'It's all nuclear work, in a way.'

'But it's not all exactly the same?'

He shook his head slowly. 'We take different angles. You

have to have something clear-cut, you know, or you won't be able to publish. We've got to get our degrees.'

He said it exactly the way you or I might say, 'We've got to make a living.' At that, maybe it's the same thing for them.

I said: 'All right. What's *your* angle?'

He said: 'I do the math. I mean, with Professor Tywood.'

'What kind of math?'

And he smiled a little, getting the same sort of atmosphere about him that I had noticed in Professor Keyser's case that morning. A sort of, 'Do-you-really-think-I-can-explain-all-my-profound-thoughts-to-stupid-little-you?' sort of atmosphere.

All he said aloud, however, was: 'That would be rather complicated to explain.'

'I'll help you,' I said. 'Is that anything like it?' And I tossed the foolscap sheet at him.

He didn't give it any once-over. He just snatched it up and let out a thin wail: 'Where'd you get this?'

'From Tywood's safe.'

'Do you have the rest of it, too?'

'It's safe,' I hedged.

He relaxed a little – just a little: 'You didn't show it to anybody, did you?'

I showed it to Professor Keyser.'

Howe made an impolite sound with his lower lip and front teeth, '*That* jackass. What did he say?'

I turned the palms of my hands upward and Howe laughed. Then he said, in an offhand manner: 'Well, that's the sort of stuff I do.'

'And what's it all about? Put it so I can understand it.'

There was distinct hesitation. He said: 'Now, look. This is confidential stuff. Even Pop's other students don't know anything about it. I don't even think *I* know *all* about it. This isn't just a degree I'm after, you know. It's Pop Tywood's Nobel Prize, and it's going to be an Assistant Professorship for me at Cal Tech. This has got to be published before it's talked about.'

And I shook my head slowly and made my words very soft: 'No, son. You have it twisted. You'll have to talk about it before it's published, because Tywood's gone and maybe he's dead and maybe he isn't. And if he's dead, maybe he's murdered. And when the department has a suspicion of murder, everybody talks. Now, it will look bad for you, kid, if you try to keep some secrets.'

It worked. I knew it would, because everyone reads murder mysteries and knows all the clichés. He jumped out of his chair and rattled the words off as if he had a script in front of him.

'Surely,' he said, 'you can't suspect *me* of ... of anything like that. Why ... why, my career —'

I shoved him back into his chair with the beginnings of a sweat on his forehead. I went into the next line: 'I don't suspect anybody of anything *yet*. And you won't be in any trouble, if you talk, chum.'

He was ready to talk. 'Now this is all in strict confidence.'

Poor guy. He didn't know the meaning of the word 'strict.' He was never out of eyeshot of an operator from that moment till the government decided to bury the whole case with the one final comment of '?' Quote. Unquote. (I'm not kidding. To this day, the case is neither opened nor closed. It's just '?')

He said, dubiously; 'You know what time travel is, I suppose?'

Sure I knew what time travel was. My oldest kid is twelve and he listens to the afternoon video programs till he swells up visibly with the junk he absorbs at the ears and eyes.

'What about time travel?' I said.

'In a sense, we can do it. Actually, it's only what you might call micro-temporal-translation —'

I almost lost my temper. In fact, I think I did. It seemed obvious that the squirt was trying to diddle me; and without subtlety. I'm used to having people think I look dumb; but not *that* dumb.

I said through the back of my throat: 'Are you going to tell me that Tywood is out somewhere in time – like Ace Rogers, the Lone Time Ranger?' (That was Junior's favorite program – Ace Rogers was stopping Genghis Khan single-handed that week.)

But he looked as disgusted as I must have. 'No,' he yelled. 'I don't know where Pop is. If you'd *listen* to me – I said micro-temporal-translation. Now, this isn't a video show and it isn't magic; this happens to be science. For instance, you know about matter-energy equivalence, I suppose.'

I nodded sourly. Everyone knows about that since Hiroshima in the last war but one.

'All right, then,' he went on, 'that's good for a start. Now, if

130

you take a known mass of matter and apply temporal translation to it – you know, send it back in time – you are, in effect, creating matter at the point in time to which you are sending it. To do that, you must use an amount of energy equivalent to the amount of matter you have created. In other words, to send a gram – or, say, an ounce – of anything back in time, you have to disintegrate an ounce of matter completely, to furnish the energy required.'

'Hm-m-m,' I said, 'that's to create the ounce of matter in the past. But aren't you destroying an ounce of matter by removing it from the present? Doesn't that *create* the equivalent amount of energy?'

And he looked just about as annoyed as a fellow sitting on a bumblebee that wasn't quite dead. Apparently laymen are never supposed to question scientists.

He said: 'I was trying to simplify it so you would understand it. Actually, it's more complicated. It would be very nice if we could use the energy of disappearance to cause it to appear, but that would be working in a circle, believe me. The requirements of entropy would forbid it. To put it more rigorously, the energy is required to overcome temporal inertia and it just works out so that the energy in ergs required to send back a mass, in grams, is equal to the mass times the square of the speed of light in centimeters per second. Which just happens to be the Einstein Mass-Energy Equivalence Equation. I can give you the mathematics, you know.'

'I know,' I waxed some of that misplaced eagerness back. 'But was all this worked out experimentally? Or is it just on paper?'

Obviously, the thing was to keep him talking.

He had that queer light in his eye that every research student gets, I am told, when he is asked to discuss his problem. He'll discuss it with anyone, even with a 'dumb flatfoot' – which was convenient at the moment.

'You see,' he said like a man slipping you the inside dope on a shady business deal, 'what started the whole thing was this neutrino business. They've been trying to find that neutrino since the late thirties and they haven't succeeded. It's a subatomic particle which has no charge and has a mass much less than even an electron. Naturally, it's next to impossible to spot, and hasn't been spotted yet. But they keep looking because, without assuming that a neutrino exists, the energetics of some nuclear reactions can't be balanced. So Pop Tywood got the idea about twenty years ago that some energy was disappearing, in the form of matter, back into time. We got working on that – or he did – and I'm the first student he's ever had tackle it along with him.

'Obviously, we had to work with tiny amounts of material and ... well, it was just a stroke of genius on Pop's part to think of using traces of artificial radioactive isotopes. You could work with just a few micrograms of it, you know, by following its activity with counters. The variation of activity with time should follow a very definite and simple law which has never been altered by any laboratory condition known.

'Well, we'd send a speck back fifteen minutes, say, and fifteen minutes before we did that – everything was arranged automatically, you see – the count jumped to nearly double what it should be, fell off normally, and then dropped sharply at the moment it was sent back below where it would have been normally. The material overlapped itself in time, you see, and for fifteen minutes we counted the double material —'

I interrupted: 'You mean you had the same atoms existing in two places at the same time.'

'Yes,' he said, with mild surprise, 'why not? That's why we use so much energy – the equivalent of creating those atoms.' And then he rushed on, 'Now I'll tell you what my particular job is. If you send back the material fifteen minutes, it is apparently sent back to the same spot relative to the Earth despite the fact that in fifteen minutes, the Earth moved sixteen thousand miles around the Sun, and the Sun itself moves more thousand miles and so on. But there are certain tiny discrepancies which I've analyzed and which turn out to be due, possibly, to two causes.

'First, there is a frictional effect – if you can use such a term – so the matter does drift a little with respect to the Earth, depending on how far back in time it is sent, and on the nature of material. Then, too, some of the discrepancy can only be explained by the assumption that passage through time itself takes time.'

'How's that?' I said.

'What I mean is that some of the radioactivity is evenly spread throughout the time of translation as if the material tested had been reacting during backward passage through time by a constant amount. My figures show that – well, if you were to be moved backward in time, you would age one day for every hundred years. Or, to put it another way, if you could watch a time dial which recorded the time outside a "time-machine," your watch would move forward twenty-four hours while the time dial moved back a hundred years. That's a universal constant, I think, because the speed of light is a universal constant. Anyway, that's my work.'

After a few minutes, in which I chewed all this, I asked: 'Where did you get the energy needed for your experiments?'

'They ran out a special line from the power plant. Pop's a big shot there, and swung the deal.'

'Hm-m-m. What was the heaviest amount of material you sent into the past?'

'Oh' – he sent his eyes upwards – 'I think we shot back one hundredth of a milligram once. That's ten micrograms.'

'Ever try sending anything into the future?'

'That won't work,' he put in quickly. 'Impossible. You can't change signs like that, because the energy required becomes more than infinite. It's a one-way proposition.'

I looked hard at my fingernails: 'How much material could you send back in time if you fissioned about ... oh, say, one hundred pounds of plutonium.' Things, I thought, were becoming, if anything, too obvious.

The answer came quickly: 'In plutonium fission,' he said, 'not more than one or two percent of the mass is converted into energy. Therefore, one hundred pounds of plutonium when completely used up would send a pound or two back into time.'

'Is that all? But could you handle all that energy? I mean, a hundred pounds of plutonium can make quite an explosion.'

'All relative,' he said, a bit pompously. 'If you took all that energy and let it loose a little at a time, you could handle it. If you released it all at once, but used it just as fast as you released it, you could still handle it. In sending back material through time, energy can be used much faster than it can possibly be released even through fission. Theoretically, anyway.'

'But how do you get rid of it?'

'It's spread through time, naturally. Of course, the minimum time through which material could be transferred would, therefore, depend on the mass of the material. Otherwise, you're liable to have the energy density with time too high.'

'All right, kid,' I said. 'I'm calling up headquarters, and

they'll send a man here to take you home. You'll stay there a while.'

'But – What for?'

'It won't be for long.'

It wasn't – and it was made up to him afterwards.

I spent the evening at Headquarters. We had a library there – a very special kind of library. The very morning after the explosion, two or three operators had drifted quietly into the chemistry and physics libraries of the University. Experts in their way. They located every article Tywood had ever published in any scientific journal and had snapped each page. Nothing was disturbed otherwise.

Other men went through magazine files and through book lists. It ended with a room at Headquarters that represented a complete Tywoodana. Nor was there a definite purpose in doing this. It merely represented part of the thoroughness with which a problem of this sort is met.

I went through that library. Not the scientific papers. I knew there'd be nothing there that I wanted. But he had written a series of articles for a magazine twenty years back, and I read those. And I grabbed at every piece of private correspondence they had available.

After that, I just sat and thought – and got scared.

I got to bed about four in the morning and had nightmares.

But I was in the Boss' private office at nine in the morning just the same.

He's a big man, the Boss, with iron-gray hair slicked down tight. He doesn't smoke, but he keeps a box of cigars on his desk and when he doesn't want to say anything for a few seconds, he picks one up, rolls it about a little, smells it, then sticks it right into the middle of his mouth and lights it in a very careful way. By that time, he either has something to say or doesn't have to say anything at all. Then he puts the cigar down and lets it burn to death.

He used up a box in about three weeks, and every Christmas, half his gift-wraps held boxes of cigars.

He wasn't reaching for any cigars now, though. He just folded his big fists together on the desk and looked up at me from under a creased forehead. 'What's boiling?'

I told him. Slowly, because micro-temporal-translation doesn't sit well with anybody, especially when you call it time travel, which I did. It's a sign of how serious things were that he only asked me once if I were crazy.

Then I was finished and we stared at each other.

He said: 'And you think he tried to send something back in time – something weighing a pound or two – and blew an entire plant doing it?'

'It fits in,' I said.

I let him go for a while. He was thinking and I wanted him to keep on thinking. I wanted him, if possible, to think of the same thing I was thinking, so that I wouldn't have to tell him —

Because I hated to have to tell him —

Because it was nuts, for one thing. And too horrible, for another.

So I kept quiet and he kept on thinking and every once in a while some of his thoughts came to the surface.

After a while, he said: 'Assuming the student, Howe, to have told the truth – and you'd better check his notebooks, by the way, which I hope you've impounded —'

'The entire wing of that floor is out of bounds, sir. Edwards has the notebooks.'

He went on: 'All right. Assuming he told us all the truth he knows, why did Tywood jump from less than a milligram to a pound?'

His eyes came down and they were hard: 'Now you're concentrating on the time-travel angle. To you, I gather, that is the crucial point, with the energy involved as incidental – purely incidental.'

'Yes, sir,' I said grimly. 'I think exactly that.'

'Have you considered that you might be wrong? That you might have matters inverted?'

'I don't quite get that.'

'Well, look. You say you've read up on Tywood. All right. He was one of that bunch of scientists after World War II that fought the atom bomb; wanted a world state – You know about that, don't you?'

I nodded.

'He had a guilt complex,' the Boss said with energy. 'He'd helped work out the bomb, and he couldn't sleep nights thinking of what he'd done. He lived with that fear for years. And even though the bomb wasn't used in World War III, can you imagine what every day of uncertainty must have meant to him? Can you imagine the shriveling horror in his soul as he

135

waited for others to make the decision at every crucial moment till the final Compromise of Sixty-Five?

'We have a complete psychiatric analysis of Tywood and several others just like him, taken during the last war. Did you know that?'

'No, sir.'

'It's true. We let up after Sixty-Five, of course, because with the establishment of world control of atomic power, the scrapping of the atomic bomb stockpile in all countries, and the establishment of research liaison among the various spheres of influence on the planet, most of the ethical conflict in the scientific mind was removed.

'But the findings at the time were serious. In 1964, Tywood had a morbid subconscious hatred for the very concept of atomic power. He began to make mistakes, serious ones. Eventually, we were forced to take him off research of any kind. And several others as well, even though things were pretty bad at the time. We had just lost India, if you remember.'

Considering that I was in India at the time, I remembered. But I still wasn't seeing his point.

'Now, what,' he continued, 'if dregs of that attitude remained buried in Tywood to the very end? Don't you see that this time-travel is a double-edged sword? Why throw a pound of anything into the past, anyway? For the sake of proving a point? He had proved his case just as much when he sent back a fraction of a milligram. That was good enough for the Nobel Prize, I suppose.

'But there was *one* thing he could do with a pound of matter that he couldn't do with a milligram, and that was *to drain a power plant*. So that was what he must have been after. He had discovered a way of consuming inconceivable quantities of energy. By sending back eighty pounds of dirt, he could remove all the existing plutonium in the world. End atomic power for an indefinite period.'

I was completely unimpressed, but I tried not to make that too plain. I just said: 'Do you think he could possibly have thought he could get away with it more than once?'

'This is all based on the fact that he wasn't a normal man. How do I know what he could imagine he could do? Besides, there may be men behind him – with less science and more brains – who are quite ready to continue onwards from this point.'

'Have any of these men been found yet? Any evidence of such men?'

A little wait, and his hand reached for the cigar box. He stared at the cigar and turned it end for end. Just a little wait more. I was patient.

Then he put it down decisively without lighting it.

'No,' he said.

He looked at me, and clear through me and said: 'Then, you still don't go for that?'

I shrugged, 'Well – It doesn't sound right.'

'Do you have a notion of your own?'

'Yes. But I can't bring myself to talk about it. If I'm wrong, I'm the wrongest man that ever was; but if I'm right, I'm the rightest.'

'I'll listen,' he said, and he put his hand under the desk.

That was the pay-off. The room was armored, sound-proof, and radiation-proof to anything short of a nuclear explosion. And with that little signal showing on his secretary's desk, the President of the United States couldn't have interrupted us.

I leaned back and said: 'Chief, do you happen to remember how you met your wife? Was it a little thing?'

He must have thought it a *non sequitur*. What else could he have thought? But he was giving me my head now; having his own reasons, I suppose.

He just smiled and said: 'I sneezed and she turned around. It was at a street corner.'

'What made you be on that street corner just then? What made her be? Do you remember just why you sneezed? Where you caught the cold? Or where the speck of dust came from? Imagine how many factors had to intersect in just the right place at just the right time for you to meet your wife.'

'I suppose we would have met some other time, if not then?'

'But you can't *know* that. How do you know whom you *didn't* meet, because once when you might have turned around, you didn't; because once when you might have been late, you weren't. Your life forks at every instant, and you go down one of the forks almost at random, and so does everyone else. Start twenty years ago, and the forks diverge further and further with time.

'You sneezed, and met a girl, and not another. As a consequence, you made certain decisions, and so did the girl, and so did the girl you didn't meet, and the man who did meet her, and the people you all met thereafter. And your family, her

137

family, their family – and your children.

'Because you sneezed twenty years ago, five people, or fifty, or five hundred, might be dead now who would have been alive, or might be alive who would have been dead. Move it to two hundred years ago: two thousand years ago, and a sneeze – even by someone no history ever heard of – might have meant that no one now alive would have been alive.'

The Boss rubbed the back of his head: 'Widening ripples. I read a story once —'

'So did I. It's not a new idea – but I want you to think about it for a while, because I want to read to you from an article by Professor Elmer Tywood in a magazine twenty years old. It was just before the last war.'

I had copies of the film in my pocket and the white wall made a beautiful screen, which was what it was meant to do. The boss made a motion to turn about, but I waved him back.

'No, sir,' I said. 'I want to read this to you. And I want you to listen to it.'

He leaned back.

'The article,' I went on, is entitled: "Man's First Great Failure!" Remember, this was just before the war, when the bitter disappointment at the final failure of the United Nations was at its height. What I will read are some excerpts from the first part of the article. It goes like this:

' "... That Man, with his technical perfection, has failed to solve the great sociological problems of today is only the second immense tragedy that has come to the race. The first, and perhaps the greater, was that, once, these same great sociological problems *were* solved; and yet these solutions were not permanent, because the technical perfection we have today did not then exist.

' "It was a case of having bread without butter, or butter without bread. Never both together. . . .

' "Consider the Hellenic world, from which our philosophy, our mathematics, our ethics, our art, our literature – our entire culture, in fact – stem ... In the days of Pericles, Greece, like our own world in microcosm, was a surprisingly modern potpourri of conflicting ideologies and ways of life. But then Rome came, adopting the culture, but bestowing, and enforcing, peace. To be sure, the *Pax Romana* lasted only two hundred years, but no like period has existed since. . . .

' "War was abolished. Nationalism did not exist. The Roman

138

citizen was Empire-wide. Paul of Tarsus and Flavius Josephus were Roman citizens. Spaniards, North Africans, Illyrians assumed the purple. Slavery existed, but it was an indiscriminate slavery, imposed as a punishment, incurred as the price of economic failure, brought on by the fortunes of war. No man was a *natural* slave – because of the color of his skin or the place of his birth.

' "Religious toleration was complete. If an exception was made early in the case of the Christians, it was because they refused to accept the principle of toleration; because they insisted that only they themselves knew truth – a principle abhorrent to the civilized Roman. . . .

' "With all of Western culture under a single *polis*, with the cancer of religious and national particularism and exclusivism absent; with a high civilization in existence – why could not Man hold his gains?

' "It was because, technologically, ancient Hellenism remained backward. It was because without a machine civilization, the price of leisure – and hence civilization and culture – for the few, was slavery for the many. Because the civilization could not find the means to bring comfort and ease to *all* the population.

' "Therefore, the depressed classes turned to the other world, and to religions which spurned the material benefits of this world – so that science was made impossible in any true sense for over a millennium. And further, as the initial impetus of Hellenism waned, the Empire lacked the technological powers to beat back the barbarians. In fact, it was not till after A.D. 1500 that war became sufficiently a function of the industrial resources of a nation to enable the settled people to defeat invading tribesmen and nomads with ease. . . .

' "Imagine, then, if somehow the ancient Greeks had learned just a hint of modern chemistry and physics. Imagine if the growth of the Empire had been accompanied by the growth of science, technology and industry. Imagine an Empire in which machinery replaced slaves, in which all men had a decent share of the world's goods, in which the legion became the armored column against which no barbarians could stand. Imagine an Empire which would therefore spread all over the world, *without* religious or national prejudices.

' "An Empire of all men – all brothers – eventually all free. . . .

' "If history could be changed. If that first great failure could have been prevented —" '

And I stopped at that point.

'Well?' said the Boss.

'Well,' I said, 'I think it isn't difficult to connect all that with the fact that Tywood blew an entire power plant in his anxiety to send something back to the past, while in his office safe we found sections of a chemistry textbook translated into Greek.'

His face changed, while he considered.

Then he said heavily: 'But nothing's happened.'

'I know. But then I've been told by Tywood's student that it takes a day to move back a century in time. Assuming that ancient Greece was the target area, we have twenty centuries, hence twenty days.'

'But can it be stopped?'

'I wouldn't know. Tywood might, but he's dead.'

The enormity of it all hit me at once, deeper than it had the night before —

All humanity was virtually under sentence of death. And while that was merely horrible abstraction, the fact that reduced it to a thoroughly unbearable reality was that I was, too. And my wife, and my kid.

Further, it was a death without precedence. A ceasing to exist, and no more. The passing of a breath. The vanishing of a dream. The drift into eternal non-space and non-time of a shadow. I would not be dead at all, in fact. I would merely never have been born.

Or would I? Would I exist – my individuality – my ego – my soul, if you like? Another life? Other circumstances?

I thought none of that in words then. But if a cold knot in the stomach could ever speak under the circumstances, it would sound like that, I think.

The Boss moved in on my thoughts – hard.

'Then, we have about two and a half weeks. No time to lose. Come on.'

I grinned with one side of my mouth: 'What do we do? Chase the book?'

'No,' he replied coldly, 'but there are two courses of action we must follow. First, you may be wrong -- altogether. All of this circumstantial reasoning may still represent a false lead, perhaps deliberately thrown before us, to cover up the real truth. That must be checked.

'Secondly, you may be right – but there may be some way of stopping the book: other than chasing it in a time machine, I mean. If so, we must find out how.'

'I would just like to say, sir, if this is a false lead, only a madman would consider it a believable one. So suppose I'm right, and suppose there's no way of stopping it?'

'Then, young fellow, I'm going to keep pretty busy for two and a half weeks, and I'd advise you to do the same. The time will pass more quickly that way.'

Of course he was right.

'Where do we start?' I asked.

'The first thing we need is a list of all men and women on the government payroll under Tywood.'

'Why?'

'Reasoning. Your specialty, you know. Tywood doesn't know Greek, I think we can assume with fair safety, so someone else must have done the translating. It isn't likely that anyone would do a job like that for nothing, and it isn't likely that Tywood would pay out of his personal funds – not on a professor's salary.'

'He might,' I pointed out, 'have been interested in more secrecy than a government payroll affords.'

'Why? Where was the danger? Is it a crime to translate a chemistry textbook into Greek? Who would ever deduce from that a plot such as you've described?'

It took us half an hour to turn up the name of Mycroft James Boulder, listed as 'Consultant,' and to find out that he was mentioned in the University Catalogue as Assistant Professor of Philosophy and to check by telephone that among his many accomplishments was a thorough knowledge of Attic Greek.

Which was a coincidence – because with the Boss reaching for his hat, the interoffice teletype clicked away and it turned out that Mycroft James Boulder was in the anteroom, at the end of a two-hour continuing insistence that he see the Boss.

The Boss put his hat back and opened his office door.

Professor Mycroft James Boulder was a gray man. His hair was gray and his eyes were gray. His suit was gray, too.

But most of all, his expression was gray; gray with a tension that seemed to twist at the lines in his thin face.

Boulder said, softly: 'I've been trying for three days to get a hearing, sir, with a responsible man. I can get no higher than

141

yourself.'

'I may be high enough,' said the Boss. 'What's on your mind?'

'It is quite important that I be granted an interview with Professor Tywood.'

'Do you know where he is?'

'I am quite certain that he is in government custody.'

'Why?'

'Because I know that he was planning an experiment which would entail the breaking of security regulations. Events since, as nearly as I can make them out, flow naturally from the supposition that security regulations have indeed been broken. I can presume, then, that the experiment has at least been attempted. I must discover whether it has been successfully concluded.'

'Professor Boulder,' said the Boss, 'I believe you can read Greek.'

'Yes, I can,' – coolly.

'And have translated chemical texts for Professor Tywood on government money.'

'Yes – as a legally employed consultant.'

'Yet such translation, under the circumstances, constitutes a crime, since it makes you an accessory to Tywood's crime.'

'You can establish a connection?'

'Can't you? Or haven't you heard of Tywood's notion on time travel, or ... what do you call it ... micro-temporal-translation?'

'Ah?' and Boulder smiled a little. 'He's told you, then.'

'No, he hasn't,' said the Boss, harshly. 'Professor Tywood is dead.'

'What?' Then – 'I don't believe you.'

'He died of apoplexy. Look at this.'

He had one of the photographs taken that first night in his wall safe. Tywood's face was distorted but recognizable – sprawled and dead.

Boulder's breath went in and out as if the gears were clogged. He stared at the picture for three full minutes by the electric clock on the wall. 'Where is this place?' he asked.

'The Atomic Power Plant.'

'Had he finished his experiment?'

The Boss shrugged: 'There's no way of telling. He was dead when we found him.'

Boulder's lips were pinched and colorless. 'That must be determined, somehow. A commission of scientists must be established, and, if necessary, the experiment must be repeated —'

But the Boss just looked at him, and reached for a cigar. I've never seen him take longer – and when he put it down, curled in its unused smoke, he said: 'Tywood wrote an article for a magazine, twenty years ago —'

'Oh,' and the professor's lips twisted, 'is *that* what gave you your clue? You may ignore that. The man is only a physical scientist and knows nothing of either history or sociology. A schoolboy's dreams and nothing more.'

'Then, you don't think sending your translation back will inaugurate a Golden Age, do you?'

'Of course not. Do you think you can graft the developments of two thousand years of slow labor onto a child society not ready for it? Do you think a great invention or a great scientific principle is born full-grown in the mind of a genius divorced from his cultural *milieu*? Newton's enunciation of the Law of Gravity was delayed for twenty years because the then-current figure for the Earth's diameter was wrong by ten percent. Archimedes almost discovered calculus, but failed because Arabic numerals, invented by some nameless Hindu or group of Hindus, was unknown to him.

'For that matter, the mere existence of a slave society in ancient Greece and Rome meant that machines could scarcely attract much attention – slaves being so much cheaper and more adaptable. And men of true intellect could scarcely be expected to spend their energies on devices intended for manual labor. Even Archimedes, the greatest engineer of antiquity, refused to publish any of his practical inventions – only mathematic abstractions. And when a young man asked Plato of what use geometry was, he was forthwith expelled from the Academy as a man with a mean, unphilosophic soul.

'Science does not plunge forward – it inches along in the directions permitted by the greater forces that mold society and which are in turn molded by society. And no great man advances but on the shoulders of the society that surrounds him —'

The Boss interrupted him at that point. 'Suppose you tell us what your part in Tywood's work was, then. We'll take your word for it that history cannot be changed.'

'Oh it can, but not purposefully – You see, when Tywood first requested my services in the matter of translating certain textbook passages into Greek, I agreed for the money involved. But he wanted the translation on parchment; he insisted on the use of ancient Greek terminology – the language of Plato, to use his words – regardless of how I had to twist the literal significance of passages, and he wanted it hand-written in rolls.

'I was curious. I, too, found his magazine article. It was difficult for me to jump to the obvious conclusion, since the achievements of modern science transcend the imaginings of philosophy in so many ways. But I learned the truth eventually, and it was at once obvious that Tywood's theory of changing history was infantile. There are twenty million variables for every instant of time, and no system of mathematics – no mathematic psychohistory, to coin a phrase – has yet been developed to handle that ocean of varying functions.

'In short, any variation of events two thousand years ago would change all subsequent history, but in *no predictable way*.'

The boss suggested, with a false quietness: 'Like the pebble that starts the avalanche, right?'

'Exactly. You have some understanding of the situation, I see. I thought deeply for weeks before I proceeded, and then I realized how I must act – *must* act.'

There was a low roar. The Boss stood up and his chair went over backward. He swung around his desk, and he had a hand on Boulder's throat. I was stepping out to stop him, but he waved me back —

He was only tightening the necktie a little. Boulder could still breathe. He had gone very white, and for all the time that the Boss talked, he restricted himself to just that – breathing.

And the Boss said: 'Sure, I can see how you decided you must act. I know that some of you brain-sick philosophers think the world needs fixing. You want to throw the dice again and see what turns up. Maybe you don't even care if you're alive in the new setup – or that no one can possibly know what you've done. But you're going to create, just the same. You're going to give God another chance, so to speak.

'Maybe I just want to live – but the world could be worse. In twenty million different ways, it could be worse. A fellow named Wilder once wrote a play called *The Skin of Our Teeth*. Maybe you've read it. It's thesis was that Mankind survived by just that skin of their teeth. No, I'm not going to give you a speech about the Ice Age nearly wiping us out. I don't know enough. I'm not even going to talk about the Greeks winning at Marathon; the Arabs being defeated at Tours; the Mongols turning back at the last minute without even being defeated – because I'm no historian.

'But take the Twentieth Century. The Germans were stopped at the Marne twice in World War I. Dunkirk happened in World War II, and somehow the Germans were stopped at Moscow and Stalingrad. We could have used the atom bomb in the last war and we didn't, and just when it looked as if both sides would have to, the Great Compromise happened – just because General Bruce was delayed in taking off from the Ceylon airfield long enough to receive the message directly. One after the other, just like that, all through history – lucky breaks. For every "if" that didn't come true that would have made wonder-men of all of us if it had, there were twenty "ifs" that didn't come true that would have brought disaster to all of us if they had.

'You're gambling on that one-in-twenty chance – gambling every life on Earth. And you've succeeded, too, because Tywood *did* send that text back.'

He ground out that last sentence, and opened his fist, so that Boulder could fall out and back into his chair.

And Boulder laughed.

'You fool,' he gasped, bitterly, 'How close you can be and yet how widely you can miss the mark. Tywood *did* send his book back, then? You are sure of that?'

'No chemical textbook in Greek was found on the scene,' said the Boss, grimly, 'and millions of calories of energy had disappeared. Which doesn't change the fact, however, that we have two and a half weeks in which to – make things interesting for you.'

'Oh, nonsense. No foolish dramatics, please. Just listen to me, and try to understand. There were Greek philosophers once, named Leucippus and Democritus, who evolved an atomic theory. All matter, they said, was composed of atoms. Varieties of atoms were distinct and changeless and by their different combinations with each other formed the various substances found in nature. That theory was not the result of experiment or observation. It came into being, somehow, full-grown.

145

'The didactic Roman poet Lucretius, in his "*De Rerum Natura*," – "On the Nature of Things" – elaborated on that theory and throughout manages to sound startlingly modern.

'In Hellenistic times, Hero built a steam engine and weapons of war became almost mechanized. The period has been referred to as an abortive mechanical age, which came to nothing because, somehow, it neither grew out of nor fitted into its social and economic *milieu*. Alexandrian science was a queer and rather inexplicable phenomenon.

'Then one might mention the old Roman legend about the books of the Sibyl that contained mysterious information direct from the gods —

'In other words, gentlemen, while you are right that any change in the course of past events, however trifling, would have incalculable consequences, and while I also believe that you are right in supposing that any random change is much more likely to be for the worse than for the better, I must point out that you are nevertheless wrong in your final conclusions.

'*Because* THIS *is the world in which the Greek chemistry text* WAS *sent back.*

'This has been a Red Queen's race, if you remember your "Through the Looking Glass." In the Red Queen's country, one had to run as fast as one could merely to stay in the same place. And so it was in this case! Tywood may have thought he was creating a new world, but it was I who prepared the translations, and I took care that only such passages as would account for the queer scraps of knowledge the ancients apparently got from nowhere would be included.

'And my only intention, for all my racing, was to stay in the same place.'

Three weeks passed; three months; three years. Nothing happened. When nothing happens, you have no proof. We gave up trying to explain, and we ended, the Boss and I, by doubting it ourselves.

The case never ended. Boulder could not be considered a criminal without being considered a world savior as well, and vice versa. He was ignored. And in the end, the case was neither solved, nor closed out; merely put in a file all by itself, under the designation '?' and buried in the deepest vault in Washington.

The Boss is in Washington now; a big wheel. And I'm Regional Head of the Bureau.

Boulder is still assistant professor, though. Promotions are slow at the University.

THE END

'The Red Queen's Race,' my fifty-eighth story, was the first to be written by *Dr*. Asimov.

In September I began another story, 'Mother Earth,' and submitted it to Campbell on October 12, 1948. After a comparatively small revision of the ending, he took that one, too.

27 : Mother Earth

'But can you be certain? Are you sure that even a professional historian can always distinguish between victory and defeat?'

Gustav Stein, who delivered himself of that mocking question with a whiskered smile and a gentle wipe at the gray moustache from the neighborhood of which he had just removed an empty glass, was not an historian. He was a physiologist.

But his companion *was* an historian, and he accepted the gentle thrust with a smile of his own.

Stein's apartment was, for Earth, quite luxurious. It lacked the empty privacy of the Outer Worlds, of course, since from its window there stretched outward a phenomenon that belonged only to the home planet – a city. A large city, full of people, rubbing shoulders, mingling sweat —

Nor was Stein's apartment fitted with its own power and its own utility supply. It lacked even the most elementary quota of positronic robots. In short, it lacked the dignity of self-sufficiency, and like all things on Earth, it was merely part of a community, a pendant unit of a cluster, a portion of a mob.

But Stein was an Earthman by birth and used to it. And after all, by Earth standards the apartment was still luxurious.

It was just that looking outward through the same windows before which lay the city, one could see the stars and among them the Outer Worlds, where there were no cities but only gardens; where the lawns were streaks of emerald, where all human beings were kings, and where all good Earthmen earnestly and vainly hoped to go some day.

Except for a few who knew better – like Gustav Stein.

The Friday evenings with Edward Field belonged to that class of ritual which comes with age and quiet life. It broke the week pleasantly for two elderly bachelors, and gave them an innocuous reason to linger over the sherry and the stars. It took them away from the crudities of life, and, most of all, it let them talk.

Field, especially, as a lecturer, scholar and man of modest

Astounding Science Fiction, May 1949
Copyright © 1949 by Street & Smith Publications, Inc.

means quoted chapter and verse from his still uncompleted history of Terrestrian Empire.

'I wait for the last act,' he explained. 'Then I can call it the "Decline and Fall of Empire" and publish it.'

'You must expect the last act to come soon, then.'

'In a sense, it has come already. It is just that it is best to wait for all to recognize that fact. You see, there are three times when an Empire or an Economic System or a Social Institution falls, you skeptic —'

Field paused for effect and waited patiently for Stein to say, 'And those times are?'

'First,' Field ticked off a right forefinger, 'there is the time when just a little nub shows up that points an inexorable way to finality. It can't be seen or recognized until the finality arrives, when the original nub becomes visible to hindsight.'

'And you can tell what that little nub is?'

'I think so, since I already have the advantage of a century and a half of hindsight. It came when the Sirian sector colony, Aurora, first obtained permission of the Central Government at Earth to introduce positronic robots into their community life. Obviously, looking back at it, the road was clear for the development of a thoroughly mechanized society based upon robot labor and not human labor. And it is this mechanization that has been and will yet be the deciding factor in the struggle between the Outer Words and Earth.'

'It is?' murmured the psychologist. 'How infernally clever you historians are. What and where is the second time the Empire fell?'

'The second point in time,' and Field gently bent his right middle finger backward, 'arrives when a signpost is raised for the expert so large and plain that it can be seen even without the aid of perspective. And that point has been passed, too, with the first establishment of an immigration quota against Earth by the Outer Worlds. The fact that Earth found itself unable to prevent an action so obviously detrimental to itself was a shout for all to hear, and that was fifty years ago.'

'Better and better. And the third point?'

'The third point?' Down went the ring finger. 'That is the least important. That is when the signpost becomes a wall with a huge "The End" scrawled upon it. The only requirement for knowing that the end has come, then, is neither perspective nor training, but merely the ability to listen to the video.'

149

'I take it that the third point in time has not yet come.'

'Obviously not, or you would not need to ask. Yet it may come soon; for instance, if there is war.'

'Do you think there will be?'

Field avoided commitment. 'Times are unsettled, and a good deal of futile emotion is sweeping Earth on the immigration question. And if there should be a war, Earth would be defeated quickly and lastingly, and the wall would be erected.'

'Can you be certain? Are you sure that even a professional historian can always distinguish between victory and defeat?'

Field smiled. He said: 'You may know something I do not. For instance, they talk about something called the "Pacific Project."'

'I never heard of it.' Stein refilled the two glasses, 'Let us speak of others things.'

He held up his glass to the broad window so that the far stars flickered rosily in the clear liquid and said: 'To a happy ending to Earth's troubles.'

Field held up his own, 'To the Pacific Project.'

Stein sipped gently and said: 'But we drink to two different things.'

'Do we?'

It is quite difficult to describe any of the Outer Worlds to a native Earthman, since it is not so much a description of a world that is required as a description of a state of mind. The Outer Worlds — some fifty of them, originally colonies, later domininions, later nations — differ extremely among themselves in a physical sense. But the state of mind is somewhat the same throughout.

It is something that grows out of a world not originally congenial to mankind, yet populated by the cream of the difficult, the different, the daring, the deviant.

If it is to be expressed in a word, that word is 'individuality.'

There is the world of Aurora, for instance, three parsecs from Earth. It was the first planet settled outside the Solar System, and represented the dawn of interstellar travel. Hence its name.

It had air and water to start with, perhaps, but on Earthly standards it was rocky and infertile. The plant life that did exist, sustained by a yellow-green pigment completely unrelated to chlorophyll and not as efficient, gave the comparatively fertile regions a decidedly bilious and unpleasant appearance to unaccustomed eyes. No animal life higher than unicellular, and the equivalent of bacteria as well, were present. Nothing dangerous, naturally, since the two biological systems, of Earth and Aurora, were chemically unrelated.

Aurora became, quite gradually, a patchwork. Grains and fruit trees came first; shrubs, flowers and grass afterward. Herds of livestock followed. And, as if it were necessary to prevent too close a copy of the mother planet, positronic robots also came to build the mansions, carve the landscapes, lay the power units. In short, to do the work, and turn the planet green and human.

There was the luxury of a new world and unlimited mineral resources. There was the splendid excess of atomic power laid out on new foundations with merely thousands, or, at most, millions, not billions, to service. There was the vast flowering of physical science, in worlds where there was room for it.

Take the home of Franklin Maynard, for instance, who, with his wife, three children, and twenty-seven robots, lived on an estate more than forty miles away, in distance, from the nearest neighbor. Yet by community-wave he could, if he wished, share the living room of any of the seventy-five million on Aurora – with each singly; with all simultaneously.

Maynard knew every inch of his valley. He knew just where it ended, sharply, and gave way to the alien crags, along whose undesirable slopes the angular, sharp leaves of the native furze clung sullenly – as if in hatred of the softer matter that had usurped its place in the sun.

Maynard did not have to leave that valley. He was a deputy in the Gathering, and a member of the Foreign Agents Committee, but he could transact all business but the most extremely essential, by community-wave, without ever sacrificing that precious privacy he had to have in a way no Earthman could understand.

Even the present business could be performed by community-wave. The man, for instance, who sat with him in his living room, was Charles Hijkman, and he, actually, was sitting in his own living room on an island in an artificial lake stocked with fifty varieties of fish, which happened to be twenty-five miles distant, in space.

The connection was an illusion, of course. If Maynard were to reach out a hand, he could feel the invisible wall.

Even the robots were quite accustomed to the paradox, and when Hijkman raised a hand for a cigarette, Maynard's robot made no move to satisfy the desire, though a half-minute passed before Hijkman's own robot could do so.

The two men spoke like Outer Worlders, that is, stiffly and in syllables too clipped to be friendly, and yet certainly not hostile. Merely undefinably lacking in the cream — however sour and thin at times — of human sociability which is so forced upon the inhabitants of Earth's ant heaps.

Maynard said: 'I have long wanted a private communion, Hijkman. My duties in the Gathering, this year —'

'Quite. That is understood. You are welcome now, of course. In fact, especially so, since I have heard of the superior nature of your grounds and landscaping. Is it true that your cattle are fed on imported grass?'

'I'm afraid that is a slight exaggeration. Actually, certain of my best milkers feed on Terrestrial imports during calving time, but such a procedure would be prohibitively expensive, I'm afraid, if made general. It yields quite extraordinary milk, however. May I have the privilege of sending you a day's output?'

'It would be most kind of you.' Hijkman bent his head, gravely. 'You must receive some of my salmon in return.'

To a Terrestrial eye, the two men might have appeared much alike. Both were tall, though not unusually so for Aurora, where the average height of the adult male is six feet one and one half inches. Both were blond and hard-muscled, with sharp and pronounced features. Though neither was younger than forty, middle-age as yet sat lightly upon them.

So much for amenities. Without a change in tone, Maynard proceeded to the serious purpose of his call.

He said: 'The Committee, you know, is now largely engaged with Moreanu and his Conservatives. We would like to deal with them firmly, we of the Independents, that is. But before we can do so with the requisite calm and certainty, I would like to ask you certain questions.'

'Why me?'

'Because you are Aurora's most important physicist.'

Modesty is an unnatural attitude, and one which is only with difficulty taught to children. In an individualistic society it is useless and Hijkman was, therefore, unencumbered with it. He simply nodded objectively at Maynard's last words.

'And,' continued Maynard, 'as one of us. You are an Independent.'

'I am a member of the Party. Dues-paying, but not very active.'

'Nevertheless safe. Now, tell me, have you heard of the Pacific Project.'

'The Pacific Project?' There was a polite inquiry in his words.

'It is something which is taking place on Earth. The Pacific is a Terrestrial ocean, but the name itself probably has no significance.'

'I have never heard of it.'

'I am not surprised. Few have, even on Earth. Our communion, by the way, is via tight-beam and nothing must go further.'

'I understand.'

'Whatever Pacific Project is – and our agents are extremely vague – it might conceivably be a menace. Many of those who on Earth pass for scientists seem to be connected with it. Also, some of Earth's more radical and foolish politicians.'

'Hm-m-m. There was once something called the Manhattan Project.'

'Yes,' urged Maynard, 'what about it?'

'Oh, it's an ancient thing. It merely occurred to me because of the analogy in names. The Manhattan Project was before the time of extra-terrestrial travel. Some petty war in the dark ages occurred, and it was the name given to a group of scientists who developed atomic power.'

'Ah,' Maynard's hand became a fist, 'and what do you think the Pacific Project can do, then?'

Hijkman considered. Then, softly: 'Do you think Earth is planning war?'

On Maynard's face there was a sudden expression of distaste. 'Six billion people. Six billion half-apes, rather, jammed into one system to a near-explosion point, facing only some millions of us, total. Don't you think it is a dangerous situation?'

'Oh, numbers!'

'All right. Are we safe despite the numbers? Tell me. I'm only an administrator, and you're a physicist. *Can* Earth win a war in any way?'

Hijkman sat solemnly in his chair and thought carefully and

slowly. Then he said: 'Let us reason. There are three broad classes of methods whereby an individual or group can gain his ends against opposition. On an increasing level of subtlety, those three classes can be termed the physical, the biological and the psychological.

'Now, the physical can be easily eliminated. Earth does not have an industrial background. It does not have a technical know-how. It has very limited resources. It lacks even a single outstanding physical scientist. So it is as impossible as anything in the Galaxy can be that they can develop any form of physico-chemical application that is not already known to the Outer Worlds. Provided, of course, that the conditions of the problem imply single-handed opposition on the part of Earth against any or all of the Outer Worlds. I take it that none of the Outer Words intends leaguing with Earth against us.'

Maynard indicated violent opposition even to the suggestion, 'No, no, no. There is no question of that. Put it out of your mind.'

'Then, ordinary physical surprise weapons are inconceivable. It is useless to discuss it further.'

'Then, what about your second class, the biological?'

Slowly, Hijkman lifted his eyebrows: 'Now, that is less certain. Some Terrestrial biologists are quite competent, I am told. Naturally, since I am myself a physicist, I am not entirely qualified to judge this. Yet I believe that in certain restricted fields, they are still expert. In agricultural science, of course, to give an obvious example. And in bacteriology. Um-m-m —'

'Yes, what about bacteriological warfare?'

'A thought! But no, no, quite inconceivable. A teeming, constricted world such as Earth cannot afford to fight an open latticework of fifty sparse worlds with germs. They are infinitely more subject to epidemics, that is, to retaliation in kind. In fact, I would say that given our living conditions here on Aurora and on the other Outer Worlds, no contagious disease could really take hold. No, Maynard. You can check with a bacteriologist, but I think he'll tell you the same.'

Maynard said: 'And the third class?'

'The psychological? Now, that is unpredictable. And yet the Outer Worlds are intelligent and healthy communities and not amenable to ordinary propaganda, or for that matter to any form of unhealthy emotionalism. Now, I wonder —'

'Yes?'

'What if the Pacific Project is just that? I mean, a huge device to keep us off balance. Something top-secret, but meant to leak out in just the right fashion, so that the Outer Worlds yield a little to Earth, simply in order to play safe.'

There was a longish silence.

'Impossible,' burst out Maynard, angrily.

'*You* react properly. *You* hesitate. But I don't seriously press the interpretation. It is merely a thought.'

A longer silence, then Hijkman spoke again: 'Are there any other questions?'

Maynard started out of a reverie, 'No ... no —'

The wave broke off and a wall appeared where space had been a moment before.

Slowly, with stubborn disbelief, Franklin Maynard shook his head.

Ernest Keilin mounted the stairs with a feeling for all the past centuries. The building was old, cobwebbed with history. It once housed the Parliament of Man, and from it words went out that clanged throughout the stars.

It was a tall building. It soared – stretched – strained. Out and up to the stars, it reached; to the stars that had now turned away.

It no longer even housed the Parliament of Earth. That had now been switched to a newer, neoclassical building, one that imperfectly aped the architectural stylisms of the ancient pre-Atomic age.

Yet the older building still held its great name. Officially, it was still Stellar House, but it only housed the functionaries of a shriveled bureaucracy now.

Keilin got out at the twelfth floor, and the lift dropped quickly down behind him. The radiant sign said smoothly and quietly: Bureau of Information. He handed a letter to the receptionist. He waited. And eventually, he passed through the door which said, 'L. Z. Cellioni – Secretary of Information.'

Cellioni was little and dark. His hair was thick and black, his mustache thin and black. His teeth, when he smiled, were startlingly white and even – so he smiled often.

He was smiling now, as he rose and held out his hand. Keilin took it, then an offered seat, then an offered cigar.

Cellioni said: 'I am very happy to see you, Mr. Keilin. It is kind of you to fly here from New York on such short notice.'

Keilin curved the corners of his lips down and made a tiny gesture with one hand, deprecating the whole business.

'And now,' continued Cellioni, 'I presume you would like an explanation of all this.'

'I wouldn't refuse one,' said Keilin.

'Unfortunately, it is difficult to know exactly how to explain. As Secretary of Information, my position is difficult. I must safeguard the security and well-being of Earth and, at the same time, observe our traditional freedom of the press. Naturally, and fortunately, we have no censorship, but just as naturally, there are times when we could almost wish we did have.'

'Is this,' asked Keilin, 'with reference to me? About censorship, I mean?'

Cellioni did not answer directly. Instead, he smiled again, slowly, and with a remarkable absence of joviality.

He said: 'You, Mr. Keilin, have one of the most widely heard and influential telecasts on the video. Therefore, you are of peculiar interest to the government.'

'The time is mine,' said Keilin, stubbornly. 'I pay for it. I pay taxes on the income I derive from it. I adhere to all the common-law rulings on taboos. So I don't quite see of what interest I can be to the government.'

'Oh, you misunderstand me. It's my fault, I suppose, for not being clearer. You have committed no crime, broken no laws. I have only admiration for your journalistic ability. What I refer to is your editorial attitude at times.'

'With respect to what?'

'With respect,' said Cellioni, with a sudden harshness about his thin lips, 'to our policy toward the Outer Worlds.'

'My editorial attitude represents what I feel and think, Mr. Secretary.'

'I allow this. You have your right to your feelings and your thoughts. Yet it is injudicious to spread them about nightly to an audience of half a billion.'

'Injudicious, according to you, perhaps. But legal, according to anybody.'

'It is sometimes necessary to place good of country above a strict and selfish interpretation of legality.'

Keilin tapped his foot twice and frowned blackly.

'Look,' he said, 'put this frankly. What is it you want?'

The Secretary of Information spread his hands out before

156

him. 'In a word – co-operation! Really, Mr. Keilin, we can't have you weakening the will of the people. Do you appreciate the position of Earth? Six billions, and a declining food supply! It is insupportable! And emigration is the only solution. No patriotic Earthman can fail to see the justice of our position. No reasonable human being anywhere can fail to see the justice of it.'

Keilin said: 'I agree with your premise that the population problem is serious, but emigration is not the only solution. In fact, emigration is the one sure way of hastening destruction.'

'Really? And why do you say that?'

'Because the Outer Worlds will not permit emigration, and you can force their hand by war only. *And we cannot win a war.*'

'Tell me,' said Cellioni softly, 'have *you* ever tried emigrating? It seems to me you could qualify. You are quite tall, rather light-haired, intelligent —'

The video-man flushed. He said, curtly: 'I have hay fever.'

'Well,' and the secretary smiled, 'then you must have good reason for disapproving their arbitrary genetic and racist policies.'

Keilin replied with heat: 'I won't be influenced by personal motives. I would disapprove their policies, if I qualified perfectly for emigration. But my disapproval would alter nothing. Their policies *are* their policies, and they can enforce them. Moreover, their policies have some reason even if wrong. Mankind is starting again on the Outer Worlds, and they – the ones who got there first – would like to eliminate some of the flaws of the human mechanism that have become obvious with time. A hay fever sufferer *is* a bad egg – genetically. A cancer prone even more so. Their prejudices against skin and hair colors are, of course, senseless, but I can grant that they are interested in uniformity and homogeneity. And as for Earth, we can do much even without the help of the Outer Worlds.'

'For instance, what?'

'Positronic robots and hydroponic farming should be introduced, and – most of all – birth control must be instituted. An intelligent birth control, that is, based on firm psychiatric principles intended to eliminate the psychotic trends, congenital infirmities —'

'As they do in the Outer Worlds —'

'Not at all. I have mentioned no racist principles. I talk only of mental and physical infirmities that are held in common by all ethnic and racial groups. And most of all, births must be held below deaths until a healthful equilibrium is reached.'

Cellioni said, grimly: 'We lack the industrial techniques and the resources to introduce a robot-hydroponic technology in anything less than five centuries. Furthermore, the traditions of Earth, as well as current ethical beliefs, forbid robot labor and false foods. Most of all, they forbid the slaughter of unborn children. Now, come, Keilin, we can't have you pouring this out over video. It won't work; it distracts the attention; it wakens the will.'

Keilin broke in, impatiently: 'Mr. Secretary, do you want war?'

'Do I *want* war? That is an impudent question.'

'Then, who are the policy-makers in the government who *do* want war? For instance, who is responsible for the calculated rumor of the Pacific Project?'

'The Pacific Project? And where did you hear of that?'

'My sources are my secret.'

'Then, I'll tell you. You heard of this Pacific Project from Moreanu of Aurora on his recent trip to Earth. We know more about you than you suppose, Mr. Keilin.'

'I believe that, but I do not admit that I received information from Moreanu. Why do you think I could get information from him? Is it because he was deliberately allowed to learn of this piece of trumpery?'

'Trumpery?'

'Yes. I think Pacific Project is a fake. A fake meant to inspire confidence. I think the government plans to let the so-called secret leak out in order to strengthen its war policy. It is part of a war of nerves on Earth's own people, and it will be the ruin of Earth in the end.'

'And I will take this theory of mine to the people.'

'You will not, Mr. Keilin,' said Cellioni, quietly.

'I will.'

'Mr. Keilin, your friend, Ion Moreanu is having his troubles on Aurora, perhaps for being too friendly with you. Take care that you do not have equal trouble for being too friendly with him.'

'I'm not worried.' The video man laughed shortly, lunged to his feet and strode to the door.

Keilin smiled very gently when he found the door blocked by two large men: 'You mean, I am under arrest right now.'

'Exactly,' said Cellioni.

'On what charge?'

'We'll think of some later.'

Kelin left – under escort.

On Aurora, the mirror image of the afore-described events was taking place, and on a larger scale.

The Foreign Agents Committee of the Gathering had been meeting now for days – ever since the session of the Gathering in which Ion Moreanu and his Conservative Party made their great bid to force a vote of no confidence. That it had failed was in part due to the superior political generalship of the Independents, and in some part due to the activity of this same Foreign Agents Committee.

For months now, the evidence had been accumulating, and when the vote of confidence turned out to be sizably in favor of the Independents, the Committee was able to strike in its own way.

Moreanu was subpoenaed in his own home, and placed under house arrest. Although this procedure of house arrest was not, under the circumstances, legal – a fact emphatically pointed out by Moreanu – it was nevertheless successfully accomplished.

For three days Moreanu was cross-examined thoroughly, in polite, even tones that scarcely ever veered from unemotional curiosity. The seven inquisitors of the Committee took turns in questioning, but Moreanu had respite only for ten-minute intervals during the hours in which the Committee sat.

After three days, he showed the effects. He was hoarse with demanding that he be faced with his accusers; weary with insisting that he be informed of the exact nature of the charges; throat-broken with shouting against the illegality of the procedure.

The Committee finally read statements at him —

'Is this true or not? Is this true or not?'

Moreanu could merely shake his head wearily as the structure spidered about him.

He challenged the competency of the evidence and was smoothly informed that the proceedings constituted a Committee Investigation and not a trial —

The chairman clapped his gavel, finally. He was a broad man of tremendous purpose. He spoke for an hour in his final summing up of the results of the inquiry, but only a relatively short portion of it need be quoted.

He said: 'If you had merely conspired with others on Aurora, we could understand you, even forgive you. Such a fault would have been held in common with many ambitious men in history. It is not that at all. What horrifies us and removes all pity is your eagerness to consort with the disease-ridden, ignorant and subhuman remnants of Earth.

'You, the accused, stand here under a heavy weight of evidence showing you to have conspired with the worst elements of Earth's mongrel population —'

The chairman was interrupted by an agonized cry from Moreanu, 'But the motive! What motive can you possibly attribute —'

The accused was pulled back into his seat. The chairman pursed his lips and departed from the slow gravity of his prepared speech to improvise a bit.

'It is not,' he said, 'for this Committee to go into your motives. We have shown the facts of the case. The Committee *does* have evidence —' He paused, and looked along the line of the members to the right and the left, then continued. 'I think I may say that the Committee has evidence that points to your intentions to use Earth manpower to engineer a coup that would leave you dictator over Aurora. But since the evidence has not been used, I will go no further into that, except to say that such a consummation is not inconsistent with your character as displayed at these hearings.'

He went back to his speech. 'Those of us who sit here have heard, I think, of something termed the "Pacific Project," which, according to rumors, represents an attempt on the part of Earth to retrieve its lost dominions.

'It is needless to emphasize here that any such attempt must be doomed to failure. And yet defeat for us is not entirely inconceivable. One thing can cause us to stumble, and that one thing is an unsuspected internal weakness. Genetics is, after all, still an imperfect science. Even with twenty generations behind us, undesirable traits may crop up at scattered points, and each represents a flaw in the steel shield of Aurora's strength.

'*That* is the Pacific Project – the use of our own criminals and traitors against us; and if they can find such in our inner councils, the Earthmen might even succeed.

'The Foreign Agents Committee exists to combat that threat. In the accused, we touch the fringes of the web. We must go on —'

The speech did, at any rate.

When it was concluded, Moreanu, pale, wide-eyed, pounded his fist, 'I demand my say —'

'The accused may speak,' said the chairman.

Moreanu rose and looked about him for a long moment. The room, fitted for an audience of seventy-five million by Community Wave, was unattended. There were the inquisitors, legal staff, official recorders – And with him, in the actual flesh, his guards.

He would have done better with an audience. To whom could he otherwise appeal? His glance fled hopelessly from each face it touched, but could find nothing better.

'First,' he said, 'I deny the legality of this meeting. My constitutional rights of privacy and individuality have been denied. I have been tried by a group without standing as a court, by individuals convinced, in advance, of my guilt. I have been denied adequate opportunity to defend myself. In fact, I have been treated throughout as an already convicted criminal requiring only sentence.

'I deny, completely and without reservation, that I have been engaged in any activity detrimental to the state or tending to subvert any of its fundamental institutions.

'I accuse, vigorously and unreservedly, this Committee of deliberately using its powers to win political battles. I am guilty not of treason, but of disagreement. I disagree with a policy dedicated to the destruction of the larger part of the human race for reasons that are trivial and inhumane.

'Rather than destruction, we owe assistance to these men who are condemned to a harsh, unhappy life solely because it was our ancestors and not theirs who happened to reach the Outer Worlds first. With our technology and resources, they can yet re-create and redevelop —'

The chairman's voice rose above the intense near-whisper of Moreanu, 'You are out of order. The Committee is quite prepared to hear any remarks you make in your own defense, but a sermon on the rights of Earthmen is outside the legitimate realm of the discussion.'

The hearings were formally closed. It was a great political victory for the Independents; all would agree to that. Of the members of the Committee, only Franklin Maynard was not completely satisfied. A small, nagging doubt remained.

He wondered —

Should he try, one last time? Should he speak once more and then no more to that queer little monkey ambassador from Earth? He made his decision quickly and acted upon it instantly. Only a pause to arrange a witness, since even for himself an unwitnessed private communion with an Earthman might be dangerous.

Luiz Moreno, Ambassador to Aurora from Earth, was, to put not too fine a point on it, a miserable figure of a man. And that wasn't exactly an accident. On the whole, the foreign diplomats of Earth tended to be dark, short, wizen, or weakly – or all four.

That was only self-protection, since the Outer Worlds exerted strong attraction for any Earthman. Diplomats exposed to the allure of Aurora, for instance, could not but be exceedingly reluctant to return to Earth. Worse, and more dangerous, exposure meant a growing sympathy with the demigods of the stars and a growing alienation from the slum-dwellers of Earth.

Unless, of course, the ambassador found himself rejected. Unless he found himself somewhat despised. And then, no more faithful servant of Earth could be imagined, no man less subject to corruption.

The Ambassador to Earth was only five foot two, with a bald head and receding forehead, a pinkish affectation of beard and red-rimmed eyes. He was suffering from a slight cold, the occasional results whereof he smothered in a handkerchief. And yet, withal, he was a man of intellect.

To Franklin Maynard, the sight and sound of the Earthman was distressing. He grew queasy at each cough and shuddered when the ambassador wiped his nose.

Maynard said: 'Your excellency, we commune at my request because I wish to inform you that the Gathering has decided to ask your recall by your government.'

'That is kind of you, councilor. I had an inkling of this. And for what reason?'

'The reason is not within the bounds of discussion. I believe

162

it is the prerogative of a sovereign state to decide for itself whether a foreign representative shall be *persona grata* or not. Nor do I think you really need enlightenment on this matter.'

'Very well, then.' The ambassador paused to wield his handkerchief and murmur an apology. 'Is that all?'

Maynard said: 'Not quite. There are matters I would like to mention. Remain!'

The ambassador's reddened nostrils flared a bit, but he smiled, and said: 'An honor.'

'Your world, excellency,' said Maynard, superciliously, 'displays a certain belligerence of late that we on Aurora find most annoying and unnecessary. I trust that you will find your return to Earth at this point a convenient opportunity to use your influence against further displays such as recently occurred in New York, where two Aurorans were manhandled by a mob. The payment of an indemnity may not be enough the next time.'

'But that is emotional overflow, Councilor Maynard. Surely, you cannot consider youngsters shouting in the streets to be adequate representations of belligerence.'

'It is backed by your government's actions in many ways. The recent arrest of Mr. Ernest Keilin, for instance.'

'Which is a purely domestic affair,' said the ambassador, quietly.

'But not one to demonstrate a reasonable spirit toward the Outer Worlds. Keilin was one of the few Earthmen who until recently could yet make their voices heard. He was intelligent enough to realize that no divine right protects the inferior man simply because he is inferior.'

The ambassador arose: 'I am not interested in Auroran theories on racial differences.'

'A moment. Your government may realize that much of their plans have gone awry with the arrest of your agent, Moreanu. Stress the fact that we of Aurora are much wiser than we have been prior to this arrest. It may serve to give them pause.'

'Is Moreanu *my* agent? Really, councilor, if I am disaccredited, I shall leave. But surely the loss of diplomatic immunity does not affect my personal immunity as an honest man from charges of espionage.'

'Isn't that your job?'

'Do Aurorans take it for granted that espionage and diplom-

163

acy are identical? My government will be glad to hear it. We shall take appropriate precautions.'

'Then, you defend Moreanu? You deny that he has been working for Earth?'

'I defend only myself. As to Moreanu, I am not stupid enough to say anything.'

'Why stupid?'

'Wouldn't a defense by myself be but another indictment against him? I neither accuse nor defend him. Your government's quarrel with Moreanu, like my government's with Keilin – whom you, by the way, are most suspiciously eager to defend – is an internal affair. I will leave now.'

The communion broke, and almost instantly the wall faded again. Hijkman was looking thoughtfully at Maynard.

'What do you think of him?' asked Maynard, grimly.

'Disgraceful that such a travesty of humanity should walk Aurora, I think.'

'I agree with you, and yet ... and yet —'

'Well?'

'And yet I can almost find myself able to think that he is the master and that we dance to his piping. You know of Moreanu?'

'Of course.'

'Well, he will be convicted, sent to an asteroid. His party will be broken. Offhand, anyone would say that such actions represent a horrible defeat for Earth.'

'Is there doubt in your mind that such is the case?'

'I'm not sure. Committee Chairman Hond insisted on airing his theory that Pacific Project was the name Earth gave to a device for using internal traitors on the Outer Worlds. But I don't think so. I'm not sure the facts fit that. For instance, where did we get our evidence against Moreanu?'

'I certainly can't say.'

'Our agents, in the first place. But how did they get it? The evidence was a little *too* convincing. Moreanu could have guarded himself better —'

Maynard hesitated. He seemed to be attempting a blush, and failing. 'Well, to put it quickly, I think it was the Terrestrian Ambassador who somehow presented us with the most evidence. I think that he played on Moreanu's sympathy for Earth first to befriend him and then to betray him.'

'Why?'

'I don't know. To insure war, perhaps – with this Pacific Project waiting for us.'

'I don't believe it.'

'I know. I have no proof. Nothing but suspicion. The Committee wouldn't believe me either. It seemed to me, perhaps, that a last talk with the ambassador might reveal something, but his mere appearance antagonizes me, and I find I spend most of my time trying to remove him from my sight.'

'Well, you are becoming emotional, my friend. It is a disgusting weakness. I hear that you have been appointed a delegate to the Interplanetary Gathering at Hesperus. I congratulate you.'

'Thanks,' said Maynard, absently.

Luiz Moreno, ex-Ambassador to Aurora, had been glad to return to Earth. He was away from the artificial landscapes that seemed to have no life of their own, but to exist only by virtue of the strong will of their possessors. Away from the too-beautiful men and women and from their ubiquitous, brooding robots.

He was back to the hum of life and the shuffle of feet; the brushing of shoulders and the feeling of breath in the face.

Not that he was able to enjoy these sensations entirely. The first days had been spent in lively conferences with the heads of Earth's government.

In fact, it was not till nearly a week had passed, that an hour came in which he could consider himself truly relaxed.

He was in the rarest of all appurtenances of Terrestrial Luxury – a roof garden. With him was Gustav Stein, the quite obscure physiologist, who was, nevertheless, one of the prime movers of the Plan, known to rumor as the Pacific Project.

'The confirmatory tests,' said Moreno, with an almost dreadful satisfaction, 'all check so far, do they not?'

'So far. *Only* so far. We have miles to go.'

'Yet they will continue to go well. To one who has lived on Aurora for nearly a year, as I have, there can be no doubt but that we're on the right track.'

'Um-m-m. Nevertheless, I will go only by the laboratory reports.'

'And quite rightly.' His little body was almost stiff with gloating. 'Some day, it will be different. Stein, you have not met these men, these Outer Worlders. You may have come

165

across the tourists, perhaps, in their special hotels, or riding through the streets in inclosed cars, equipped with the purest of private, air-conditioned atmospheres for their well-bred nostrils; observing the sights through a movable periscope and shuddering away from the touch of an Earthman.

'But you have not met them on their own world, secure in their own sickly, rotting greatness. Go, Stein, and be despised a while. Go, and find how well you can compete with their own trained lawns as something to be gently trod upon.

'And yet, when I pulled the proper cords, Ion Moreanu fell – Ion Moreanu, the only man among them with the capacity to understand the workings of another's mind. It is the crisis that we have passed now. We front a smooth path now.'

Satisfaction! Satisfaction!

'As for Keilin,' he said suddenly, more to himself than to Stein, 'he can be turned loose now. There's little he can say, hereafter, that can endanger anything. In fact, I have an idea. The interplanetary Conference opens on Hesperus within the month. He can be sent to report the meeting. It will be an earnest of our friendliness – and keep him away for the summer. I think it can be arranged.'

It was.

Of all the Outer Worlds, Hesperus was the smallest, the latest settled, the furthest from Earth. Hence the name. In a physical sense, it was not best suited to a great diplomatic gathering, since its facilities were small. For instance, the available community-wave network could not possibly be stretched to cover all the delegates, secretarial staff, and administrators necessary in a convocation of fifty planets. So meetings in person were arranged in buildings impressed for the purpose.

Yet there was a symbolism in the choice of meeting place that escaped practically nobody. Hesperus, of all the Worlds, was furthest removed from Earth. But the spatial distance – one hundred parsecs or more – was the least of it. The important point was that Hesperus had been colonized not by Earthmen, but by men from the Outer World of Faunus.

It was therefore of the second generation, and so it had no 'Mother Earth.' Earth to it was but a vague grandmother, lost in the stars.

As is usual in all such gatherings, little work is actually done on the session floors. That space is reserved for the official soundings of whatever is primarily intended for home ears. The actual swapping and horse-trading takes place in the lobbies and at the lunch-tables and many of irresolvable conflict has softened over the soup and vanished over the nuts.

And yet particular difficulties were present in this particular case. Not in all worlds was the community-wave as paramount and all-pervading as it was on Aurora, but it was prominent in all. It was, therefore, with a certain sense of outrage and loss that the tall, dignified men found it necessary to approach one another in the flesh, without the comforting privacy of the invisible wall between, without the warm knowledge of the breakswitch at their fingertips.

They faced one another in uneasy semi-embarrassment and tried not to watch one another eat; tried not to shrink at the unmeant touch. Even robot service was rationed.

Ernest Keilin, the only accredited video-representative from Earth, was aware of some of these matters only in the vague way they are described here. A more precise insight he could not have. Nor could anyone brought up in a society where human beings exist only in the plural, and where a house need only be deserted to be feared.

So it was that certain of the most subtle tensions escaped him at the formal dinner party given by the Hesperian government during the third week of the conference. Other tensions, however, did not pass him by.

The gathering after the dinner naturally fell apart into little groups. Keilin joined the one that contained Franklin Maynard of Aurora. As the delegate of the largest of the Worlds, he was naturally the most newsworthy.

Maynard was speaking casually between sips at the tawny Hesperian cocktail in his hand. If his flesh crawled slightly at the closeness of the others, he masked the feeling masterfully.

'Earth,' he said, 'is, in essence, helpless against us if we avoid unpredictable military adventures. Economic unity is actually a necessity, if we intend to avoid such adventures. Let Earth realize to how great an extent her economy depends upon us, on the things that we alone can supply her, and there will be no more talk of living space. And if we are united, Earth would never dare attack. She will exchange her barren longings for atomic motors – or not, as she pleases.'

And he turned to regard Keilin with a certain hauteur as the other found himself stung to comment:

'But your manufactured goods, councilor – I mean those you ship to Earth – they are not *given* us. They are exchanged for agricultural products.'

Maynard smiled silkily. 'Yes, I believe the delegate from Tethys has mentioned that fact at length. There is a delusion prevalent among some of us that only Terrestrial seeds grow properly —'

He was interrupted calmly by another, who said: 'Now, I am not from Tethys, but what you mention is not a delusion. I grow rye on Rhea, and I have never yet been able to duplicate Terrestrial bread. It just hasn't got the same taste.' He addressed the audience in general, 'In fact, I imported half a dozen Terrestrians five years back on agricultural laborer visas so they could oversee the robots. Now, they can do wonders with the land, you know. Where they spit, corn grows fifteen feet high. Well, that helped a little. And using Terrestrian seed helped. But even if you grow Terrestrian grain, its seed won't hold the next year.'

'Has your soil been tested by your government's agricultural department?' asked Maynard.

The Rhean grew haughty in his turn: 'No better soil in the sector. And the rye is top-grade. I even sent a hundredweight down to Earth for nutritional clearance, and it came back with full marks.' He rubbed one side of his chin, thoughtfully: 'It's flavor I'm talking about. Doesn't seem to have the right —'

Maynard made an effort to dismiss him: 'Flavor is dispensable temporarily. They'll be coming to us on our terms, these little-men-hordes of Earth, when they feel the pinch. We give up only this mysterious flavor, but they will have to give up atom-powered engines, farm machinery, and ground cars. It wouldn't be a bad idea, in fact, to attempt to get along without the Terrestrian flavors you are so concerned about. Let us appreciate the flavor of our home-grown products instead – which could stand comparison if we gave it a chance.'

'That so?' the Rhean smiled. 'I notice you're smoking Earth-grown tobacco.'

'A habit I can break if I have to.'

'Probably by giving up smoking. I wouldn't use Outer World tobacco for anything but killing mosquitoes.'

He laughed a trifle too boisterously, and left the group. Maynard stared after him, a little pinch-nosed.

To Keilin, the little byplay over rye and tobacco brought a

certain satisfaction. He regarded such personalities as the tiny reflection of certain Galactopolitical realities. Tethys and Rhea were the largest planets in the Galactic south, as Aurora was the largest in the Galactic north. All three planets were identically racist, identically exclusivist. Their views on Earth were similar and completely compatible. Ordinarily, one would think that there was no room to quarrel.

But Aurora was the oldest of the Outer Worlds, the most advanced, the strongest militarily – and, therefore, aspired to a sort of moral leadership of all the Worlds. That was sufficient in itself to arouse opposition, and Rhea and Tethys served as focal points for those who did not recognize Auroran leadership.

Keilin was somberly grateful for that situation. If Earth could but lean her weight properly, first in one direction, then in the other, an ultimate spilt, or even fragmentation—

He eyed Maynard cautiously, almost furtively, and wondered what effect this would have on the next day's debate. Already, the Auroran was more silent than was quite polite.

And then some under-secretary or sub-official threaded his way through the clusters of guests in finicking fashion, and beckoned to Maynard.

Keilin's following eyes watched the Auroran retreat with the newcomer, watched him listen closely, mouth a startled 'What!' that was quite visible to the eye, though too far off to be heard, and then reach for a paper that the other handed him.

And as a result, the next day's session of the conference went entirely differently than Keilin would have predicted.

Keilin discovered the details in the evening video-casts. The Terrestrian government, it seemed, had sent a note to all the governments attending the conference. It warned each one bluntly that any agreement among them in military or economic affairs would be considered an unfriendly act against Earth and that it would be met with appropriate counter-measures. The note denounced Aurora, Tethys and Rhea all equally. It accused them of being engaged in an imperialist conspiracy against Earth, and so on – and on – and on.

'Fools!' gritted Keilin, all but butting his head against the wall out of sheer chagrin. 'Fools! Fools! Fools!' And his voice died away still muttering that same, one word.

*

The next session of the conference was well and early attended by a set of angry delegates who were only too eager to grind into nothingness the disagreements still outstanding. When it ended, all matters concerning trade between Earth and the Outer Worlds had been placed in the hands of a commission with plenary powers.

Not even Aurora could have expected so complete and easy a victory, and Keilin, on his way back to Earth, longed for his voice to reach the video, so that it could be to others, and not to himself only, that he could shout his disgust.

Yet, on Earth, some men smiled.

Once back on Earth, the voice of Keilin slowly swirled under and down – lost in the noisier clamor that shouted for action.

His popularity sank in proportion as trade restrictions grew. Slowly, the Outer Worlds drew the noose tighter. First, they instituted a strict application of a new system of export licensing. Secondly, they banned the export to Earth of all materials capable of being 'used in a war effort.' And finally they applied a very broad interpretation indeed of what could be considered usable in such a connection.

Imported luxuries – and imported necessities, too, for that matter – vanished or priced themselves upwards out of the reach of all but the very few.

So the people marched, and the voices shouted and the banners swung about in the sunlight, and the stones flew at the consulates —

Keilin shouted hoarsely and felt as if he were going mad.

Until, suddenly, Luiz Moreno, quite of his own accord, offered to appear on Keilin's program and submit to unrestricted questioning in his capacity as ex-Ambassador to Aurora and present Secretary without Portfolio.

To Keilin it had had all the possibilities of a rebirth. He knew Moreno – no fool, he. With Moreno on his program, he was assured an audience as great as his greatest. With Moreno answering questions, certain misapprehensions might be removed, certain confusions might be straightened. The mere fact that Moreno wished to use his – *his* – program as sounding board might well mean that already a more pliant and sensible foreign policy might have been decided upon. Perhaps Maynard was correct, and the pinch was being felt and was working as predicted.

The list of questions had, of course, been submitted to Moreno in advance, but the ex-Ambassador had indicated that he would answer all of them, and any follow-up questions that might seem necessary.

It seemed quite ideal. Too ideal, perhaps, but only a criminal fool could worry over minutiae at this point.

There was an adequate ballyhoo – and when they faced one another across the little table, the red needle that indicated the number of video sets drawing power on that channel hovered well over the two hundred million mark. And there was an average of 2.7 listeners per video set. Now the theme; the official introduction.

Keilin rubbed his cheek slowly, as he waited for the signal.

Then, he began:

Q. Secretary Moreno, the question which interests all Earth at the moment, concerns the possibility of war. Suppose we start with that. Do you think there will be war?

A. If Earth is the only planet to be considered, I say: No, definitely not. In its history, Earth has had too much war, and has learned many times over how little can be gained by it.

Q. You say, 'If Earth is the only planet to be considered —' Do you imply that factors outside our control will bring war?

A. I do not say 'will'; but I could say 'may.' I cannot, of course speak for the Outer Worlds. I cannot pretend to know their motivations and intentions at this critical moment in Galactic history. They *may* choose war. I hope not. If so be that they do, however, we will defend ourselves. But in any case, *we* will never attack; *we* will not strike the first blow.

Q. Am I right in saying, then, that in your opinion there are no basic differences between Earth and the Outer Worlds, which cannot be solved by negotiation?

A. You certainly are. If the Outer Worlds were sincerely desirous of a solution, no disagreement between them and us could long exist.

Q. Does that include the question of immigration?

A. Definitely. Our own role in the matter is clear and beyond reproach. As matters stand, two hundred million human beings now occupy ninety-five percent of the available land in the universe. Six billions – that is, ninety-seven percent of all mankind – are squeezed into the other five percent. Such a situation is obviously unjust and, worse, unstable. Yet Earth, in the face of such injustice, has always been willing to treat this problem as soluble by degrees. It is still so willing. We should agree to reasonable quotas and reasonable restrictions. Yet the Outer Worlds have refused to discuss this matter. Over a space of five decades, they have rebuffed all efforts on the part of Earth to open negotiations.

Q. If such an attitude on the part of the Outer Worlds continues, do you *then* think there will be war?

A. I cannot believe that this attitude will continue. Our government will not cease hoping that the Outer Worlds will eventually reconsider their stand on the matter; that their sense of justice and right is not dead, but only sleeping.

Q. Mr. Secretary, let us pass on to another subject. Do you think that the United Worlds Commission set up by the Outer Worlds recently to control trade with Earth represents a danger to peace?

A. In the sense that its actions indicate a desire on the part of the Outer Worlds to isolate Earth, and to weaken it economically, I can say that it does.

Q. To what actions do you refer, sir?

A. To its actions in restricting interstellar trade with Earth to the point where, in credit values, the total stands now at least than ten percent of what it did three months ago.

Q. But do such restrictions really represent an economic danger to Earth? For instance, it is not true that trade with the Outer Worlds represents an almost insignificant part of total Terrestrian trade? And is it not true that the importations from the Outer Worlds reach only a tiny minority of the population at best?

A. Your questions now are representative of a profound fallacy which is very common among our isolationists. In credit values, it is true that interstellar trade represents only five percent of our total trade, but ninety-five percent of our atomic engines are imported. Eighty percent of our thorium, sixty-five percent of our cesium, sixty percent of our molybdenum and tin are imported. The list can be extended almost indefinitely, and it is quite easy to see that the five percent is an extremely important, a vital, five percent. Furthermore, if a large manufacturer receives a shipment of atomic steel-shapers from Rhea, it does not follow that the benefit redounds only to him. Every man on Earth who uses steel implements or objects manufactured by steel implements benefits.

Q. But is it not true that the current restrictions on Earth's interstellar trade have cut our grain and cattle exports to almost nothing? And far from harming Earth, isn't this really a boon to our own hungry people?

A. This is another serious fallacy. That Earth's good food supply is tragically inadequate is true. The government would be the last to deny it. But our food exports do not represent any serious drain upon this supply. Less than one fifth of one percent of Earth's food is exported, and in return we obtain, for instance, fertilizers and farm machinery which more than make up for that small loss by increasing agricultural efficiency. Therefore, by buying less food from us, the Outer Worlds are engaged, in effect, in cutting our already inadequate food supply.

Q. Are you ready to admit, then, Secretary Moreno, that at least part of the blame for this situation should rest with Earth itself? In other words, we come to my next question: Was it not a diplomatic blunder of the first magnitude for the government to issue its inflammatory note denouncing the intentions of the Outer Worlds before those intentions had been made clear at the Interplanetary Conference?

A. I think those intentions were quite clear at the time.

Q. I beg pardon, sir, but I was at the conference. At the time the note was issued, there was almost a stalemate among the Outer World delegates. Those of Rhea and Tethys strongly opposed economic action against Earth, and there was considerable chance that Aurora and its block might have been defeated. Earth's note ended that possibility instantly.

A. Well, what is your question, Mr. Keilin?

Q. In view of my statements, do you or do you not think Earth's note to have been a criminal error of diplomacy which can now be made up only by a policy of intelligent conciliation?

A. You use strong language. However, I cannot answer the question directly, since I do not agree with your major premise. I cannot believe that the delegates of the Outer Worlds could behave in the manner you describe. In the first place, it is well known that the Outer Worlds are proud of their boast that the percentage of insanity, psychoses and even relatively minor maladjustments of personality are almost at the vanishing point in their society. It is one of their strongest arguments against Earth, that we have more psychiatrists than plumbers and yet are more pinched for want of the former. The delegates to the conference represented the best of this so-stable society. And now you would have me believe that these demigods would, in a moment of pique, have reversed their opinions and instituted a major change in the economic policy of fifty worlds. I cannot believe them capable of such childish and perverse activity, and must therefore insist that any action they took was based not upon any note from Earth, but upon motivations that go deeper.

Q. But I saw the effect upon them with my own eyes, sir. Remember, they were being scolded in what they considered to be insolent language from an inferior people. There can be no doubt, sir, that as a whole, the men of the Outer Worlds are a remarkably stable people, despite your sarcasm, but their attitude toward Earth represents a weak point in this stability.

A. Are you asking me questions, or are you defending the racist views and policies of the Outer Worlds?

Q. Well, accepting your viewpoint that Earth's note did no harm, what good could it have done? Why should it have been sent?

A. I think we were justified in presenting our side of the question before the bar of Galactic public opinion. I believe we have exhausted the subject. What is your next question, please? It is the last, isn't it?

Q. It is. It has recently been reported that the Terrestrian government will take stern measures against those dealing in smuggling operations. Is this consistent with the government's view that lowered trade relations are detrimental to Earth's welfare?

A. Our primary concern is peace, and not our own immediate welfare. The Outer Worlds have adopted certain trade restrictions. We disapprove of them, and consider them a great injustice. Nevertheless, we shall adhere to them, so that no planet may say that we have given the slightest pretext for hostilities. For instance, I am privileged to announce here for the first time that in the past month, five ships, traveling under false Earth registry, were stopped while being engaged in the smuggling of Outer World matériel into Earth. Their goods were confiscated and their personnel imprisoned. This is an earnest of our good intentions.

Q. Outer World ships?

A. Yes. But traveling under false Earth registry, remember.

Q. And the men imprisoned are citizens of the Outer Worlds?

A. I believe so. However, they were breaking not only our laws, but those of the Outer Worlds as well, and therefore doubly forfeited their interplanetary rights. I think the interview had better close, now.

Q. But this —

It was at this point that the broadcast came to a sudden end. The conclusion of Keilin's last sentence was never heard by anyone but Moreno. It ended like this:

'— means war.'

But Luiz Moreno was no longer on the air. So as he drew on his gloves, he smiled and, with infinite meaning, shrugged his shoulders in a little gesture of indifference.

There were no witnesses to that shrug.

The Gathering at Aurora was still in session. Franklin Maynard had dropped out for the moment in utter weariness. He faced his son, whom he now saw for the first time in naval uniform.

'At least *you're* sure of what will happen, aren't you?'

In the young man's response, there was no weariness at all, no apprehension; nothing but utter satisfaction. 'This is it, dad!'

'Nothing bothers you, then? You don't think we've been maneuvered into this.'

'Who cares if we have? It's Earth's funeral.'

Maynard shook his head: 'But you realize that we've been put in the wrong. The Outer World citizens they hold are lawbreakers. Earth is within its rights.'

His son frowned: 'I hope you're not going to make statements like that to the Gathering, dad. I don't see that Earth is justified at all. All right, what if smuggling was going on? It was just because some Outer Worlders are willing to pay black market prices for Terrestrial food. If Earth had any sense, she could look the other way, and everyone would benefit. She makes enough noise about how she needs our trade, so why doesn't she do something about it? Anyway, I don't see that we ought to leave any good Aurorans or other Outer Worlders in the hands of those apemen. Since they won't give them up, we'll make them. Otherwise, none of us will be safe next time.'

'I see that you've adopted the popular opinions, anyway.'

'The opinions are my own. If they're popular opinion also, it's because they make sense. Earth *wants* a war. Well, they'll get it.'

'But why do they want a war, eh? Why do they force our hands? Our entire economic policy of the past months was only intended to force a change in their attitude without war.'

He was talking to himself, but his son answered with the final argument: 'I don't care why they wanted war. They've *got* it now, and we're going to smash them.'

Maynard returned to the Gathering, but even as the drone of debate re-filled the room, he thought, with a twinge, that there would be no Terrestrian alfalfa that year. He regretted the milk. In fact, even the beef seemed, somehow, to be just a little less savory —

The vote came in the early hours of the morning. Aurora declared war. Most of the worlds of the Aurora bloc joined it by dawn.

In the history books, the war was later known as the Three Weeks' War. In the first week, Auroran forces occupied several of the trans-Plutonian asteroids, and at the beginning of the third week, the bulk of Earth's home fleet was all but completely destroyed in a battle within the orbit of Saturn by an Aurora fleet not one-quarter its size, numerically.

Declarations of war from the Outer Worlds yet neutral followed like the *pop-pop* of a string of firecrackers.

On the twenty-first day of the war, lacking two hours, Earth surrendered.

The negotiations of peace terms took place among the Outer Worlds. Earth's activities were concerned with signing only. The conditions of peace were unusual, perhaps unique, and under the force of an unprecedented humiliation, all the hordes of Earth seemed suddenly struck with a silence that came from a shamed anger too strong for words.

The terms mentioned were perhaps best commented upon by a voice on the Auroran video two days after they were made public. It can be quoted in part:

'... There is nothing in or on Earth that we of the Outer Worlds can need or want. All that was ever worthwhile on Earth left it centuries ago in the persons of our ancestors.

'They call us the children of Mother Earth, but that is not

so, for we are the descendants of a Mother Earth that no longer exists, a Mother that we brought with us. The Earth of today bears us at best a cousinly relation. No more.

'Do we want their resources? Why, they have none for themselves. Can we use their industry or science? They are almost dead for lack of ours. Can we use their man power? Ten of them are not worth a single robot. Do we even want the dubious glory of ruling them? There is no such glory. As our helpless and incompetent inferiors, they would be only a drag upon us. They would divert from our own use food, labor and administrative ability.

'So they have nothing to give us but the space they occupy in our thought. They have nothing to free us from but themselves. They cannot benefit us in any way other than in their absence.

'It is for that reason that the peace terms have been defined as they have been. We wish them no harm, so let them have their own solar system. Let them live there in peace. Let them mold their own destiny in their own way, and we will not disturb them there by even the least hint of our presence. But we in turn want peace. We in turn would guide our own future in our own way. So we do not want *their* presence. And with that end in view, an Outer World fleet will patrol the boundaries of their system, Outer World bases will be established on their outermost asteroids, so that we may make sure they do not intrude on our territory.

'There will be no trade, no diplomatic relationships, no travel, no communications. They are fenced off, locked out, hermetically sealed away. Out here we have a new universe, a second creation of Man, a higher Man —

'They ask us: What will become of Earth? We answer: That is Earth's problem. Population growth can be controlled. Resources can be efficiently exploited. Economic systems can be revised. We know, for we have done so. If they cannot, let them go the way of the dinosaur, and make room.

'Let them make room, instead of forever demanding room!'

And so an impenetrable curtain swung slowly shut about the Solar System. The stars in Earth's sky became only stars again, as in the long-dead days before the first ship had penetrated the barrier of light's speed.

The government that had made war and peace resigned, but

there was no one, really, to take their place. The legislature elected Luiz Moreno – ex-Ambassador to Aurora, ex-Secretary without Portfolio – as President *pro tem*, and the Earth as a whole was too numbed to agree or disagree. There was only a widespread relief that someone existed who would be willing to take the job of trying to guide the destinies of a world in prison.

Very few realized how well-planned an ending this was, or with what calculation Moreno found himself in the president's chair.

Ernest Keilin said hopelessly from the video screen: 'We are only ourselves now. For us, there is no universe and no past – only Earth, and the future.'

That night he heard from Luiz Moreno once again, and before morning he left for the capital.

Moreno's presence seemed incongruent within the stiffly formal president's mansion. He was suffering from a cold again, and snuffled when he talked.

Keilin regarded him with a self-terrifying hostility; an almost singeing hatred in which he could feel his fingers begin to twitch in the first gestures of choking. Perhaps he shouldn't have come — Well, what was the difference; the orders had been plain. If he had not come, he would have been brought.

The new president looked at him sharply: 'You have to alter your attitude toward me, Keilin. I know you regard me as one of the Gravediggers of Earth – isn't that the phrase you used last night? – but you must listen to me quietly for a while. In your present state of suppressed rage, I doubt if you could hear me.'

'I will hear whatever you have to say, Mr. President.'

'Well – the external amenities, at least. That's hopeful. Or do you think a video-tracer is attached to the room?'

Keilin merely lifted his eyebrows.

Moreno said: 'It isn't. We are quite alone. We *must* be alone; otherwise, how could I tell you safely that it is being arranged for you to be elected president under a constitution now being devised? Eh, what's the matter?'

Then he grinned at the look of bloodless amazement in Keilin's face. 'Oh, you don't believe it. Well, it's past your stopping. And before an hour is up, you'll understand.'

'I'm to be president?' Keilin struggled with a strange, hoarse voice. Then, more firmly: 'You are mad.'

'No. Not I. Those out there, rather. Out there in the Outer Worlds.' There was a sudden vicious intensity in Moreno's eyes, and face, and voice, so that you forgot he was a little monkey of a man with a perpetual cold. You didn't notice the wrinkled, sloping forehead. You forgot the baldish head and ill-fitting clothes. There was only the bright and luminous look in his eyes, and the hard incision in his voice. *That* you noticed.

Keilin reached blindly backward for a chair, as Moreno came closer and spoke with increasing intensity.

'Yes,' said Moreno. 'Those out among the Stars. The godlike ones. The stately supermen. The strong, handsome master-race. *They* are mad. But only we on Earth know it.

'Come, you have heard of the Pacific Project. I know you have. You denounced it to Cellioni once, and called it a fake. But it isn't a fake. And almost none of it is a secret. In fact, the only secret about it was that almost none of it was a secret.

'You're no fool, Keilin. You just never stopped to work it all out. And yet you were on the track. You had the feel of it. What was it you said that time you were interviewing me on the program? Something about the attitude of the Outer Worldling toward the Earthman being the only flaw in the former's stability. That was it, wasn't it? Or something like that? Very well, then; good! You had the first third of the Pacific Project in your mind at the time, and it was no secret after all, was it?

'Ask yourself, Keilin – what was the attitude of the typical Auroran to a typical Earthman? A feeling of superiority? That's the first thought, I suppose. But, tell me, Keilin, if he really felt superior, *really* superior, would it be so necessary for him to call such continuous attention to it? What kind of superiority is it that must be continuously bolstered by the constant repetition of phrases such as "apemen," "submen," "half-animals of Earth," and so on? That is not the calm internal assurance of superiority. Do you waste epithets on earth-worms? No, there is something else there.

'Or let us approach it from another tack. Why do Outer World tourists stay in special hotels, travel in inclosed ground-cars, and have rigid, if unwritten, rules against social inter-mingling? Are they afraid of pollution? Strange, then, that they are not afraid to eat our food and drink our wine and smoke our tobacco.

'You see, Keilin, there are no psychiatrists on the Outer Worlds. The supermen are, so they say, too well adjusted. But here on Earth, as the proverb goes, there are more psychiatrists than plumbers, and they get lots of practice. So it is we, and not they, who know the truth about this Outer World superiority-complex, who know it to be simply a wild reaction against an overwhelming feeling of *guilt*.

'Don't you think that can be so? You shake your head as though you disagree. You don't see that a handful of men who clutch a Galaxy while billions starve for lack of room *must* feel a subconscious guilt, no matter what? And, since they won't share the loot, don't you see that the only way they can justify themselves is to try to convince themselves that Earthmen, after all, are inferior, that they do not deserve the Galaxy, that a new race of men have been created out there and that we here are only the diseased remnants of an old race that should die out like the dinosaur, through the working of inexorable natural laws?

'Ah, if they could only convince themselves of that, they would no longer be guilty, but merely superior. Only, it doesn't work; it never does. It requires constant bolstering; constant repetition, constant reinforcement. And still it doesn't quite convince.

'Best of all, if only they could pretend that Earth and its population do not exist at all. When you visit Earth, therefore, avoid Earthmen; or they might make you uncomfortable by not looking inferior enough. Sometimes they might look miserable instead, and nothing more. Or worse still, they might even seem intelligent – as I did, for instance, on Aurora.

'Occasionally, an Outer Worlder like Moreanu did crop up, and was able to recognize guilt for what it was without being afraid to say so out loud. He spoke of the duty the Outer Worlds owed Earth – and so he was dangerous to us. For if the others listened to him and had offered token assistance to Earth, their guilt might have been assuaged in their own minds; and that without any lasting help to Earth. So Moreanu was removed through our web-weaving, and the way left clear to those who were unbending, who refused to admit guilt, and whose reaction could therefore be predicted and manipulated.

'Send them an arrogant note, for instance, and they automatically strike back with a useless embargo that merely gives us the ideal pretext for war. Then lose a war quickly, and you are sealed off by the annoyed supermen. No communication, no contact. You no longer exist to annoy them. Isn't that simple? Didn't it work out nicely?'

Keilin finally found his voice, because Moreno gave him time by stopping. He said: 'You mean that all this was planned? You *did* deliberately instigate the war for the purpose of sealing Earth off from the Galaxy? You sent out the men of the Home Fleet to sure death because you wanted defeat? Why, you're a monster, a . . . a —'

Moreno frowned: 'Please relax. It was not as simple as you think, and I am not a monster. Do you think the war could simply be – instigated? It had to be nurtured gently in just the right way and to just the right conclusion. If we had made the first move, if we had been the aggressor, if we had in any way put the fault on our side – why, they of the Outer Worlds would have occupied Earth and ground it under. They would no longer feel guilty, you see, if *we* committed a crime against *them*. Or, again, if we fought a protracted war, or one in which we inflicted damage, they could succeed in shifting the blame.

'But we didn't. We merely imprisoned Auroran smugglers, and were obviously within our rights. They had to go to war over it because only so could they protect their superiority, which in turn protected them against the horrors of guilt. And we lost quickly. Scarcely an Auroran died. The guilt grew deeper and resulted in exactly the peace treaty our psychiatrists had predicted.

'And as for sending men out to die, that is a commonplace in every war – and a necessity. It was necessary to fight a battle, and, naturally, there were casualties.'

'But why?' interrupted Keilin, wildly. 'Why? *Why?* Why does all this gibberish seem to make sense to you? What have we gained? What can we possibly gain out of the present situation?'

'Gained, man? You ask what we've gained? Why, we've gained the universe. What has held us back so far? *You* know what Earth has needed these last centuries. You yourself once outlined it forcefully to Cellioni. We need a positronic robot society and an atomic power technology. We need chemical farming and we need population control. Well, what's prevented that, eh? Only the customs of centuries which said robots were evil since they deprived human beings of jobs, that population control was merely the murder of unborn children, and so on. And worse, there was always the safety valve of emigration either actual or hoped-for.

'But now we cannot emigrate. We're *stuck* here. Worse than that, we have been humiliatingly defeated by a handful of men out in the stars, and we've had a humiliating treaty of peace forced upon us. What Earthman wouldn't subconsciously burn for revenge? Self-preservation has frequently knuckled under to that tremendous yearning to "get even."

'And that is the second third of the Pacific Project, the recognition of the revenge motive. As simple as that.

'And how can we know that this is really so? Why, it has been demonstrated in history scores of times. Defeat a nation, but don't crush it entirely, and in a generation or two or three it will be stronger than it was before. Why? Because in the interval, sacrifices will have been made for revenge that would not have been made for mere conquest.

'Think! Rome beat Carthage rather easily the first time, but was almost defeated the second. Every time Napoleon defeated the Europen coalition, he laid the groundwork for another just a little bit harder to defeat, until he himself was crushed by the eighth. It took four years to defeat Wilhelm of medieval Germany, and six much more dangerous years to stop his successor, Hitler.

'There you are! Until now, Earth needed to change its way of life only for greater comfort and happiness. A minor item like that could always wait. But now it must change for revenge, and that will not wait. And I want that change for its own sake.

'Only – I am not the man to lead. I am tarred with the failure of yesteryear, and will remain so until, long after I am bone-dust, Earth learns the truth. But you ... *you,* and others like you, have always fought for the road to modernization. *You* will be in charge. It may take a hundred years. Grandchildren of men unborn may be the first to see its completion. But at least you will see the start.

'Eh, what do you say?'

Keilin was fumbling at the dream. He seemed to see it in a misty distance – a new and reborn Earth. But the change in attitude was too extreme. It could not be done just yet. He shook his head.

He said: 'What makes you think the Outer Worlds would allow such a change, supposing what you say to be true? They will be watching, I am sure, and they will detect a growing danger and put a stop to it. Can you deny that?'

Moreno threw his head back and laughed noiselessly. He gasped out: 'But we have still a third left of the Pacific Project, a last, subtle and ironic third —

'The Outer Worlders call the men of Earth the subhuman dregs of a great race, but *we* are the men of *Earth*. Do you realize what that means? We live on a planet upon which, for a billion years, life – the life that has culminated in Mankind – has been adapting itself. There is not a microscopic part of Man, not a tiny working of his mind, that has not as its reason some tiny facet of the physical make-up of Earth, or of the biological make-up of Earth's other life-forms, or of the sociological make-up of the society about him.

'No other planet can substitute for Earth, *in Man's present shape.*

'The Outer Worlders exist as they do, only because pieces of Earth have been transplanted. Soil has been brought out there; plants; animals; men. They keep themselves surrounded by an artificial Earth-born geology which has within it, for instance, those traces of cobalt, zinc and copper which human chemistry must have. They surround thmselves by Earth-born bacteria and algae which have the ability to make those inorganic traces available in just the right way and in just the right quantity.

'And they maintain that situation by continued imports – luxury imports, they call it – from Earth.

'But on the Outer Worlds, even with Terrestrian soil laid down to bedrock, they cannot keep rain from falling and rivers from flowing, so that there is an inevitable, if slow, admixture with the native soil; an inevitable contamination of Terrestrian soil bacteria with the native bacteria, and an exposure, in any case, to a different atmosphere and to solar radiations of different types. Terrestrian bacteria disappear or change. And then plant life changes. And then animal life.

'No great change, mind you. Plant life would not become poisonous or nonnutritious in a day, or year, or decade. But already, the men of the Outer Worlds can detect the loss or change of the trace compounds that are responsible for that infinitely elusive thing we call "flavor." It has gone that far.

'And it will go further. Do you know, for instance, that on

Aurora, nearly one half the native bacterial species known have protoplasm based on the fluorocarbon rather than hydrocarbon chemistry? Can you imagine the essential foreignness of such an environment?

'Well, for two decades now, the bacteriologists and physiologists of Earth have studied various forms of Outer World life – the only portion of the Pacific Project that has been truly secret – and the transplanted Terrestrian life is already beginning to show certain changes on the subcellular level. *Even among the humans.*

'And here is the irony. The Outer Worlders, by their rigid racism and unbending genetic policies are consistently eliminating from among themselves any children that show signs of adapting themselves to their respective planets in any way that departs from the norm. They are maintaining – they *must* maintain as a result of their own thought-processes – an artificial criterion of "healthy" humanity, which is based on Terrestrian chemistry and not their own.

'But now that Earth has been cut off from them; now that not even a trickle of Terrestrian soil and life will reach them, change will be piled on change. Sicknesses will come, mortality will increase, child abnormalities will become more frequent —'

'And then?' asked Keilin, suddenly caught up.

'And then? Well, they are physical scientists – leaving such inferior sciences as biology to us. And they cannot abandon their sensation of superiority and their arbitrary standard of human perfection. They will never detect the change till it is too late to fight it. Not all mutations are clearly visible, and there will be an increasing revolt against the mores of those stiff Outer World societies. There will be a century of increasing physical and social turmoil which will prevent any interference on their part with us.

'We will have a century of rebuilding and revitalization, and at the end of it, we shall face an outer Galaxy which will either be dying or changed. In the first case, we will build a second Terrestrian Empire, more wisely and with greater knowledge than we did the first; one based on a strong and modernized Earth.

'In the second case, we will face perhaps ten, twenty, or even all fifty Outer Worlds, each with a slightly different variety of Man. Fifty humanoid species, no longer united against us, each increasingly adapted to its own planet, each with a sufficient tendency toward atavism to love Earth, to regard it as the great and original Mother.

'And racism will be dead, for variety will then be the great fact of Humanity, and not uniformity. Each type of Man will have a world of its own, for which no other world could quite substitute, and on which no other type could live quite as well. And other worlds can be settled to breed still newer varieties, until out of the grand intellectual mixture, Mother Earth will finally have given birth not to merely a Terrestrian, but to a *Galactic* Empire.'

Keilin said, fascinated, 'You foresee all this so certainly.'

'Nothing is *truly* certain; but the best minds on Earth agree on this. There may be unforeseen stumbling blocks on the way, but to remove those will be the adventure of our great-grand-children. Of *our* adventure, one phase has been successfully concluded; and another phase is beginning. Join us, Keilin.'

Slowly, Keilin began to think that perhaps Moreno was not a monster after all —

THE END

What interests me most about 'Mother Earth' is that it seems to show clear premonitions of the novels *Caves of Steel* and *The Naked Sun*, which I was to write in the 1950s.

One thing about the story that I can't explain is the fact that I have two characters in it, one of whom is named Moreno and one Moreanu. I haven't the slightest idea why I used such similiar names. There was no significance in it, I assure you, only carelessness. There was also a Maynard.

Somehow, in reading and rereading the manuscript, the sloppiness of the situation never struck me. It did, however, just as soon as I saw the story in print. Why Campbell didn't notice and make me change the names, I haven't the faintest idea.

I had no sooner sold 'Mother Earth' than I began a new 'Foundation' story entitled '. . . And Now You Don't.' It was to be the last. Like 'The Mule,' it was fifty thousand words long, and I didn't finish it till March 29, 1949. I submitted it to Campbell the next day and he took it at once. At two cents a word, it netted me a check for one thousand dollars, the first four-figure check I ever received.

It appeared as a three-part serial in the November 1949,

December 1949 and January 1950 issues of *Astounding*, and it made up the final two thirds of my book *Second Foundation*.

By then, though, a great change was coming over the field of science fiction. The atom bomb had altered science fiction from a disregarded field of crazy stories into a literature of dreadful perception. Slowly, it was mounting in readership and esteem. New magazines were about to come into being, and the large publishing houses were about to consider putting out regular lines of hardback science fiction novels (hitherto the domain of small specialty houses no more affluent than the magazines and no more hopeful as a source of income).

The matter of hardback novels was of particular interest to Doubleday & Company, Inc. (though, of course, I didn't know it at the time). On February 5, 1949, while I was working on the last of the 'Foundation' stories, I attended a meeting of the Hydra Club – a group of science fiction professionals who lived in New York. There I met a Doubleday editor, Walter I. Bradbury, for the first time. It was he who was trying to build up a science fiction line for Doubleday, and he expressed some interest in 'The Mule.'

I paid little attention to this, however. The thought of publishing a *book*, a real *book*, as opposed to magazine stories, was so outlandish that I simply couldn't cram it into my head.

But Fred Pohl could. He had been in the Army, serving in Italy and rising to the rank of sergeant. After discharge, he became an agent again. I had indignantly told him the story of Merwin's rejection of 'Grow Old with Me,' so when Bradbury continued searching, Pohl suggested to him that he look at that story of mine.

Bradbury was interested and, after considerable trouble, Pohl managed to pry the story out of me. ('It's no good,' I kept saying – having never really recovered from the double rejection.)

But on March 24, 1949, I received the word that Bradbury wanted 'Grow Old with Me' if I would expand it to seventy thousand words. What's more, he paid me a $250 option, which I could keep even if the revision was unsatisfactory. That was the first time anyone had paid me anything *in advance*, and I was flabbergasted.

On April 6, I began the revision, and on May 25, 1949, I finished it and retitled it *Pebble in the Sky*. On May 29,

Doubleday accepted it, and I had to grasp the fact that I was going to have a *book* published.

But even as I struggled with that, another change was taking place simultaneously.

There was still the matter of a job. All the time I was working for Professor Elderfield, I was still searching for one that I could take after that temporary position reached its natural end in May 1949. I was having no success at all.

But then, on January 13, 1949, Professor William C. Boyd of Boston University School of Medicine was visiting New York, and we met.

Professor Boyd was a science fiction reader of long standing and had liked my stories. For a couple of years we had been corresponding and we had grown quite friendly. Now he told me that there was an opening in the biochemistry department at his school and would I be interested? I *was* interested, of course, but Boston is twice as far from New York as Philadelphia is, and I hated to leave New York again.

I refused the offer, but not very hard.

And I continued to look for a job, and I continued to fail.

I therefore reconsidered my refusal of the position at Boston University School of Medicine and wrote a letter to Professor Boyd, saying that perhaps I might be interested, after all.

On March 9, 1949, I traveled to Boston for the first time in my life (on a sleeper – but I didn't sleep). I met Professor Burnham S. Walker, head of the department of biochemistry, the next day and he offered me a position on the faculty at five thousand per year. I saw no way out of my jobless dilemma but to accept.

Did I have to? Was there no chance that I might have made my living as a writer?

How could I honestly come to a decision that I could? In mid-1949, I had been writing for exactly eleven years. In all that time, my *total* earnings had come to $7,821.75, averaging a little over $710 per year, or $13.70 per week. In my better years, such as the seventh (mid-1944 to mid-1945, when I had sold four stories, including 'The Mule'), I had earned $1,600, and in the tenth and eleventh together I had earned $3,300. It looked as though, even in good years, I could not count on much more than thirty dollars per week, and that just wasn't enough.

Of course, now that I was going to be publishing a *book* —

But books were unknown quantities. Besides, the book sale had come too late. By the time Bradbury accepted *Pebble in the Sky,* I was committed to the new job, and two days later, on June 1, 1949, I left for Boston.

It is at this point I must come to a halt, for the multiple changes put a final end to the first stage of my writing career.

I had left Campbell, this time forever. Oh, I saw him occasionally, and we corresponded, but the steady drizzle of near-weekly visits was never to take place again. Though I wrote for him and continued to publish in *Astounding,* new magazines appeared, including *The Magazine of Fantasy and Science Fiction* in 1949, *Galaxy Science Fiction* in 1950, and others. My market broadened, and the word rate went up still further, to three cents and even four cents a word.

The appearance of my first book, *Pebble in the Sky,* on January 19, 1950, introduced a new dimension to my self-image, to my prestige in the field and to my earnings. Other books followed – some new novels, some collections of older stories.

My position at Boston University School of Medicine led me to publish non-fiction. The first attempt was a textbook for medical students called *Biochemistry and Human Metabolism.* This was begun in 1950 in collaboration with Professors Walker and Boyd. It went through three editions and, though rather a failure, allowed me to discover that I enjoyed non-fiction writing at least as much as fiction writing and helped me start on a new phase of my writing career.

With all this taken into account, it is not surprising that my earnings as a writer began to rise rapidly almost as soon as I came to Boston. By 1952 I was making considerably more money as a writer than as a professor, and the discrepancy grew larger – in favor of writing – each succeeding year. By 1957, I'd decided (still somewhat to my surprise) that I had been a writer all along and that that was all I was.

On July 1, 1958, I gave up my salary and my duties but, with the agreement of the school, kept my title, which was then Associate Professor of Biochemistry. I keep that title to this day. I give an occasional lecture at the school when asked to do so, and I also lecture elsewhere when asked to do so (and charge a fee). For the rest, I became a full-time free-lance writer.

Writing is easy now, and is ever more satisfying. I keep what amounts to a seventy-hour week, if you count all the ancillary jobs of proofreading, indexing, research and so on. I average seven or eight books a year, and this book, *The Early Asimov,* is my 125th book.

And yet, I must admit there has never been, since 1949, anything like the real excitement of those first eleven 'Campbell years,' when I wrote only in my spare time, and sometimes not even then, when every submission meant unbearable suspense, when every rejection meant misery and every acceptance ecstasy, and every fifty-dollar check was the wealth of Croesus.

And on July 11, 1971, John Campbell, at the still-early age of sixty-one, while watching television, died at 7.30 P.M. quietly and peacefully, without any pain at all.

There is no way at all to express how much he meant to me and how much he did for me except, perhaps, to write these books evoking, once more, those days of a quarter century ago.

APPENDIX – The Sixty Stories of the Campbell Years

STORY (WORDS)	MAGAZINE ISSUE	COLLECTION
1. Cosmic Corkscrew (9,000)	—	—
2. THE CALLISTAN MENACE (6,500)	*Astonishing Stories* April 1940	*The Early Asimov* (Vol. I)
3. Marooned off Vesta (6,400)	*Amazing Stories* March 1939	*Asimov's Mysteries*
4. This Irrational Planet (3,000)	—	—
5. RING AROUND THE SUN (5,000)	*Future Fiction* March 1940	*The Early Asimov* (Vol. I)
6. The Weapon (4,000)	—	—
7. Paths of Destiny (6,000)	—	—
8. Knossos in Its Glory (6,000)	—	—
9. THE MAGNIFICENT POSSESSION (5,000)	*Future Fiction* July 1940	*The Early Asimov* (Vol. I)
10. TRENDS (6,900)	*Astounding Science Fiction* July 1939	*The Early Asimov* (Vol. I)
11. THE WEAPON TOO DREADFUL TO USE (6,500)	*Amazing Stories* May 1939	*The Early Asimov* (Vol. I)
12. The Decline and Fall (6,000)	—	—
13. BLACK FRIAR OF THE FLAME (16,000)	*Planet Stories* Spring 1942	*The Early Asimov* (Vol. I)
14. Robbie (Strange Playfellow) (6,500)	*Super Science Stories* September 1940	*I, Robot*
15. HALF-BREED (9,000)	*Astonishing Stories* February 1940	*The Early Asimov* (Vol. I)
16. THE SECRET SENSE (5,000)	*Cosmic Stories* March 1941	*The Early Asimov* (Vol. I)
17. Life Before Birth (6,000)	—	—
18. The Brothers (6,000)	—	—
19. HOMO SOL (7,200)	*Astounding Science Fiction* September 1940	*The Early Asimov* (Vol. II)

STORY (WORDS)	MAGAZINE ISSUE	COLLECTION
20. HALF-BREEDS ON VENUS (10,000)	*Astonishing Stories* December 1940	*The Early Asimov* (Vol. II)
21. THE IMAGINARY (7,200)	*Super Science Stories* November 1942	*The Early Asimov* (Vol. II)
22. The Oak (6,000)	—	—
23. HEREDITY (10,500)	*Astonishing Stories* April 1941	*The Early Asimov* (Vol. II)
24. HISTORY (5,000)	*Super Science Stories* March 1941	*The Early Asimov* (Vol. II)
25. Reason (7,000)	*Astounding Science Fiction* April 1941	*I, Robot*
26. CHRISTMAS ON GANYMEDE (6,000)	*Startling Stories* January 1942	*The Early Asimov* (Vol. II)
27. THE LITTLE MAN ON THE SUBWAY (4,000)	*Fantasy Book* Vol. 1, No. 6	*The Early Asimov* (Vol. II)
28. Liar! (7,000)	*Astounding Science Fiction* May 1941	*I, Robot*
29. Masks (1,500)	—	—
30. THE HAZING (5,000)	*Thrilling Wonder Stories* October 1942	*The Early Asimov* (Vol. II)
31. SUPER-NEUTRON (5,000)	*Astonishing Stories* September 1941	*The Early Asimov* (Vol. II)
32. Nightfall (13,200)	*Astounding Science Fiction* September 1941	*Nightfall and Other Stories*
33. NOT FINAL! (7,000)	*Astounding Science Fiction* October 1941	*The Early Asimov* (Vol. II)
34. LEGAL RITES (7,500)	*Weird Tales* September 1950	*The Early Asimov* (Vol. II)
35. Robot AL-76 Goes Astray (5,000)	*Amazing Stories* February 1942	*The Rest of the Robots*
36. Foundation (12,500)	*Astounding Science Fiction* May 1942	*Foundation*
37. Runaround (7,000)	*Astounding Science Fiction* March 1942	*I, Robot*
38. Bridle and Saddle (18,000)	*Astounding Science Fiction* June 1942	*Foundation*
39. Big Game (1,000)	—	—
40. First Law (1,000)	*Fantastic Universe* October 1956	*The Rest of the Robots*
41. TIME PUSSY (1,000)	*Astounding Science Fiction* April 1942	*The Early Asimov* (Vol. II)

STORY (WORDS)	MAGAZINE ISSUE	COLLECTION
42. Victory Unintentional (7,000)	*Super Science Stories* August 1942	*The Rest of the Robots*
43. AUTHOR! AUTHOR! (12,000)	—	*The Early Asimov* (Vol. III)
44. DEATH SENTENCE (7,000)	*Astounding Science Fiction* November 1943	*The Early Asimov* (Vol. III)
45. Catch That Rabbit (7,000)	*Astounding Science Fiction* February 1944	*I, Robot*
46. The Big and the Little (22,500)	*Astounding Science Fiction* August 1944	*Foundation*
47. The Wedge (6,000)	*Astounding Science Fiction* October 1944	*Foundation*
48. Dead Hand (25,000)	*Astounding Science Fiction* April 1945	*Foundation and Empire*
49. BLIND ALLEY (8,500)	*Astounding Science Fiction* March 1945	*The Early Asimov* (Vol. III)
50. Escape (Paradoxical Escape) (7,000)	*Astounding Science Fiction* August 1945	*I, Robot*
51. The Mule (50,000)	*Astounding Science Fiction* November 1945 December 1945	*Foundation and Empire*
52. Evidence (7,000)	*Astounding Science Fiction* September 1946	*I, Robot*
53. Little Lost Robot (10,000)	*Astounding Science Fiction* March 1947	*I, Robot*
54. Now You see It— (25,000)	*Astounding Science Fiction* January 1948	*Second Foundation*
55. NO CONNECTION (7,000)	*Astounding Science Fiction* June 1948	*The Early Asimov* (Vol. III)
56. THE ENDOCHRONIC PROPERTIES OF RESUBLIMATED THIOTIMOLINE (3,000)	*Astounding Science Fiction* March 1948	*The Early Asimov* (Vol. III)
57. Grow Old with Me (Pebble in the Sky) (70,000)	—	*Pebble in the Sky*
58. THE RED QUEEN'S RACE (7,000)	*Astounding Science Fiction* January 1949	*The Early Asimov* (Vol. III)
59. MOTHER EARTH (15,000)	*Astounding Science Fiction* May 1949	*The Early Asimov* (Vol. III)
60. —And Now You Don't (50,000)	*Astounding Science Fiction* November 1949 December 1949 January 1950	*Second Foundation*

(*Note: Stories in capital letters appear in the Early Asimov.*)